ORGANIZED

for

MURDER

by
Ritter Ames

Organized for Murder
By Ritter Ames
print edition
Copyright © 2014 by Ritter Ames
Cover design by Lyndsey Lewellen
http://www.ritterames.com

BOOKS by RITTER AMES

• • • •

The Frugal Lissa Mysteries cozy series
Frugal Lissa Finds a Body
Coming soon—
Frugal Lissa Digs Up a Body
Frugal Lissa Hunts a Body

• • • •

The Organized Mysteries cozy series
Organized for Murder
Organized for Homicide
Organized for Scheduled Sabotage
Organized for S'more Death
Organized for Masked Motives
Organized for Picnic Panic

• • • •

The Bodies of Art Mysteries traditional series
Counterfeit Conspiracies
Marked Masters
Abstract Aliases
Fatal Forgeries
Bronzed Betrayals

• • • •

DEDICATION

TO THE BEST CRITIQUE group in the world, because you all helped Kate be the best she could be. And to all the other great critique groups out there who tirelessly help fellow authors shape and hone and shine their WIPs (works in progress) into something a publisher wants to release.

• • • •

KATE MCKENZIE'S 5-STEP ORGANIZATIONAL START METHOD

BEGIN ANY DE-CLUTTER PROJECT BY COLLECTING AND LABELING FIVE LARGE BOXES:

__REJECT__—items un-repairable, missing parts, past expiration, or like half-a-dozen others already in the house.

__RECYCLE__—gently used, unwanted items for charitable organizations or Freecycle.

__RESELL__—through consignment shops, tag sales, eBay, Craigslist, or newspaper ads.

__RETURN__—sporting goods, toys, books, tools, etc. that belong to family members, neighbors, or friends.

__REVIEW__—things requiring extra thought before fate is determined.

.

Completely unload the room or closet, distributing discarded items into correct boxes. Return only "keepers" to the target area.

CHAPTER ONE

Memo
STACKED IN YOUR FAVOR, LLC,
KATE MCKENZIE, PRES.
BUSINESS PLANNER FOR JOB # <u>1</u>

· · · ·

DATE <u>Wed., April 7th</u>

· · · ·

9:00 A.M. TO 3:00 P.m.—Meet with Miss Amelia Nethercutt at her <u>mansion</u> to organize her and her late husband's exotic collections. Magnificent sprawling home and grounds. On phone seemed eager to learn organizational techniques. Says she scrapbooks and keeps a daily journal. Spend time telling how to develop her vision, to make a date with herself each day to keep living space organized and de-cluttered. Also, since she's a collector, offer the "One-in/One-Out Rule" so old replaced item always goes out when new item is purchased.

· · · ·

"ON THE SECOND DAY, I decided widowhood was infinitely better than divorce."

"Miss Amelia!" Kate McKenzie caught herself, and her teacup, an instant before the Lapsang Souchong escaped over the gold rim and onto the Aubusson rug. While the cream and sienna tones of the carpet would have accepted the tea stain like a distant relative, such an accident threatened to be an uneasy alliance. Especially as Kate courted this new, and particular, client.

Amelia Nethercutt took the still-clattering china from Kate's hands and settled the pieces on the gleaming rosewood coffee table, then said, "It isn't as if I don't know the pros and cons of both marital dissolution options, my dear. My marriage to Daniel was my fifth, no, sixth marriage. I keep forgetting Joey. And receiving an inheritance is much more liberating than monthly alimony."

Kate stiffened on the white-on-white Victorian sofa and hoped her smile didn't look like a grimace. She again swatted the irritating peacock feather and gilt-streaked twig arrangement that invaded the personal space around her left shoulder. Where had common sense fled when she agreed to work sight-unseen in this procurement madhouse?

Façades could be most deceiving—Amelia's and the mansion's. The woman's exterior resembled that of her home—sweeping luxury and professional styling. Even Kate's first look inside of the house, the foyer with its elegant mahogany collectibles cabinet standing guard against taupe-colored grass-cloth, fooled her.

Then she'd seen this parlor, the study, the bedrooms, the conservatory, the library, and... well...all the other "treasure rooms."

This first workday revolved in a repetitive nightmare of list making, supply ordering, prioritizing, and attempts to stem the overwhelming need to hyperventilate. Even her never-fail categorizing system of REJECT, RECYCLE, RESELL, RETURN, and REVIEW periodically failed to keep Kate's panic at bay. Finally, for the first time ever, she gave up and began dividing the upstairs by what rooms were wholly trash and which might be salvageable. Of course, this never meant she would actually be allowed to throw out anything, but she persevered. Until Amelia had called from downstairs and said it was time for a "tea moment."

Kate's last ally disappeared as Mrs. Baxter, the Nethercutts' cotton-haired cook, had bustled in bringing the tea tray and placed it near Amelia. "Nice meeting you, dearie," Mrs. Baxter said, before straightening her pink pillbox hat and telling her employer, "I'm going to the market and the drugstore. There's a cab waiting. I'll be back as quickly as I can."

Amelia nodded, pouring tea as she spoke, "That's fine. I left some budgeting papers on the front table for the garden club vice-president. Please drop them off while doing your errands." She had smiled at Kate then and added, "I'm president again this year, you know." Kate assumed the comment was rhetorical, but she offered a smile for insurance.

"The material is out in the foyer," Amelia called to Mrs. Baxter, and as she waved toward the front door her spicy, nose-tickling scent perfumed the air. "I've made some exciting suggestions and changes. They will require a few club members to reflect a bit before complete acceptance, especially our esteemed vice-president, Gabriella Cavannah-Wicker. Your taking the packet will expedite matters admirably, so everyone has adequate ruminative time."

Mrs. Baxter rolled her eyes heavenward behind her thick lenses. She left via the front door, just as Kate performed her teacup juggle in response to Amelia's disturbing pronouncement. A statement particularly unsettling in light of her late-husband Daniel Nethercutt's recent demise.

Amelia picked up the sugar bowl and offered, "There's nothing like a few minutes for tea."

The smoky smelling brew looked dark. Kate added a liberal dose of milk and worried about the exquisite teacup, musing whether the liquid was capable of eating through the fragile porcelain.

Once more she should have listened to her instincts, but, as usual, decided to focus on the positive side and be nice and agreeable. Landing a rich client seemed a godsend for her new organizing business, STACKED IN YOUR FAVOR. Besides, it wasn't difficult to believe her initial unease due to the fact only a week had passed since Mr. Daniel drifted off to whatever heavenly reward a compulsive collector deserved. At first, Kate worried Amelia was one of those bereaved spouses who too quickly decided to "clean house." But Amelia insisted. Amelia insisted on everything, and Kate's backbone turned to butter.

In this room alone, the front parlor, majolica plates competed with marble busts and conch shells. A stuffed and seriously flaking crocodile, missing its right glass eye, crouched in one corner. Beside the door, a stack of piano sheet music stood as high as Kate's waist, but she'd yet to find any kind of keyboard instrument in the house. The outdoors was brought inside with a collection of faded garden gnomes simulating hopscotch near an overgrown spider plant.

Jeez! What had she gotten herself into? Could she even finish the job by the time her first-grade twins graduated from high school? Amelia didn't need an organizational expert as much as a designer with the balls of General Patton. Or a bulldozer.

And how should she respond to a comment contrasting spousal death with divorce? She decided to ignore it and try wiggling out of the mess she'd let her size eight flats walk into. "Miss Amelia, I'm not sure I'm the best person for this job. My business *is* organizing spaces and archiving items. However, you have many precious treasures here needing—"

"Nonsense, Kate. I picked you because you are perfect for this chore." Amelia rose to her full six-foot stature and glided to the bookcase by the door, the silvery silks of her caftan trailing like the wake behind the QEII. "I first met your mother-in-law at college," she said, flipping pages of a ragged yearbook as she navigated back. "You couldn't find a woman more in control of things than Jane, whatever the task. So, I knew I had to hire you."

Kate's mother-in-law, Jane McKenzie, did indeed know how to keep things in their place, but this did not mean her son's wife possessed superhuman talents. With the elder McKenzies currently finishing a Caribbean cruise, Jane had been unavailable for consultation prior to her daughter-in-law accepting this assignment.

Kate opened her mouth to try to explain family ties and genetic capabilities to Amelia, but she stopped as the scent of Chanel No. 5 preceded a voice in the hall.

"Yoo-hoo, Mummy, where are you?"

A shadow flitted across Amelia's patrician face and disappeared so swiftly Kate couldn't be sure she hadn't imagined it.

"Ah, my stepdaughter Sophia." Amelia smiled as she called, "Darling, in the parlor."

Seconds later, a trim figure sashayed into the room and Kate suddenly felt fat and shabby in her working twills. Though no taller than Kate's fit five-and-a-half feet, and brunette to the organizer's blond, Sophia's lean frame and personal trainer-esque, toned body gave the appearance of runway perfect, with no hint of any past pregnancies. Dressed in simple black slacks, a white blouse that whispered money—lots of it—and dark glasses resting atop long, dark tresses, Kate was reminded of a reincarnated Jacqueline Kennedy Onassis. Until the woman smiled. To her knowledge, Jackie O never resembled a cobra when greeting people.

"Sophia Nethercutt-White." The viper strode forward and extended an impeccably manicured hand. "And you are?"

Kate forced herself to move toward the woman, instead of yielding to an instinct to cower back. "I'm Ka—"

"This is Kate McKenzie, Sophia, dear." Amelia wrapped a protective arm around her shoulders. "You remember my saying I wanted to get an expert to help me categorize and organize. It's time I put this house into working order. I haven't seen dozens of my own things for a decade and can't possibly fathom everything your father collected before our marriage. There are probably untold riches in here."

"No doubt." Sophia raised an eyebrow and turned piercing black eyes on Kate. "I had no idea you were going to act so quickly, Mummy. I would prefer strangers not paw through Father's things."

Amelia waved the comment away like an irritating insect. "Daniel was an open book about his possessions and loved to share them. I know he would welcome Kate to this project."

Sophia folded her arms. "We need to discuss this. There are a number of things I can't locate of Father's, and I don't think having a stranger—"

"Nonsense. Missing items give more credence for needing Kate's expertise. My decision has been made, Sophia." Amelia's light blue eyes turned icy. "Which reminds me. I have Charles Webster Walker coming later."

"Your lawyer?" Sophia uncrossed her arms. "Why?"

"I'm making a few revisions to my will. With Daniel gone it's the responsible thing to do. Your father and I agreed on most things, but how we distributed our estate was always a compromised affair. Now, of course, I can do things any way I like." Amelia displayed a frightening smile that personified the Grimm Brothers' "better to eat you with" line.

Kate shivered.

Bending to pick up the tray, Kate freed herself, both physically and figuratively, from the scene by saying, "I'll take these tea things into the kitchen. Or would you like some, Sophia? The pot feels heavy enough for another cup."

"No, thank you."

"Well, it's nice meeting you." Kate nodded as she passed the angry young woman on the way out the door.

"And you," Sophia returned, arms again locked across her chest, her gaze trained on Amelia.

The large kitchen was the only clutter-free area in the house, likely due to heroic efforts by Mrs. Baxter. Kate was convinced the mansion had been purchased solely because it was the only residence in town large enough to accommodate the extensive Nethercutt collection. The place brought to mind an eBay warehouse.

She dropped the tray a bit too heavily on the tiled island, near a sleek crystal vase holding fragrant lily of the valley blooms. Because the outside of the teapot still felt warm, she used a small towel to cover it in case Amelia wanted another fortifying cup after dealing with her evil stepchild. Two steps to the sink, and she was soaping her fingernails one more time. She knew all lingering dust and grime was probably gone, but...

"Hi."

Startled, she jumped back and upset the tall vase with an elbow. The clear glass rocked at the counter's edge, and Kate, heart in her throat, grabbed the base, making the rescue just milliseconds before a shattering disaster.

"Sorry, didn't mean to scare you. I'm Danny."

The vase was safe, but Kate felt lingering adrenaline still pumping. She snatched a towel from the countertop, then swiped at her hands and took two deep breaths. Feeling calmer, she turned and smiled at the teen who filled the back doorway. "Oh, hello, I'm Kate McKenzie."

Danny looked about sixteen, at the gangly stage where all the pizzas and junk food in the world couldn't possibly fill out that final burst of height. He wore baggy jeans and a flapping flannel shirt over a T-shirt imprinted with the multi-washed logo of a local heavy metal band. He removed the lid from a Hansel-and-Gretel styled cookie jar and added, "Saw the Wicked Witch of the West go in the front door, so I slipped around back."

"You mean—"

"My Aunt Sophia." Danny bit into a chocolate chip cookie. He poked the rest of the cookie in his mouth and lifted the jar, offering a muffled, "You want one?"

"No, thanks." Kate waved a hand over the tray. "I had tea with your grandmother."

He made a face. "Did she give you the awful stuff?"

"It was Lap—"

"Yeah, that's the awful stuff." He stuck out his tongue. "She always drinks it too strong."

Kate couldn't resist. "There's a little more in the pot if you'd like some." They both laughed.

"Well, nice to meet you, Kate McKenzie." He snatched three more cookies from the jar and clunked down the lid, then nabbed a can of soda out of the refrigerator. "My dad and uncle should be here soon. Gramma gave me her old roadster, an MG, and Dad wants Uncle Thomas to check everything out before I drive it." He flashed a dark look. "'Course, that wouldn't be necessary if Gramma would buy me a new one." Then he flashed Kate a grin like he was kidding all along.

Or being a smart-aleck teen. Someone in the Nethercutt family was obviously trying to instill a little character in the lad. Despite the grin, she noticed the humor never reached his cloudy green eyes. Aloud, she asked, "Is Thomas your Aunt Sophia's husband?" Danny snorted.

"Sophia would never live with a man who doesn't mind grease under his fingernails."

Danny shook his head, slipping the cola under an arm to free a hand for the doorknob. "Besides, Auntie is into old geezers who die quickly. Has her current husband locked away right now, drooling in his oatmeal and telling his private nurse about his childhood during the Great War.

Uncle Thomas is Gramma's son. You should see us all together at family holidays."

I think I'd rather not.

The door slammed shut, and Kate smiled, wondering about this teen and his talkative nature, and she couldn't help but suspect he was up to something. He demonstrated none of the antisocial, sullen behavior other moms warned was in the not-too-distant future for

Kate with her own twins. However, she didn't completely trust this first impression persona was the dominant one for Amelia's grandson either.

Her twins! If Danny was out of school, then her daughters Samantha and Suzanne had already been dismissed as well. What kind of organizational expert didn't keep track of the time? She should have checked her master list. Kept up with the time. Too many things to remember, so much running through her head. She took a deep breath and snapped the rubber band on her left wrist. *Number five for today.* Sanity restored, she inhaled one more time.

The corner cuckoo clock set her in motion, and she pulled the daily master list from her pocket. No stops on the way home, just hurry to relieve her husband, Keith, from his after-school parental responsibilities, get dinner on the table, and send him off to his job on time. She scooped up her purse and dashed through the swinging kitchen door, offering the women in the parlor a hasty goodbye before streaking out the front, with Amelia calling, "Hug those sweet darlings of yours for me."

Yet, even as she hustled to her blue van, Kate relished for a moment the heightened view boasted from the Tudor mansion's lofty setting, the tiny town below gaining a doll-like quality. She saw the distant radio tower for local talk station WHZE, where Keith was evening sports anchor. The station was small, but the management's commitment to New England sports was rock solid, and as a homegrown hockey hero, Keith was approached for the job soon after the new format became public.

The four McKenzies had moved to his hometown of Hazelton, Vermont six months earlier, and lived a few miles from his parents. The move had been a good one so far. With Kate's parents deceased, she appreciated having a doting set of grandparents nearby to help out, and the girls loved being spoiled.

Keith had played B-string goalie ten seasons with various major league hockey teams, eight while the couple was married, before blowing out a knee and calling it quits. The timing had definitely been right. All the moving and politics kept a steady strain on their marriage. Before the move she only knew Hazelton from sporadic Currier and Ives-like Christmas visits, but loved its winding rural roads and the picturesque Main Street that unfolded in open friendliness as travelers emerged from a centuries-old covered bridge at the town's eastern boundary. Kate also found being married to the returning prodigal citizen automatically made her a local. Or close enough, anyway.

Unfortunately, sports-talkers in small New England cities did not make what even moderately-successful hockey players did. With the twins in school all day, Kate finally persuaded Keith to take on more duties around the house and allow her time to start a business. He'd balked at first, but she'd found an advocate in her mother-in-law. Once Jane McKenzie stepped into the discussion, her son didn't have a chance. When he'd looked to his father, George, for moral support, the elder McKenzie just shook his head and ducked out the back door with his pipe.

Kate smiled as she merged into traffic for the short drive home. It's always said men marry their mothers. At first, she'd felt a little uneasy about the idea, but no longer.

A red Jeep parked at the head of their cul-de-sac barred her from entering. The vehicle was Keith's, and he had the neighborhood kids whooping and hollering as they used the paved circle for an impromptu Rollerblading rink. Two teams, players distinguished by the mismatched shirts they wore of either blue or red, battled a hard rubber puck with street sticks toward opposite goals. Kate's blond-curled daughters were the masked and dueling goalies. She parked and took her place alongside other parents watching their helmeted offspring, all clapping and whistling over the triumphs and groaning for the mis-skates.

Meg Berman, hair fiery bright in the spring sun and still wearing garden grubbies, waved Kate over and called, "You just missed Sam dive for the puck. She saved the red team." Kate's daughter Samantha turned at the words and waved at her mom. The puck flew Sam's way again, courtesy of Jamey Hendricks, daughter Suzanne's crush of the week, and this time the hard plastic flew unhindered into the net.

"Blue team wins!" Half the kids cheered, skating to form a middle line for the best sportsmanship handshake Keith always mandated.

Her husband took off his helmet, his wavy brown hair tumbling free, and joined one end. "Congratulations, blue team. Red team, nice effort on your part, too. Sam, we have to work on that attention span, though. Don't forget."

"But, Daddy, Mommy is here."

Keith turned his hundred-watt smile Kate's way. Even after almost nine years of marriage she felt the familiar flutter in her heart.

"Hi, honey. We're about finished." He reached out and grabbed a twin with each hand.

"That's fine. I'll go in and start dinner. It's sloppy joes, so hurry." Kate pointed to her watch. "You don't have much time."

The other kids and parents dispersed. Kate walked with Meg. "Looks like you've been gardening." She motioned toward her friend's gloves and the claw-like hand tool.

"The only way to stay optimistic that something flowery will eventually come up is to keep acting like Mother Nature is on-track." Meg sighed, slipping her hand under one arm to remove a glove. "It's been too chilly this year, but I have faith the pastels will pop out soon. More important, what's the Nethercutt mansion like inside?"

Kate rolled her eyes. "You're not going to believe it. Let me decompress for a bit, then I'll try to find words to describe the place."

"Maybe I could come help you on the job and see it for myself," Meg coaxed, wiggling thin brows in a hopeful look that made her freckles dance.

"You can't imagine what you're volunteering for."

Meg's two boys, five-year-old Ben and eight-year-old Mark skated up, their wheels making a sizzling sound across the asphalt, then silence and synchronized *thunks* as they jumped in tandem to the sidewalk. Ben might have been smaller, but was already a match for his big bro. "Mom, can we go out for pizza?" Mark begged, screeching to a stop just inches from Kate's toes.

"Please, Mom, since Dad's not gonna be home tonight?" Ben backed him up, his head just grazing Mark's shoulder. Meg's husband, Gil, a columnist for the Bennington paper, covered state government and often had to stay in Montpelier.

Meg frowned, but Kate saw a tiny smile fighting to break free. "How can I say no when you tag team me like this?"

"You're welcome to come share sloppy joes with us," Kate said, knowing how much the boys loved to talk hockey with Keith.

"Can we?" they chorused.

When their mom nodded, Kate sent everyone toward her house. "Just let me get the van in the garage."

Five minutes later it was controlled chaos in the kitchen. The kids alternately relived successes and defeats, filling Kate in on the action she'd missed while she browned hamburger and laid out the other ingredients. She handed Suzanne a stack of place mats, then frisbeed paper plates to the boys. "You guys set the table together, okay? Get extra napkins, Sam."

Everything was simmering nicely, both food and conversation, when the business line rang.

"Stacked in Your Favor. Kate McKenzie speaking."

"Mrs. McKenzie," an acid voice responded. "This is Sophia Nethercutt-White. We met today. You were working for my stepmother."

"Yes." Kate noted how the woman's greeting neatly put her into her place. "Can I help you?"

"Actually, no," Sophia said. "And my stepmother no longer requires your services, either. The police are here. Amelia Nethercutt is dead."

CHAPTER TWO

SAY GOODBYE TO FRANTIC A.M.s

Stop cluttered, crazy mornings by setting a bookcase beside the door and designating a shelf for each family member. Make sure all backpacks, lunches, homework projects, sports items, purses, briefcases, etc. are in place before bedtime. Assign each person a color and put small plastic baskets in his/her assigned color on shelves for keys and personal items.

• • • •

KATE STAYED AT LOOSE ends as she shuttled her girls and the Berman boys to school the next day. When the kids piled out at the neat bricked elementary building, she wanted to go along as well, to feel she belonged somewhere. Several times she touched her pocket notebook like it was a talisman, knowing she wouldn't complete the Nethercutt job lists prepared for the rest of the week, but wanting to do something to fill the void created by Amelia's death.

This is ridiculous. Stop being maudlin.

She couldn't understand why she stayed rattled. While shocked about Amelia's death, she was ecstatic about the job ending, yet a little depressed about being let go. Out of sync, out of place, and out of sorts.

The vacillating Vermont spring weather matched her frame of mind. She flipped the heater to its highest setting and resolved to drag herself out of the doldrums. Her mood lighted upon her return home to find Meg at the McKenzie front door with freshly brewed mocha lattes.

Hot mocha lattes.

"What is wrong with me?" They faced each other across the kitchen table, their hands cradling warm cups. Kate wished self-esteem heated up as easily. "Even though I've gotten what I wanted, to be free of the job, I'm still feeling dissatisfied. And crazed about not finishing what I'd started. Not to mention guilty for being happy that I don't have to go back. Ugh!"

"You can't wish a person dead just to get out of a crazy project," Meg said, smiling to soften her words. "Get off the guilt train."

"No. I'm not sure what I'm thinking exactly. Maybe selfish I get to quit, but what a heavy price to pay. Guilt. Selfishness. Even confusion about her death."

"Confused? Why?"

"She was such a formidable woman. Everything about her seemed strong, from her strength of character to physical presence." Kate thought back to the exchange between Amelia and Sophia. "You should have been there the moment she told her stepdaughter she was bringing in the family lawyer to change her will. And dropping the verbal bombs to Mrs. Baxter and me about the papers for the garden club. Amelia positively radiated power. No way you would expect the woman to drop dead just a few hours later. I wonder how she died."

She rose and grabbed the cookie jar from the countertop. "Oh, I'm just being silly. I tried to quit the job, and now I'm trying to concoct some kind of conspiracy. Why do I have all these conflicting emotions?"

"It's the strange way closure works." Meg grabbed the first Oreo. "I remember Gil once got laid off from a job he absolutely hated. He experienced the same ambivalent feelings you're having. The only thing to do is keep busy. Get your mind working farther down your to-do list."

"Well, there's plenty to get done," Kate moaned. "I focused earlier on what I couldn't finish and forgot all the things I needed to accomplish to put an end to this job."

In the next few hours she un-ordered all of the organizing materials ordered the previous afternoon and confirmed how to return anything already shipped. She mailed an itemized invoice of time and supplies used, assuming it would get forwarded to the estate's lawyer. Her cell phone felt like a permanent extension of her left hand by the time she got through to the last vendor.

"Hey, honey." Keith walked into her home office about two o'clock, dressed in khakis and a golf shirt. "Considering you have this free day and all, would you pick up the girls so I can meet the guys for nine holes?"

A *free* day? Was he kidding? Luckily Keith pulled her into an embrace before she had a chance to splutter a reply. When her mouth was no longer otherwise occupied, she said, "Okay, go. Just don't make any bets you can't win."

He grinned and gave her shoulders a squeeze. "Thanks, Katie, I owe you one." He disappeared out the door, then called back from down the hall, "Oh, and I promised to help the girls with after school soccer practice. The assistant coach isn't going to be there."

"In that case, you owe me more than 'one', buster."

The only response she received in reply was her husband laughing as he closed the front door.

• • • •

SHE MAY HAVE BEEN HOODWINKED to help out with the team, but the exercise and the girls' high energy were the best tonic for Kate's soul. They all arrived back home at four-thirty, sweaty and grass-stained, and ready for a quiet evening.

Nearly an hour later, with everyone finally fed and her kitchen back to normal, Kate pretreated and washed a load of sports clothes before retiring to the living room with a diet soda, settling on the couch next to Keith to watch the twins play Barbies. Or, in her daughters' case, argue over who had "the real" Barbie.

Keith looked at the clock and stretched. "Guess I should head for the station." He clicked off ESPN and added, "Watching sports on TV is different since I started the radio show. I used to watch for entertainment, but now I focus more for information and technique."

"Maybe we can deduct cable on our taxes," Kate suggested.

He kneeled to kiss each twin goodbye. Suzanne added an extra hug before the girls resumed their argumentative play. The doorbell rang, and Keith moved to answer it. Kate glanced out the front window and saw a Hazelton police cruiser sitting at the curb.

"Honey," Keith called. "You need to come here."

In the foyer beside her husband loomed a fifty-ish looking man wearing a dark suit. A uniformed police officer remained on the porch.

"This is Lieutenant Johnson of the Vermont State Police and Constable Banks of Hazelton PD," Keith introduced the pair.

"Mrs. McKenzie, we'd like to talk with you about Amelia Nethercutt," Lieutenant Johnson cut in, dragging his vowels out in a husky drawl. "You'll have to come with us to the police station. We need to take your fingerprints and get a DNA sample."

"DNA? What's this all about?" Keith demanded.

"My fingerprints? Why?" Kate asked at the same time.

"For elimination purposes." The lieutenant trained a steely-gray gaze on Kate. "As I believe you are already aware, Amelia Nethercutt was found dead yesterday. The death looked suspicious when the constable here," he nodded toward Banks, "responded to the call. Given his concerns about the nature of the death and evidence at the scene, we managed to expedite the autopsy, and the results corroborated his suspicions. It's a murder case, and we've been called in to handle the investigation." Turning to Keith, he added, "Your wife is a material witness in our investigation. She was at the scene, so we need her fingerprints and DNA for elimination purposes."

"I'm calling a lawyer." Keith grabbed the cordless phone.

"No, don't." Kate pulled her husband into the hallway for a little privacy. "This can't be a big deal. Get a babysitter, and I'll go answer their questions. Don't worry."

"I don't like the sound of 'material witness,'" he whispered. "It usually means the police suspect a person, but don't yet have enough evidence to make an arrest."

She shook her head. "It means no such thing. We can't afford the extra expense of a lawyer, and I have nothing to hide. I'll answer the lieutenant's questions, and he can quickly move on to other leads."

Keith frowned as he phoned a colleague to cover for him that night. Hours later, he waited for her in the police department lobby as she sat alone in one of the eight-by-eight interrogation rooms. The door was locked. She'd already checked three times and stopped herself from making another trip across the room to check again. She made herself breathe deeply and snapped the rubber band on her left wrist instead. Number six for the day.

The Hazelton PD was compact and functional. The officers had ushered her through a small waiting area, past the hallway that led to the jail cells, and into this windowless box that contained nothing more than a heavy table and two chairs. The room needed a thorough cleaning, as did her hands. Kate pulled a packet of moist towelettes from her purse. She worked the table over as best she could, but it showed little improvement. The effort and feel of the cool wipe in her hand did lift her spirits a bit, however.

She'd remembered the town constable, Jim Banks, from his easygoing manner at PTA meetings, but had never actually met him, just recognized his bushy mustache and knew two Banks teens attended Hazelton High. The oldest, a daughter, used to babysit for Meg. The state police lieutenant, Walter Johnson, looked the older of the two law enforcement officials by a good half-decade, and was unfamiliar to her. His slow drawl claimed roots to some distant place like Tennessee or Texas.

Kate looked at her watch. After ten already. Why had they brought her in so early, only to make her wait? She'd heard doors opening and closing periodically, and assumed others were being interviewed. At least she hoped so. Her stomach knotted. They couldn't really believe she had anything to do with Amelia's murder, could they?

An eternity passed before Lieutenant Johnson walked in with a manila folder clasped under an arm, and a steaming coffee in each hand. He offered her a cup and forced a smile. She sipped the bitter liquid and watched Johnson extract a printout of the swirls and whorls that tagged Kate to her fingerprints.

"Yours matched those on the teapot, Mrs. McKenzie." Johnson pulled a pen from his pocket, as Constable Banks silently entered the room. The men nodded at one another. The local officer remained near the door.

"I don't doubt what you say, Lieutenant." Kate found herself nervously twisting the dirty towelette and dropped the cloth onto the table. "I worked there most of the day, so you'll find my fingerprints throughout the house. The bigger question you should be asking is what possible reason I might have to kill Amelia Nethercutt. I can't get paid for a job if I murder my client."

"A witness tells us the victim said you implied you wanted out of this particular arrangement."

"Quitting is much simpler than killing someone."

"Which implies you did want out of the job."

Kate blinked. The way he said it sounded ominous. Obviously, logic wasn't going to work here, at least not hers. Best to go with the original plan and simply answer the questions. "Yes, I did want out of the situation, Lieutenant, but we hadn't signed a contract. Given the sheer magnitude of the chore, coming up with a total job price was impossible. Amelia agreed to pay me by the hour. Without a contract, I could leave at any time, and I planned to do exactly that within a few days."

Johnson made a series of lengthy notes on the pad sandwiched in the folder, stopping several times to study the wall above her head before adding more scribbles onto the hidden page. Constable Banks remained straight and silent. She shifted in her chair, wondering whether they were doing this to get her to talk.

If so, it can't work. I have nothing to say. She did have a question, though. "How did Amelia die?"

"The family cook found her," Johnson said. "Mrs. Baxter let Mrs. Nethercutt's lawyer in the front door and found her employer's body when she went to announce his arrival."

"Yes, Amelia mentioned her attorney was coming later in the day." Kate wondered whether she should elaborate on the conversation between stepmother and stepdaughter and decided there was no harm in stating facts. "She said she was updating her will now that her husband had passed on."

Johnson nodded. "Always a good idea. You'd be surprised how many people don't change their wills after the death of a spouse. Can make for a big family fight after the remaining spouse finally dies and the will is ambiguous. What do you think?"

Behind him, Constable Banks's dark head nodded in agreement.

What did this guy want from her? First he left her to sit for hours, and then starts a gab fest about wills? She had her own thoughts on this, of course, given the undertones of Amelia's words, she but didn't believe he truly wanted her opinion. Kate settled for an impartial shrug.

"The cook came back from grocery shopping and saw the lawyer at the door," Constable Banks added his deep voice to the conversation for the first time. "They walked into the parlor together, and the cook screamed her head off. The 9-1-1 operator reported hearing her in the background while Miss Amelia's death was reported by the lawyer."

"Oh, poor Mrs. Baxter." Kate thought about that grandmotherly-looking soul coming back to see such a sight. Then she realized she didn't know what kind of sight it was. Though the lawmen had turned uncharacteristically talkative, their words veered sharply away from her question. She tried once more. "But how did Amelia die?"

Johnson closed down again and returned his gaze to the area above her head. He tapped a pen against the table's edge.

Different murder scenarios tripped through her mind like a super-speed movie, and Kate realized she was holding her breath. *Stop it!* They were trying to psych her out. Focusing, she forced air in and out of her lungs in a slow, regular pattern. *That's better.* No way were they going to think her guilty of a murder she knew nothing about. She smiled. Miss Calm—that was Kate McKenzie.

So, it was a shock when she once more found herself unconsciously winding the towelette through her fingers. She swallowed a scream of dismay, and shoved the soiled cloth into a pocket, filth and all. Total calm—*right*.

Lieutenant Johnson redirected his sharp-gray eyes her way, evidently settled on his next interrogation tack. "Your prints are the only ones on the teapot, and the only prints on the poison."

She blinked in confusion. Impossible! Mrs. Baxter's and Amelia's fingerprints should have been on the teapot as well, and Kate hadn't touched anything that resembled poison. Then she remembered seeing Amelia grasp the thin wooden handle to pour the tea and the matching wooden button-top on the pot's lid. "Didn't the handle show any fingerprints?"

"Wood isn't helpful at transferring print evidence."

Meaning hers, as she'd checked the temperature of the remaining brew, left the only available prints for comparison. What bad luck.

Still, this didn't explain the rest of his statement. "I touched the sides of the pot to see if it needed emptying. The tea was still warm, so I wrapped a towel around the teapot. But I never touched any poison."

"Another witness told us you did. Watched you return the container to the kitchen island, as your fingerprints at the base verify."

"You mean the vase of flowers?" Kate was incredulous.

"Lily of the valley. After several days the water becomes poisonous to humans," the lieutenant explained. "In this case, the same water was added to Mrs. Nethercutt's covered teapot and killed her with that one last cup."

A chill raced up Kate's spine. She'd only touched the vase when Danny came into the kitchen. He must be the witness who gave her over to the police. *The little rat.*

"Do you have something you'd like to tell us, Mrs. McKenzie?" Johnson interrupted her thoughts.

"Huh?"

"You were frowning."

"Oh." Kate straightened in the chair, her gaze meeting his as she took a steadying breath. She touched her pocket notebook to shore up her psyche. "Just thinking. I assume Amelia's grandson told you about me to divert suspicion from his family. I nearly knocked the vase to the floor when Danny opened the back door and startled me."

Johnson's face stayed as impassive as the area's native granite, but Constable Banks showed surprise at her words.

Teach these two for getting complacent and taking the word of some self-possessed rich kid. Then, ashamed of herself, she amended the thought. She was a stranger. It was natural for a teenager to throw her over to save his kith and kin. "Did you speak to her stepdaughter?"

"Sophia Nethercutt-White left right after you. Said Amelia Nethercutt mentioned she was going to the kitchen for more tea. Ms. Nethercutt-White only returned after the death was discovered."

"In updating her will, might Amelia have included changes the heirs weren't happy with or expecting?" Kate asked.

"The attorney said everything was standard," Johnson responded. "Mostly differences in how the late woman's greenhouse and flower stock were taken care of, and the means for setting value on everything else. A few new bequests added, but nothing significant or likely to cause a fight. It's really none of your business, ma'am."

Kate felt her face redden. Didn't the man realize she didn't care who got what, as long as she wasn't charged with murder? "That's not why I asked."

"I'm listening, Mrs. McKenzie."

"Well..." She felt shaky, realizing how confrontational this interview was becoming. "Did Sophia tell you she had a problem with my working among the various collections in the house? She didn't like the idea of Amelia signing a new will either."

The men exchanged startled looks, and she recounted the conversation that occurred in the front parlor. Johnson's expression returned to stone before she finished.

"As you probably know from all the cop shows on television, Mrs. McKenzie—"

"Those aren't my cup of tea, Lieutenant." Kate shook her head, before realizing what expression she'd used, and amended, "I mean, my video viewing is usually limited to whatever my six-year-olds watch in the evening."

Johnson rolled the page containing her fingerprints into a tube and tapped it several times on the tabletop. "What I'm trying to get across is how, no matter the crime, but especially murder, we must follow a number of leads before settling on a final suspect."

"In that case, why didn't you question me at my home?" She knew an edge was creeping into her voice but didn't care. "Let's face it. I'm the person least likely to gain from her murder."

"Like all the other witnesses in the case, we needed you here to take your fingerprints," he explained. "Get a hair sample to eliminate trace evidence."

"So, everyone else has come in?"

"Well, most." His expression changed, admitting he was telling her more than he wanted. "This is just a first step in the investigation. And since your story follows a logical path and you clearly have no inheritance motive—"

"Then, I'm not under arrest?"

"You are a lead we needed to question," he said. "Not to say we won't have more questions for you later, but you've satisfied what we need to know at the present time."

Kate almost congratulated herself, thinking all misunderstanding was cleared away, until she remembered the ride in the police cruiser and wondered whether HPD had offered chauffeur services to any of the other 'leads.' She didn't want to ask. "Am I free to leave?"

"Yes." Lieutenant Johnson put the fingerprint card atop his notes and closed the folder. Rising, he added, "But don't leave the area."

"That sounds like I'm still a suspect."

"Everyone who was in that house remains a suspect." Johnson tapped the file twice on the tabletop, then turned and signaled Constable Banks, concluding the interview.

Keith enveloped her in a hug as soon as she entered the vacant lobby, and Kate found herself tearing up. "Honey, it's okay. It's over." He stroked her hair.

She nodded, unable to answer, still worried about the suspect label hanging like neon over her head. Nevertheless, this wasn't the place to discuss it. She whispered, "Let's go home."

The Jeep's dashboard gave off a comforting glow as they drove down Main Street. The two-hundred-year-old First Episcopal Church stood stately white in the moonlight, its steeple pointing the way to heaven, with the darkened maple trees behind creating a perfect, inky backdrop. They passed Tucker's Hardware and the Country Store, alive during the day to serve residents' needs and now shut tight. Only the dozen or so streetlights fought the darkness. Midnight was fast approaching, and Kate wanted to be home, snuggled under the down comforter in the couple's king-sized bed.

"Did Meg take the girls home with her?"

Keith shook his dark head in the dim light. "They didn't want to go, and dug in their heels to be home whenever we came back. Meg promised to either get a sitter or stay up and trek between the two houses."

"Poor Meg." There was plenty of room in their house for the boys to sleep over, but the youngest Berman refused to bed down anywhere but his own bunk.

Yet, as much as she trusted her neighbor with the twins, she was glad the girls were snug in their own room. The Berman place was a bit of a madhouse with two large dogs, an equal number of cats, a snake, a bearded dragon, an ant farm, two rambunctious boys, and an entirely different household routine. Besides reawakening the pleadings for a pet of their own, something Kate continued to fend off as long as possible, the change in bedtime venue would likely have been too much for Samantha and Suzanne. Especially after watching their mother escorted away by the local constabulary. In a Berman bed, the girls would have no doubt been lying awake in the darkness, worried and wired, set to be tired and cranky the next evening—when Keith could escape to the radio station.

Kate didn't want her kids cranky. She'd reserved that emotion for herself.

Her exhausted mind still labored through roller-coaster feelings evoked from the grief of learning her client had been killed, followed by the nerves of being interrogated about the murder.

Keith reached across the center console and laced his fingers with hers. She felt huge tears swell and fall. One hit the back of his hand, and he looked over. Wordlessly, he pulled to the shoulder of the road in front of the Winstons' small apple farm and wrapped his arms around her.

"I'm okay. Angry more than anything." She sniffed, and counted off fingers as she continued, "I mean, first I get overwhelmed by Amelia and dissed by her stepdaughter. Next, I lose income I was kind of counting on, at least for a while, and have to un-order supplies for the job I'm not going to finish. Finally, I can't even spend a quiet evening with my kids because the police haul me away in a squad car like a suspect. Me! The one person with nothing to gain from Amelia's death except the 'benefit' of not having to quit. Can you think of a more stupid motive?"

"It's their job, Katie." When she glared at him, he quickly added, "Not that I disagree with you."

She had to laugh then but reached for the tissues on the dash. "Just drive us home. Please."

He used one finger to raise her chin. "You okay?"

"Absolutely." She sniffed again. "But, I didn't thank you for coming tonight. Knowing you were in the building really did make the whole situation easier."

"Where else would I be?" His teeth reflected bright white.

"I love you too," she said, returning the smile. "But, I really want to go home."

"That is one wish I can definitely grant, my lady." Keith kissed her forehead, then settled back into his seat and checked for traffic.

The Berman house sat unlit and shut tight as they entered the cul-de-sac of the tiny neighborhood, but Kate could see the kitchen light sifting through the windows of their own, otherwise darkened, home. Keith grabbed a stray hockey stick off the front porch, and she pushed through the door. A lamp clicked on in the living room, and Tiffany James, the most reliable of the neighborhood crew of rotating teen sitters, and the daughter of Kate's local nemesis, interior decorator Valerie James, bolted up from the couch.

"Mrs. McK! They let you go free!" Tiffany shot across the room and surprised Kate with a hug. "Mom was afraid you'd be in the big house for *days*. Murderers rarely get out on bail."

I'll just bet your mom was worried about me. Kate's mental sarcasm matched her irritation level, but she kept her voice light as she told the teen, "They only wanted to question me as a witness. Nothing more serious."

"The police interview many people and follow a lot of leads at the beginning of any investigation," Keith cut in, propping the hockey stick against one wall and hanging their jackets in the closet. "Kate was happy to help in any way."

Tiffany pulled out of the hug and studied Kate's face. "You're so brave. I hope I have your courage if I ever find myself in equally dire straits."

Kate felt pressure building in her chest and wanted to snap, 'I need more courage to handle whatever stories you and your mother concoct about me,' but Keith jumped in first. He pulled out his wallet and said, "We appreciate your pitching in tonight, Tiff. Come on and I'll take you home."

"The twins were *angels*," Tiffany effused. She slipped the money into her back pocket and shrugged into a burgundy leather jacket she scooped off the end of the couch. "So *brave*, so—"

"Thank you, Tiffany." Kate nearly ran up the stairs to escape.

She felt soiled from sitting in the interrogation room. After checking on her sleeping "angels," she hit the shower. She came out wearing her favorite, pink silk pajamas. Comfort was suddenly everything to her. Keith was already in bed, propped up on pillows and reading *Sports Illustrated*.

"The girl can't help it that her mother's a bitch, honey," Keith said softly, dropping the magazine on the night stand before drawing the covers back for Kate.

"I know, but now the talk of Hazelton will be how I'm up for capital murder charges or something equally ridiculous." She tugged the comforter straight, then scrunched down into a fetal position. "I'm tempted to keep the girls home from school tomorrow. I don't want them to hear any crazy stories."

"Which will make people talk all the more." He touched the rubber band on Kate's wrist. "This week has been pretty stressful. How've you been doing?"

"Six by the time I was released from the police station. Another two in the shower once I started obsessing about Amelia's death and the interrogation, and after hearing Tiffany's effusive words of support."

She punched her pillow, visualizing Valerie James's smug face. "*Grrr.* I don't know how Valerie knew where I was, but no doubt she's the one who told Tiffany. Meg wouldn't have said anything."

"Honey, we had a police cruiser in front of our house." Keith pulled her into his arms. "You can bet behind each set of our neighbors' curtains were eager pairs of eyes watching you climb in and drive off with the officers. News like that is too juicy to keep quiet, especially after everyone's been gossiping today about Amelia's death. All it takes is one busybody making a phone call, and soon the news is viral. Besides, Valerie is probably still steamed that Amelia gave the job to you instead of choosing her design company."

"It isn't even what the witch does," Kate argued. "Organizing can entail some design, especially in reducing household items that don't meet the design theme. But what I was hired to do was more quantifying and codifying. Why would she want the hassle? All I hear out of her is how many *referrals* she gets from satisfied customers."

His chest muscles rippled as he shrugged a shoulder. "Probably wanted the job to get into the house, then she could have made other suggestions afterward for additional commissions."

"Well, given what happened because I was awarded the great honor, Valerie should be thanking me rather than spreading malicious rumors."

"Go figure." His brown eyes were at half-mast. "Don't worry about the twins. They think you walk on water. Sam will probably punch anyone who tries to say something bad about her mom, and Suze will wither them with one of her looks."

It was good hearing his words. Not because Sam might get into another scrape—that would simply lead to more of the same kind of parent/daughter/teacher talks they'd too often had following the move to Hazelton. Sam's first grade teacher assured them this was nothing more than a phase while their daughter got used to her new home, but it was still worrisome. However, Kate took solace in knowing the golden-curled pair remained capable of handling most anything as long as they stuck together. "They're quite a team."

"You bet," Keith seconded. "I'll take them to school in the morning and explain things to their teacher."

"You're such a good husband." She patted his bare chest.

"And a tired one."

"Go to sleep."

Within minutes, his breathing changed, and she knew he was lost to REM eye movements and dreams reliving past hockey glories, while she lay wide awake. After half an hour she decided to give in and get up.

Chamomile tea was her first thought, but at the reminder of Amelia's death she chose warm milk instead. The intermittent stirring gave her time to circle the living room and kitchen, picking up and replacing the flotsam and jetsam that signaled an active family lived in the house. She straightened the skates in their utility room cubbies, glanced at the hockey stick rack and noticed Keith had replaced the one he'd brought in from the front porch.

Still moving, she set the girls' backpacks on the wooden bench in the entry and closed a book someone had left face down on the coffee table. She moved back to the kitchen and added ingredients to the crock-pot, guaranteeing hot, cinnamon oatmeal by morning. Finally, the steaming white liquid was ready. She poured it into the floral decorated *Mom* cup Suzanne gave her for Mother's Day two years back and grabbed an Oreo from the jar.

The food and normalcy of the activities seemed to do the trick, and soon Kate noticed the comforting impression of heavy lids. Before sleep, though, she decided to start another load of laundry. She hated this chore but doing a bit each day kept the blasted baskets from overwhelming her.

She transferred wet sports clothes to the dryer. While most of the sorting baskets were nearly empty, there was always enough for a white load. One of the organizing techniques she lived by was the White Rule—everything plain white for everyday items, from towels, to T-shirts, to socks and underwear. That way she not only avoided having to match socks but could get a whole load of washing together at any time. She filled the machine, added a cup of soap and bleach, and things were soon churning nicely. She reached into the overhead cabinet for the softener, and her fingers froze as she touched a smooth, glassy surface. This had definitely not been in the house earlier.

Kate withdrew her hand, the object firmly in her grasp. A highly polished, ebony box inlaid with ivory. She gasped. The sleep of moments before faded to distant memory. This was the second time she had seen the little treasure. The first was yesterday in Amelia Nethercutt's late husband's upstairs study.

CHAPTER THREE

A RECIPE FOR ORGANIZATION – Crock Pot Oatmeal

Nothing's better than waking up in the morning to an already prepared breakfast and more time. *Measure rolled oats (not quick oats) into a crock-pot using a ratio of one cup oats to two cups water. Cinnamon, dehydrated apples, brown sugar, maple syrup (from Vermont, of course), or chunky walnuts can be added for additional flavoring. Turn the crock-pot on low overnight (about eight hours) and wake knowing breakfast is ready and waiting and oh, so yummy.*

• • • •

KATE DROPPED THE BOX as if it were on fire and watched the ebony object sink into the sudsy tub, disappearing amid her whites and woes. She opened her mouth to scream, but nothing came out. She bolted for the stairs. Halfway up, she tripped.

She couldn't wake Keith. Not after the horrendous evening they'd already gone through. And why? So they could worry together?

The company would be nice, but it's not fair. Someone should get a little sleep.

A wave of unaccountable shivers gripped her body, and she grabbed the knitted mauve afghan in the living room. She knew her chills stemmed from terror, rather than temperature, and not a little bit of paranoia.

Coming to her senses, she retraced her steps and dipped a hand in the washing machine tub, blindly searching through the waves until two fingertips brushed a sharp corner. The soapsuds had eliminated any of the perpetrator's prints. She dried the box with a kitchen towel and sat at the table to contemplate her fate, turning it several times to study this new curse.

Something hard was imprisoned inside and made a solid clinking sound when Kate shook it. The top lipped over each side and held fast. There were no visible hinges, but something kept the pieces together and tight. A nearly invisible line ran within the lid's shadows and proved the presence of an opening. But no matter how much Kate pressed on spots and tugged the lid, the box refused to give up its secret. She pulled the afghan tighter around her shoulders and bit her lip.

Who was setting her up, and what might he or she try next? Of course, Danny had thrown her to the wolves, and she understood his motive. But did he also slip into her house and leave the incriminating little tchotchke?

This was completely unfair. No, it was more than unfair. It was freaking insane and downright scary as hell!

Kate's backbone stiffened as something even more frightening occurred to her. Did Tiffany let him in the house? Had the little drama queen opened the front door and congratulated herself on a visit from the richest male at Hazelton High? Kate imagined Tiffany fluttering around the living room, fawning over Danny, carrying out his every whim. But wouldn't Meg have investigated if a strange MG sat in front of the house? For that matter, if Danny did plant the evidence, was he saving his hide or someone else's?

It took all her willpower to not snatch up the phone and punch the James' number, and demand to speak to Tiffany. Instead, something made her drag her huge security blanket across the tile floor to check the rear entrance of the house. Yes, the back door was closed tight, and the cherry-cluster print curtain remained drawn against the evening's earlier western light. But the deadbolt latch stood tall in the unlocked position.

Damn! Kate chewed on her lip. She needed a plan.

Her office, once a back bedroom, was neatly stacked to the rafters with shelves and supplies for the business. She carried the ebony box to the worktable next to the window and found brown wrapping paper and packing tape. The afghan fell to the floor as she grabbed a tissue and busily wiped her fingerprints from the outside. Then, employing the tissue as protection from further prints, she set the dreaded thing in the dead middle of one dark page and began wrapping. Minutes later, Kate realized she'd not only left prints on the paper but also the packing tape she'd planned to use.

Double damn! Too bad she hadn't watched those police television shows the lieutenant mentioned earlier. She needed to figure out how to get rid of this thing without creating a path of bread crumbs pointing right back to her.

Though she would have to redo it later, she went ahead and wrapped the box, hid it in one cardboard carton, then another, and finally stashed the whole enchilada atop a high shelf.

Talk about OCD. Like adding container layers will make the thing invisible.

She perched on a stool at the worktable and took a few deep breaths, then pulled a notepad and pen from one of the rolling Rubbermaid drawer sets. Someone had a reason for killing Amelia Nethercutt. Kate's only gift over law enforcement officials resided in her organizational skills.

And my powers to obsess 24/7. If she organized the facts, maybe the murderer would be revealed. *Okay, that sounds simplistic, but a girl's got to start somewhere.*

She divided the page into columns: Suspects, Motive, Opportunity

Danny was at the mansion on the day of the murder, and so was Sophia. Kate wrote quickly. Moreover, Danny's father and uncle were supposedly checking out the car. Yes, she was rolling now. Four suspects. Motive was easy; all were family and expected to inherit. Ditto for opportunity; everyone again. The lawyer was coming with a new will. What if Amelia planned to disinherit someone? The lieutenant said the changes were minimal, but his comment could have been an attempt to curb gossip. Until Kate knew more about the will, opportunity seemed the best avenue of investigation. After she'd left the mansion that afternoon, any of the men could have entered unobserved through the back door to poison the tea. And Sophia could have slipped into the kitchen before her departure.

Kate sighed. Nothing pointed at one person that didn't point equally toward everyone else. Hers were the only fingerprints found. No matter what Lieutenant Johnson said before he let her leave the station, his parting comment meant the police hadn't yet struck her absolutely from the suspect roster.

Of course, the box would change everything if they found it. Her gaze strayed to the nesting boxes holding the knickknack. Getting rid of it had to be top priority, or at least she had to find out what lay inside. A diamond ring? A safe deposit key to a cache of cash?

Sudden exhaustion overwhelmed her, and Kate shoved the notepad aside to head back to bed. The knitted blanket still lay puddled in the middle of the room, and she almost left it, then changed her mind. One disadvantage of being a professional organization expert was everyone expected her home to always be in perfect condition, everything in its place.

"So all's right with the world." Kate shook her head.

A quick trip to the living room, and the afghan landed back on the couch where it belonged. Seconds later she again slipped between the covers and inched closer to Keith. The sheets on her side might be cold, but her husband—a born and bred Vermonter who'd chosen to attend the frigid University of Wisconsin as his alma mater—radiated a kind of extra internal heat that Kate, a native Oregonian, envied. He'd never understood how she was always cold in the northern U.S. and Canadian cities they had moved to during his hockey career. San Jose had stayed at the top of her wish list, but none of the warmer-weathered clubs had ever traded for him.

Vancouver had been the closest in climate to what she was used to, but he'd been traded again after one season.

Lying motionless, she absorbed his heat, willing the stress to ebb out as warmth enveloped her within the bed's cocooned environment. Safe, that's how he always made her feel. Keith rolled over and pulled her close. She lay her head on his shoulder and promptly fell asleep.

• • • •

SHE WOKE ALONE IN THE huge bed, lists of tasks and worries already running through her head as she leapt out and was shocked to see the time. Nine-fifteen! And no noise in the house. It was sweet of Keith to let her sleep, but how had he accomplished it? Their daughters never had less than three arguments before getting belted up in the van.

A tour of the girls' bedroom and bath showed the normal detritus flung aside in the morning routine—right down to the four complete outfit changes Suze left by the closet door and cap off the toothpaste to prove Sam had brushed her teeth. As Kate returned the toothpaste cap, she wondered, not for the first time, if Samantha took on her tomboy attitude due to her nickname and whether Suzanne compensated by over-employing the feminine prerogative to change her mind. She hung, folded, and replaced everything back to some semblance of order, vowing once more to retrain her daughters to pick up after themselves.

Yeah, right.

The note Keith left on the kitchen counter said he'd gone in early to cover for last night's replacement. The last line explained how he'd managed the impossible. *Promised the girls ice cream after school if you didn't wake up. Love, Keith.*

A quick swipe with a rag and the crock was ready for the dishwasher. One cup of coffee still sat in the pot. The brew had the burnt smell and bitter taste of being hours old, but it was warm, and she wrapped her chilled fingers around the mug while considering what to do next.

First thought was to phone Keith. But if she called he would probably run right home, which would lead to more speculation by his colleagues. Speculation about her. He hadn't been at the radio station long, and, though he had a contract, the McKenzies hadn't bought their house to just live in it one year. No, calling her husband was not an option. Last night guaranteed enough turmoil for WHZE to know about for some time, thank you very much. The crew didn't need a whiff of any more.

She grabbed a blank grocery pad and outlined a plan.

1) Talk to Tiffany after school.
2) Try to figure out what is in the you-know-what.

It seemed silly to not just say *the box*, but she didn't want to write anything to possibly later incriminate her. A sip of coffee gave her a new idea.

3) Visit Mrs. Baxter

The Nethercutt cook may hesitate reliving the incident of finding her employer poisoned, but Kate had no choice other than to try. She remembered Amelia saying something about Mrs. Baxter and her parents being in service to the family for generations. She assumed Amelia meant her own family, since she was from Hazelton originally, and Mr. Daniel was not, but the information needed to be confirmed. Yes, the cook definitely required an interview.

Kate wanted to get more of an idea, too, about how Amelia was poisoned. Hard to believe simply pouring water from a vase of lily of the valley would kill someone. How long did it take? What happened after Amelia drank the tea? Had death come slowly and tortuously, or fast and easy?

The last question was a bit too gruesome on an empty stomach. She put a piece of bread in the toaster.

How could she get information on poisons without setting off alarms? There was the Internet, but, while search engines functioned as the Web's natural organizers, they always seemed to want to show off for Kate, pointing up all the hundreds of thousands of sites available on any subject. She'd heard of ways to winnow down the data, but she hadn't yet mastered the technique.

"Plus, who wants to start getting spam emails from assassins or Homeland Security?" She snapped her fingers and wrote:

4) Visit library

The perfect place to research poisons—just hide in the shelves and read. She'd begin with books today, then gear up for a big Internet safari in the evening if she came home emptyhanded. Though all bravado aside, at the moment she felt very alone. Before the urge for pity overcame her good intentions, the toast popped up, and the doorbell rang. She slipped the notepad into her sweatshirt's big front pocket and went to see who was calling.

Meg fidgeted on the front porch, looking great in emerald sweats, and waving a newspaper. "Gil went in early and grabbed a morning edition of the paper. Not much in it yet, but I thought you might like to read what the police have released. Meanwhile, I'm dying to learn the inside scoop. I've worked my flowerbeds outside and made the human beds inside. I even washed the breakfast dishes and stacked newspapers for recycling. Basically, I'm out of ways to waste time, and I have to know all about last night."

"You cannot imagine how happy I am to see you."

"Good."

Yet as she ushered her friend into the house, Kate panicked for a moment. Yes, they'd become increasingly closer friends in the last six months, sharing recipes and mothering tips, but the women had only recently reached the sharing-your-load plateau. Was this too big a load? Should she explain the predicament she found herself in? Could she? Looking into her friend's bright green eyes and questioning smile, Kate let her heart override her brain. More than anything, she needed a friend's help, and when one showed up at exactly the right time, she recognized she should just accept fate's gift. "Come into the kitchen, and I'll tell you everything."

Meg made a new pot of coffee while Kate spread jam on her toast and spilled her troubles. Fifteen minutes later the aromatic brew was forgotten, and breakfast sat stone cold, but all of the new skeletons had been trotted out of the McKenzie closet. Or in this case, the washing supplies cupboard.

"That's incredible." Meg shook her head, her gaze straying toward the mud room doorway. "You say the box is now in your office?"

"Yes."

"And you can't get it open?"

"I tried everything last night."

A glint appeared in Meg's green eyes. "Even a hammer?"

"Oh, I couldn't. It's not my property."

"You're being set up to take the fall for murder. The box's owner is dead. You're in no position to quibble about the care and handling of something whose presence may railroad you into a life sentence in prison."

Kate couldn't argue with her friend's logic. They needed to find out the contents and get rid of the thing, no matter what. "But it belongs to one of Amelia's heirs."

"One who, in all likelihood, probably killed her and is trying to frame you for the crime." Meg placed her hands resolutely on her hips. "Come on. Show it to me."

The ebony box remained inside its cardboard nest. At first, Kate felt relieved to find everything as she'd left it, but after withdrawing the object disappointment shot through her. "I keep thinking I must have dreamed everything. Hoping, I guess."

Meg turned it end-over-end, attempting the same techniques Kate had already tried to open the lid. "You're not dreaming, and something is definitely inside."

"But do we have to break it?"

"I would, but with two boys I'm used to more wreckage than you are. Broken items are a way of life in our house." Meg sighed, holding the box at arm's length. "If what you say is true, though, we don't have the right. The person this thing goes to may not be the person we're looking for. No matter how much I want to smash the scary thing into a billion pieces. How about if I lock it up in my safe deposit box?"

"Too dangerous. I couldn't ask you to do that."

"Nonsense." Meg slipped the item into her jacket pocket. "I'll go by the bank on my way to lunch with Mother, leaving nary a clue to anyone I have it. Or that you don't."

Kate chewed her lip. "I don't know—"

"Well, I do." Meg smiled and gave her arm a squeeze. "You need a plan. Consider this a start."

"Actually, I already started one." She pulled out the list. "Task number five was going to be deciding what to do with it, but I guess that's covered."

Meg scanned the items on the page and nodded in agreement, adding, "Sounds like exactly the right plan, but I can almost guarantee no one came to your front door last night. I sat at my living room window all evening waiting for you to come home and doing cross-stitch until my eyes gave out during the late news."

Kate grinned, and the redhead added, "No, I'm not a nosy neighbor. Just a concerned one."

"Absolutely." Kate wrapped her newest best friend in a hug.

The moment passed, and Meg cleared her throat. "I'll find out what I can from Mother about Amelia. News of the murder has definitely hit every gossip circuit by now, so it won't be an unusual topic to bring up at a Hazelton ladies' luncheon. Two of her garden club members are joining us. We may have a real hen party by the time the salad plates get whisked away."

Meg's mother had owned a local dress shop for years, retiring the previous fall to grow hybrid roses and get reacquainted with an ex-salesman husband who'd traveled too much during their four decades of marriage. Lunch out had become a weekly event, chiefly to give Meg's mother a break from her father.

Talk of the midday mother-daughter event made Kate miss her own mom even more. Hers, though, had been more likely to plan an environmental protest than a ladies' day out.

"Great." She swallowed the lump in her throat. "We'll meet and trade information after school."

CHAPTER FOUR

NEWS UPDATE—

Wealthy Socialite Murdered

Hazelton, VT., (AP)—*Authorities called a press conference to report the murder of millionaire heiress, Amelia Nethercutt, née Lane. Death is reported due to poisoning, and Vermont State Police Lieutenant Walter Johnson says authorities are pursuing a number of leads. Law enforcement spokespersons acknowledge the autopsy was put on expedited status by the governor and showed death was a result of poisoning. Johnson would not elaborate on suspects, however sources reveal a number of local residents already questioned as material witnesses. Preceded in death by the recent demise of husband Daniel, the couple was known for strong ties to the arts and philanthropic work. A well-known local garden club supporter...*

• • • •

MEG LEFT TO PREPARE for her lunch mission, and Kate pulled the phone book from the desk drawer. Three Baxters made up the total listings for the area, but after dialing all three, she found herself exactly where she'd started. Nowhere. Men answered at two of the numbers, but neither had any idea who her quarry was. The third hung up before she'd had a chance to ask.

Kate grabbed the spiral notepad she'd mentally labeled her "casebook." No need to add the "put you-know-what in a safer place" chore, though she still felt guilty about letting Meg assume the responsibility.

"Darn it. I'm obsessing again." Another snap of the rubber band added to her weekly total, but it was still better than one would imagine under the circumstances. At least that was what Kate told herself as she took a couple of slow, deep breaths. Then she bit her lip and brainstormed on the blank lines.

1) Go by Amelia's mansion—see if someone is living in and can tell me how to reach Mrs. B.

2) Check with local employment services to see if Mrs. B signed on for a new position.

Of course, the last would be unlikely. The murder had occurred too recently. And who's to say the family planned to terminate Mrs. Baxter at all? One of Amelia's children might employ her. Yes, a mansion visit offered the better option, but what could she use as a cover story? A condolence call? Given the circumstances, wouldn't it be more appropriate for Kate to make her condolences at the funeral home?

Well, forget social convention, I need to know now.

She pulled off her hoodie and detoured into the bedroom. Her peach-colored, light wool suit was perfect for a Vermont spring day, pastel for the season, but warmer than it looked. A quick trip by Hazelton Flowers, and Kate was soon wending her way up and around the mountainous country lane. Dazzling sunlight played peek-a-boo behind the dense tree line, and no neighbors' homes were visible as the van moved in and out of the wooded switchbacks toward the Nethercutt gates. Kate frowned as she realized how isolated the mansion was, hidden from outsiders by its surrounding stone walls and forests of near fully-leafed hardwoods and evergreen pines. She knew other people lived on this mountain, along the fringes of the Nethercutt property, but neighbors obviously guarded their privacy as much as Amelia and Daniel had.

Kate set the hand brake and rolled her shoulders to relieve her stress, once more wishing she'd gotten something close to a full night's sleep. She stepped from the vehicle, potted gladioli in hand and words of sympathy running through her head. But she lost her train of thought when a man in a gray suit raced through the side yard and disappeared around the back of the mansion.

Who was that, and why was he running? Had something else happened?

She shoved the plant back onto the floorboard and tore off in pursuit as fast as her beige pumps allowed. Rounding the corner of the house she almost collided with Gray Suit. A bit above six-foot, the middle-aged man stood arguing with Danny in front of a Deco-inspired greenhouse.

"Don't disappear while I'm talking to you, young man," Gray Suit ordered. He and the teen traded laser-fueled looks.

Danny's face flushed at Kate's sudden appearance. His arms were crossed tightly enough to meld together, but he wiggled a thumb in her direction. "Um, Dad, we have company."

The man whirled, his surprise at seeing was her replaced a split-second later by a calm that bespoke years of practice.

Danny made the introductions. "This is the lady Gramma hired to organize the place.

Name's Kate something. I forget." He jerked his head in Gray Suit's direction and addressed Kate. "My father, William Nethercutt."

Extending a manicured hand, Danny's father said, "Nice to meet you. Kate McKenzie, right? Mother spoke about hiring you. Call me Bill."

Kate shook his hand. "Hello...Bill, I apologize for the intrusion. I just wanted to come by and say how sorry I am about Amelia. I have a plant..." She waved toward the front. "In my van."

Bill smiled, but Kate didn't like the look in his eyes. Not cold, exactly, but definitely calculating. His voice, on the other hand, could only be described as too-immediately-friendly. "Very nice of you. I'll walk you around. We have cake and coffee inside. The neighbors have been..." Then turning to Danny, he finished instead with, "Come along, son. We'll continue our discussion later."

They split up at the walk. Bill went to unlock the front door, and Danny followed Kate.

"I appreciate the help, but I really can manage." She opened the sliding door.

"No problem." The teen hefted the pot and grinned. "I've always been taught a Nethercutt man helps lovely ladies whenever he can."

Ooh, a player today. Kate returned the smile. "Well, I do appreciate it. So, did your uncle give the MG a clean bill of health?"

His expression fell. "Dad said, uh, I gotta wait for a while."

"Oh, I am sorry. Is it because of your grandmother's death?"

Relief flashed across the young man's face. "Yes. Yes, but things'll work out soon."

"I'm sure they will." Kate placed a hand on his arm.

His response was anything but grieving, and Kate figured he'd better forget any hope at a career in poker playing. Danny was clearly not mourning the loss of his grandmother. True, Amelia had been his *step*-grandmother, but given the fact she'd been in the family most of his life, *and* had gifted him a car, didn't that naturally presume some closeness between the two? On the other hand, it seemed as if he wasn't getting that car after all now. Something else to dig into.

Danny moved ahead of her in a loose lope.

The teen was cool and charming. Talking with the person he'd fingered to the police the night before didn't seem to prey at all on his conscience. Kate caught up to him again on the broad steps and added, "I'd like to offer my condolences to the cook, Mrs. Baxter, too. It must have been horrible for her yesterday. You don't happen to know where she lives, do you?"

"Gatehouse." Danny used his free hand to point to a cottage near the east end of the property. "Gramma let her live there so she could walk to work. She can't drive."

"But how did she get to and from the grocer's?"

"Took a cab."

Yes, Kate remembered Mrs. Baxter saying a cab was waiting before she'd left for her errands. The neat little gatehouse seemed perfect for a single woman. At least she had the impression Mrs. Baxter was widowed. Where had she gotten that idea?

Kate turned back to Danny, as he added, "When she was ready to come home she called, and Gramma told Dad to go pick her up."

So, Bill was definitely around at the time the body was found. It didn't prove he was onsite as the poison was administered, but he could have added the water to the teapot on his way back through the kitchen after receiving his chauffeuring orders.

"Did your dad help check out the car with your Uncle Thomas yesterday?"

Danny shrugged. "He wasn't much help. Tax attorneys aren't really comfortable around motor oil. Not like he was in any hurry to get back to me and Uncle Thomas, either."

Warning bells sounded in Kate's head. "I'm sure he was helpful carrying in the groceries for Mrs. Baxter."

Another shrug. "Mostly Uncle Thomas did. We hadn't realized how close to five it was, and I reminded Dad about meeting Mom for dinner. She and Gramma don't...didn't get along. Divorce didn't change anything. Mom always made it a practice to schedule something to screw things up whenever she knew Dad and I were coming here. Anyway, we unloaded the bags to the side porch, and Uncle Thomas took stuff into the kitchen. Mrs. B's screams kind of made everything come to a halt."

"I can't imagine how horrible..."

Danny twitched one shoulder, shrugging off the thought, and ushered her inside. The interior seemed much as Kate remembered, but not quite. She tried to decide on the difference and realized a lighted display case was missing from the foyer. "Wasn't a collection of porcelain here?"

"Yeah, Aunt Sophia snatched that early this morning. She had two guys and a truck in the driveway at eight. Said it was Grandpop's, and he'd always promised it to her. Dad tried to argue with her, you know, wait 'til the will is read and all, but she didn't listen. Big surprise."

"Danny..." Bill Nethercutt exited the kitchen, tray in hand. "Let's not rattle the family skeletons." He smiled at Kate. "I'm sure you know the way to the parlor." With an inward sigh, she headed back to the room of the damned.

• • • •

KATE BROKE FREE FROM the Nethercutt men as soon as niceties allowed. As her tires bounced over the cobblestone drive she glanced in her rearview mirror and saw the pantomime of their argument resume. Too bad there wasn't any way to overhear without being obvious. Both father and son required further investigation.

The converted gatehouse sat nestled under tall hemlocks and could be a model for the grandmother's cottage in Little Red Riding Hood. At Kate's knock, Mrs. Baxter opened the door, her eyes huge and watery blue behind a pair of wire-rimmed glasses. It took a second for the plump woman to realize who Kate was, but she quickly recovered. "Oh, yes, you were the organizing lady at Miss Amelia's." Mrs. Baxter smiled and waved her into a seat, then left the room promising refreshment.

Comfortable in an overstuffed chair, Kate glanced around the small cottage and imagined herself swaddled in a tea cozy. Chintz covered the furniture, and cat figurines posed on small shelves and across the narrow windowsills. It completely clashed with the streamlined kitchen work area at the Nethercutt mansion. She wondered about the incongruity but didn't have much time to think further as Mrs. Baxter bustled in carrying a tray of cups and a tall stainless-steel carafe. A rich coffee aroma filled the crowded room.

"I must apologize." Mrs. Baxter passed a sugar bowl and tongs. "Normally I would offer tea and scones, but...after..."

Kate's words rushed, "No, I should be the one apologizing, showing up here today of all days." She set the sugar bowl next to her cup and saucer, and then wrapped Mrs. Baxter's hand in her own. "I had such a horrible ordeal with the police yesterday, I think I needed to find someone who could help make some sense of it all. But like you, tea is anathema to me. When I couldn't sleep last night, I chose warm milk for the exact same reason you brought coffee. Oh, I'm rambling. I should never have come."

Mrs. Baxter used her free hand to pat Kate's. "Nonsense. You're entirely right to be here. How else to get to the bottom of this silliness? Hauling everyone into the station like common criminals! They *fingerprinted* me. Of course, my fingerprints covered the house." The snowy head shook in indignation. Mrs. Baxter pulled free and took a tissue from her peacock-blue dress pocket.

"I didn't mind the printing," Kate said, savoring the unusually nutty flavor of the coffee's rich blend. "Like you, however, I did feel uneasy having to defend myself. I had no motive to kill Amelia."

The cook's mouth formed a straight line. "Isn't that the truth? Like the woman's heirs haven't been itching to grab their inheritances for years. And, of course, Sophia blamed Miss Amelia for Mr. Daniel's death."

"What?"

"Oh, yes." Mrs. Baxter added two sugar cubes to her own coffee and stirred. "For the past year, Mr. Daniel's heart condition had been worrying everyone. His poor doctor had a devil of a time trying to get his medicine stabilized. But Miss Amelia tired of our Vermont winter and decided it was imperative they go to Washington in time for the cherry blossoms and another few days to jaunt around

Georgetown searching for *new collectibles*. Followed it all up with the silly homecoming party. Completely wore out the poor man's heart. He died the same night, as if... Well, I hate to mention anything that hints of gossip, but it was..." Mrs. Baxter motioned Kate closer, lowering her voice, "Almost as if Amelia had planned the whole thing as a kind of...a send-off."

While Mrs. Baxter's hesitant speech and affected actions suggested discomfort at the revelation, Kate couldn't miss the light that gleamed deep in the woman's eyes. Mrs. Baxter's bitter words echoed the comment Amelia made the day she died about widowhood versus divorce. Had Amelia said it more than the one time? The words had come right after Mrs. Baxter's departure for the store, but had the cook actually left? It would have been easy for her to stay out of sight in the hall and overhear the conversation. Did she really know something about Mr. Daniel's death that threw a shadow of suspicion on the murdered woman? "Did the doctor tell them not to go?"

"Not exactly." Mrs. Baxter took an exploratory sip of coffee. "But it's no secret whatever Miss Amelia wanted, Miss Amelia got."

"Did anyone in her family resent her for being controlling?"

"Resent her?" Mrs. Baxter laughed so hard she had to put down her cup. "They didn't resent her. They *despised* her."

"Everyone?"

"Except for Mr. Daniel." Mrs. Baxter took a ladyfinger from the cookie plate. "He adored Miss Amelia. Even after ten years of marriage, he wanted to do whatever made her happy. Infuriated his son and daughter. Would you like a cookie, dear? I made them fresh this morning."

Kate accepted a melt-in-the-mouth butter cookie from the plate and planned her next question. "So, did you begin working for the Nethercutts once they returned to Hazelton?"

"I've always worked for the Lane family. That's Miss Amelia's maiden name," she explained. A well-fed calico sauntered in, melding beautifully with the surroundings. "Ah, Lady Puss, you're gracing us with your presence, I see."

"What a beautiful cat."

"Yes, a gift from Miss Amelia." Mrs. Baxter leaned down to scratch the cat's chin. "Rescued from one of the backyard trees, and she didn't have the heart to call the animal shelter."

"You've been a longtime friend, then?"

"All my life, dear. My mother was the family cook. My father tended the automobiles. I was scullery maid, pastry assistant, and childhood friend, whichever was appropriate to the moment. Miss Amelia had to let everyone go after her parents died, what with her getting married and living abroad. But once she remarried this last time to Mr. Daniel, and returned to Hazelton, I was the first person she called."

"Sounds like she thought a lot of you."

"Of my talents, you mean." Mrs. Baxter gave a brisk nod. "Knew I learned beside my mother, and Miss Amelia always adored her cooking. We needed more help around the place, to dust and straighten everything, but Miss Amelia was tight regarding daily people. Only had a crew come in once a week."

Here was a new angle. "When were they last in the house?"

"The Friday after Mr. Daniel's funeral." Mrs. Baxter sighed. "A lovely service. The minister did Mr. Daniel right, though the Nethercutts' idea of church attendance was to do little more than send in the tithes they wrote off on their taxes at year-end. But, I never knew a man better than Mr. Daniel, and he deserved every fine word spoken over him."

Okay, the cleaning people were out unless one of them had a key. Made a wax impression at some time? Was anything taken? She couldn't remember hearing anything like that in the police station, but Sophia said something the day they'd met. "Did the officers mention missing items when they interviewed you?"

"I was traumatized over finding the body." Mrs. Baxter answered in non sequitur fashion, her drifting gaze showing a mind firmly elsewhere, across time and space to the previous day, standing once more in the deadly parlor. Kate shivered as she watched the age-spotted hands shake at the memory and return the cup to its saucer.

"I'm sorry—"

"Such an agonized expression." Mrs. Baxter's eyes glossed over. Her right hand covered her own face at temple and cheek.

Kate recognized the signs. Mrs. Baxter was revisiting a trauma to which the cook had never meant to return and now couldn't forget. She tried to switch the subject, but Mrs. Baxter blazed on, apparently past any diverting effort. Her need for exorcising the memory remained too great to easily overcome.

"Miss Amelia had been in tremendous pain, clutching her middle. I'll forever associate the smell of vomit with the poor woman," Mrs. Baxter recounted. "Overpowering, I tell you. I grabbed Mr. Walker's arm. He was her attorney and just arrived for an appointment. If he hadn't helped me to a chair I think I would have fainted dead away. Oh!"

Kate patted Mrs. Baxter's hand in sympathy. She remembered what the lieutenant had said the night before about the body's discovery. While she knew it was unreasonable and unfair, she wished the attorney had seen Amelia first and stopped this poor woman from stumbling onto the sight.

Mrs. Baxter shook her head. "Mr. Walker took charge. We saw him ringing the front bell as Mr. William and I drove up. But, of course, Miss Amelia never answered the door herself. I called from the car window, and he walked around the back to come in with Mr. Thomas and myself."

"You mean Amelia's son," Kate clarified. "Why didn't he let the lawyer inside?"

"Couldn't hear the door chimes out in the garage." Mrs. Baxter's gaze drifted out the window, toward the mansion, and her voice grew softer. "Mr. Walker made all the necessary phone calls. It seemed mere seconds before the police arrived, though likely much longer. Time's tricky like that. Thank goodness Mr. Walker hadn't given up and left. Everyone fell to pieces once Miss Amelia was discovered."

Silence reigned for several seconds. The coffee had gone cold, and Kate gathered the cups and saucers, returning them to the tray. "It must have been devastating. I'm truly sorry."

"We were close as children you know." Mrs. Baxter stared vacantly out the front bow window. "Gave me all her hand-me-down clothes and toys. Always thought of me first whenever she got something new."

"She was a dear friend."

Mrs. Baxter's head pivoted sharply, and her gaze bore into Kate's. "Most people don't realize that."

Kate was at a loss, wondering where to lead the conversation. She thought of Danny. "I met Miss Amelia's grandson right before I left that day. He seemed to really like your cookies."

With a snort, Mrs. Baxter topped off the cups with hot coffee from the carafe. "He just had the *munchies*."

"Well, he is a teenage boy. I don't have one myself, but I'm told they eat like herds of horses and grow nonstop."

"Oh, Danny's growing all right." Mrs. Baxter pursed her lips, like she would let go of a secret if the right question was asked.

"I don't understand."

"Danny's into plants and...things." Mrs. Baxter moved her lips, almost like a fish.

"Things *organic*."

"Yes, I noticed the greenhouse, and a lot of teens are into natural foods."

"Not that kind of organic." Mrs. Baxter took a sip of coffee, then raised the plate and offered another cookie. Kate held up a hand, smiling her thanks-but-no-thanks, and the older woman continued, "Oh, he claims he's just growing flowers in the greenhouse, and carts around those bottles of supplements. Always trying to get me to take some of them hocus pocus pills. But he can't fool me." She leaned closer again and whispered, "I've smelled marijuana smoke on his clothes."

Interesting. The daily headlines screamed about rising teen drug use. *Look at all the Ecstasy stories, and the date rape drugs. Roofies.* The thought made Kate want to run to find the twins and lock them in their room until they turned twenty-five. "Did you ask Danny about it?"

"No need." The well-nourished cat returned and performed a graceful leap into Mrs. Baxter's ample lap. "Miss Amelia smelled it, too. Recognized the nasty smell from the days she dealt with her ne'er-do-well son, Thomas. In fact, the bum dropped by that afternoon because he wanted to get more money off his mother."

"I thought Thomas came to check over the car for Danny," Kate prodded.

Mrs. Baxter sniffed. "The man doesn't mind getting his hands dirty, that's for sure. Could have told Miss Amelia he wasn't a good influence on Danny. Not my place, of course."

"What happened when she smelled the marijuana on Danny?"

"Miss Amelia took her grandson by the ear and marched him right into the study." Mrs. Baxter gave a decisive nod. "Even with the door closed their yelling came through. Then the boy slammed out of the house a half-hour later."

"Exactly what day was that?" Kate asked.

"Monday."

Two days before Amelia's murder.

"With them yelling, did you understand any of what they said?" Kate prompted, feeling creepily voyeuristic despite this being a mission of self-preservation.

As her hand stroked the purring cat, Mrs. Baxter's face took on the same self-satisfied expression the feline wore. "I could only pick up the stray word, but I definitely heard 'lawyer' and 'inheritance.' Both of which were in Miss Amelia's voice."

CHAPTER FIVE

To stay motivated:
STACKED IN YOUR FAVOR, LLC
KATE MCKENZIE, PRES.

• • • •

Friday afternoon, April 9th

• • • •

WORDS TO STAY ON-TRACK:
"The person who makes a success of living is the one who sees his goal steadily and aims for it unswervingly. That is dedication."
— Cecil B. De Mille —

• • • •

GOAL(S) FOR THE DAY:

- *Need to get in touch with Jane—ship enters Port of Miami, Sat. a.m.*
- *Trade info with Meg—find out what she learned at lunch.*
- *Take meat out of freezer to make cheeseburger potatoes for dinner.*
- *Call Keith—see if he'll be home during his afternoon break to talk.*
- *Find Tiffany*
- *MOST IMPORTANT—Take girls for ice cream or my name is Mud!*

• • • •

DESPITE HAZELTON'S tiny, bucolic aesthetics, lunchtime along Main Street was always a busy place, with steady, brisk trade. A tour bus stood in the parking lot of Molly's Café, its passengers offloaded for food and a stretch. A nearby auction meant droves of antique hunters prowled the shops. Kate wasn't sure which direction to head after leaving Mrs. Baxter's but felt she needed to find someplace that seemed normal.

Like the Book Nook.

Saree Modine was a Jamaican transplant by way of a New Orleans marriage. She'd arrived in Hazelton after her husband, Marcel, a professor of art history, gained a position at nearby Bennington College. Her bookstore and coffee bar, as eclectic as her life's journey, boasted cheerful ambiance, comfy chairs, offbeat inventory, and the best hot drinks in town. Kate found it instantly charming, and the special kinship the women shared for why they'd moved to the area created another bonus. When Kate asked how the couple adapted to the Vermont climate, a blush had colored the young woman's café au lait cheekbones, and Saree had said with a giggle, "We be newlyweds forever, we keep livin' here, no? Nothin' better for stayin' warm than keepin' those sheets dancin' these cold northern nights."

Kate vowed then and there to spend all her free time in the shop with the upbeat, curly-haired sprite.

The van's clock read nearly one o'clock, and Kate looked forward to more than a haven from conflicting thoughts and theories. She hoped a bite of lunch and cup of caffeine might settle her stomach as well.

In the store entry, a poster on an easel displayed a smiling shot of Kate. She grinned and read the announcement for "A Night with an Organizational Expert." Months earlier Saree had asked her to speak on spring cleaning and clutter-busting and scheduled the event at what had seemed far into the future.

But the future is a few days away!

Though Kate had faithfully prepared, writing succinct notes on index cards, it was a bit of a shock to realize her fifteen minutes of fame were fast approaching. More jitters to abate. She turned toward the café section of the shop.

Three couples lingered over their meals, but another pair showed signs of leaving. Kate dropped her purse at the table in the far corner and ordered a cup of green tea with mango and a vegetarian muffaletta from the young man at the counter. She planned on splitting the decadent sandwich into thirds and taking two parts home for the girls to eat over the weekend. While her twins would live on pizza, hotdogs, and hamburgers if given the chance, they never failed to eat anything from Saree's. Kate intended to put the huge sandwich's good nutrition to excellent use.

Said storekeeper, wrapped in a dress of swirling kaleidoscopic colors, stood at the main register ringing up a book sale, but she headed to Kate's table as soon as her happy customer jingled out the door.

"Ah, Kate McKenzie." Saree flashed a smile. "Did you see your sign?"

"I did, Saree. It made me feel truly professional."

Saree laughed. "You are that, chickie." She checked back over her shoulder, then added, "I believe I join you a moment."

"Tea and company." Kate nodded, and Saree's calm embraced her. She'd been right to come here. "Yes, please join me."

Bringing back a java brew smelling of cinnamon, Saree cocked an eyebrow and asked, "What troubles your soul, chickie?"

Kate reviewed her options. Once again divulge the whole sad tale to someone else before she told it all to Keith? Or shrug off her friend's concern and claim overwork and motherhood? A split second later she decided the latter wasn't an option. Her psyche had chosen the Book Nook for a reason. Still, telling Saree everything didn't seem the best plan either. Kate improvised. "I lost a client yesterday."

Saree waved her hand in a graceful gesture. "Their loss, chickie. I lose customers, I say I find more. You be good at your job."

"You don't understand." Kate took a sip of the fruity tea and contemplated her next words. "My client and I didn't part ways, she died. No, she was murdered."

The lithe dark hands flew to the flawless cheeks. "Miss Amelia?"

Kate nodded. "Apparently right after I left for the day."

"Such nastiness in this world." Saree pursed her lips, her forehead creasing with thought. "Miss Amelia, she grew beautiful flowers."

Kate recalled the elegant greenhouse behind the mansion, where she'd discovered Danny and Bill Nethercutt arguing. She considered what Mrs. Baxter alluded to regarding Danny's growing habits.

"Chose many books on flowers, she did." Saree smiled again, and her accented lilt rose with the memory. "Her grandson, he come with her often. She come alone sometimes, too, lookin' for new books and such."

"You know Danny?" Kate's muffaletta arrived, along with her requested takeout container.

"I know him, yes. Know most the family." Saree gestured toward the white box. "Takin' my good food home to your little beauties, eh?"

Kate nodded as she divided the sandwich and picked up a wedge. "I can always get the twins to eat veggies if I say they came from you."

"Sweet things." Saree made a tsking sound. "Too bad Miss Amelia didn't have such sweet chicks."

The muffaletta suddenly tasted like cardboard. Kate put it back on the plate and wiped her mouth with a napkin. "What are your impressions of Miss Amelia's family?"

Saree shook her tight curls, and sadness washed over her face. She leaned close and whispered, "They not really care about her, no.

I hear them, grandson and son, talkin' when they come to get her order. Orchids, them books were. I walk away a moment. Come back and hear them call her names, the nasty b-word. Complain about tight purse, how she greedy, stingy. Cannot wait for her to die." Her hand flew up and covered her mouth. A second later she said, "I misspeak. I not mean to say—"

Kate squeezed Saree's arm. "We're just talking here. Two friends. What can you tell me about lily of the valley?"

"You're plantin' them?"

Kate smoothed her napkin as she bit her lower lip. The police hadn't said she couldn't say anything. "That's how someone poisoned Amelia. In a cup of tea."

Saree rose, shaken, and lifted her nearly full cup from the table. "I have much work to do."

"Saree, I—"

As if to validate her escape, a young mother and tow-headed son moved to the register cradling armloads of brightly-colored board books. "I must go."

At a loss, Kate watched the retreating figure, then loaded the white box with muffaletta and pulled out her casebook. Everything Saree said confirmed what she had already heard from Mrs. Baxter and surmised for herself. She was no longer hungry but taking time to jot down notes would allow the crowd to clear and give her an opportunity to speak to Saree again before leaving. Plus, whatever she got onto paper spent less time rolling around as obsessive thoughts later.

Turning to a fresh page, she headed it "General Info & Witness Statements."

General Info & Witness Statements (and New Questions)
William "Bill" Nethercutt:
Is Amelia's stepson—Sophia's brother—Danny's father.

Seems to be in huge disagreement with son over MG. Why?

As a tax attorney, how much did Bill know about Amelia's estate? How would Mr. Daniel's portion of the estate get divided? Kate needed to learn if everything sat in trust for Amelia's lifetime, or if it all went directly to his loving wife. And what about the missing hall display case? Bill hadn't liked Danny telling Kate that Sophia swiped it.

Danny:

Is Amelia's step-grandson.

Huge fight with father this a.m. Is that this father/son usual dynamic?

Seems ready to implicate everyone as possible murder suspect.

Doesn't act at all nervous about pointing the finger in my direction—if he did.

At the police station Kate thought Danny had labeled her top suspect and chief patsy, but her field trip told her she was one of many. The teen had no compunction at pointing a finger at his father's disappearance. His Uncle Thomas hadn't gotten a break either. The way Danny told it, Thomas made several trips into the kitchen with groceries, presumably without supervision.

Funny, though, the teen never said anything to implicate Sophia. Why? His comments in the kitchen were anything but complimentary toward his aunt.

It would help to know the details of the changing will. Lieutenant Johnson alluded to minor alterations, but Kate remembered the way Amelia spoke to Sophia. *People like the viper don't sweat over minor alterations.*

Nothing was more fiscally responsible than dealing with matters like wills as soon as a change became necessary, but was it a coincidence Miss Amelia changed hers a week after Sophia mentioned disappearing household treasures? Were they stolen and hoarded? Sold? Or just used to incriminate Kate? She considered Mrs. Baxter's information about Danny's row with his grandmother mere days before her death. Did the police have a list of the missing pieces? Did Danny steal and sell the items? Or did Bill? Was that why he didn't want Danny talking about Sophia taking the foyer collection, worried it would draw attention to other missing pieces?

Logic told Kate she was on the right track. She just needed to get everything on paper and look for a pattern.

General:

Could any of the male Nethercutt clan have spiked the tea and gotten Amelia to drink it in time for the lawyer and Mrs. B to find her dead?

How long does the poison take to work?

At exactly what time was she found?

Kate dropped her pen, irritated with herself for neglecting to ask Mrs. Baxter the last question.

Another reason to visit the cottage again. Yes, I definitely should watch some detective shows. I stink at investigating.

As irritated as she was with her follow-through of the morning, she couldn't give up yet. A little logical deduction, noting everything that cropped up, and next time she would be ready.

Mrs. Baxter:

Longtime friend of Miss Amelia—family worked for Amelia's parents, the Lanes.

Hired immediately after Amelia returned to Hazelton

Says Amelia's family wanted her money & hated her for having a controlling manner

Overheard closed-door/marijuana row between Amelia & Danny two days before murder

All kinds of things lay buried in Mrs. B's revelations, but Kate couldn't be sure if the weirdness of their conversation was due to it being two days after Amelia's death or because the cook always spoke a bit duplicitously. She should have taken Meg along. Even if her neighbor didn't know Mrs. Baxter personally, she might have been more on point when reading the longtime Hazeltonite. Kate puzzled over how to interpret the dismissive tone the cook used speaking of Amelia's and Mr. Daniel's collections. Resentment could be a powerful force.

The weekly cleaning crew angle was promising. Kate remembered Mrs. Baxter never said whether anything was missing at the time of Miss Amelia's death, either.

She saw Saree conclude business with her customer and move on to straightening shelves.

Saree:

Heard Thomas (son) & Danny (grandson) grumbling over Amelia's thrift

Danny often to Book Nook with Amelia for new purchases. Was she training him to assume her gardening pursuits, or does he truly have an interest in flowers & plants?

Need to find out what kind of books Danny is interested in.

Saree might hold the answer to the last inquiry on her list. Could the gardening books Danny perused to share his grandmother's passion have provided the means of killing her?

Kate left a tip and headed for the back shelves where she'd seen Saree disappear. She found the shopkeeper sitting on the floor of the hobby section, a large gardening book in her lap.

"Authors try to save heartache, tell things in books to keep folks from hurtin'." Saree brushed fingers across an open page, a small, full-color photo of lily of the valley in one corner.

"Instead, words give strength to meanness, help curious ones deal death."

Kate knelt beside her. "Looks like we've been thinking along the same lines. I came to ask if one of Amelia's gardening books had information that included potential poisons." Saree turned the book, and Kate read the opened text.

Beware that all parts of lily of the valley are poisonous, as well as the water stems have sat in. Reaction is immediate. If anyone is suspected of ingesting any part of this plant, especially the leaves, victim should be immediately transported to the nearest medical facility.

The words "reaction is immediate" swam before Kate's eyes. At least she finally had proof anyone with an opportunity to slip into the kitchen could have killed Amelia. She could also forget stopping by the library. She had her answer.

"I never thought my books be bad," Saree said, sighing heavily as she took back the massive volume and slid it into the empty spot on the shelf.

"Nothing you could do." Kate patted her shoulder, then rose. "Anyone with a murderous heart will search until a means is found."

The women walked to the front of the store, silent until Kate reached for the doorknob.

"You take care, Kate McKenzie," Saree warned. "This mischievous one has put you within touchin' distance of a nasty deed. Take care you not smacked into its center."

The tinkling door chimes only heightened Saree's warning as Kate left the bookstore. She was already "smack into its center" and would remain there until the murderer was found.

She might lack faith in her detecting abilities, but Kate knew her organizing skills could help compensate for those deficiencies. It was too early to pick up the girls or interrogate Tiffany. The cruise ship wouldn't hit port in Miami until the next morning, but Jane might be reachable by cell phone. Besides, she didn't want her mother-in-law to get the tragic information at sea from an impersonal television source.

Kate whipped out her Android and punched in the number, but a mechanical voice delivered the "not currently in the calling area" message. Sighing, she headed for home. Maybe Meg would be back from lunch with her mother.

• • • •

MEG MET KATE BEFORE she could get out of the van. The emerald sweats had been exchanged for a flowing floral skirt in spring colors to accommodate her ladies' luncheon and spy mission, but green remained her blouse color of choice, only now in a sage hue. Waving a

sheet torn from a legal pad, Meg crowed, "The old girls really dished."

Kate motioned her inside. "Come on, we'll sit in the kitchen."

They traded information, Meg reading over the casebook while Kate studied the yellow page. Apparently, Amelia belonged to every gardening group in New England, and Danny had indeed been "crowned heir," happily assuming responsibility for the greenhouse whenever his grandparents left town. Additionally, one of the ladies remembered Miss Amelia worried right before Mr. Daniel's death, about Sophia campaigning to divert her father's attentions away from his wife.

"Did Amelia actually call Sophia a witch, and say she was working to alienate Mr. Daniel's affections from her? From Miss Amelia, I mean?" Kate asked, tapping the line with a fingertip.

"That's what Hyacinth told us."

"Hyacinth? Really?"

"Yep." Meg grinned. "Guess with that name she had to be in the gardening group. The Harley club wouldn't take her."

Kate laughed. It still seemed a little strange trusting someone else like this, but true friendship had been sorely missing from her life.

"You've set this all out in order, haven't you?" Meg mused as she turned a page in the casebook. "I just jotted everything down willy-nilly on a pad in my car."

Alarmed, Kate asked, "But they didn't know why you were interested, right?"

Meg shook her head. "Like I said, I wrote the notes in the car after I'd left. At the table, all I had to do was mention Amelia Nethercutt's name, and the *ladies* did the rest. I sat back and listened."

"What did your mother say?"

"Are you kidding? She was the worst gossip of the bunch. Nearly embarrassed me, until she gave the choicest tidbit of all."

Meg leaned across the table and pointed to a line near the bottom. Kate read:

Amelia discovered items in an antique store last week that should have been in an upstairs room of her home. Determined to unmask the criminal stealing and selling her possessions. Said she'd see the 'filthy thief' in jail if it was the last thing she ever did.

CHAPTER SIX

HOW TO KEEP A HAPPILY Organized Home
(for the organization presentation)

Unless you live alone, don't try to organize your home by yourself. Involve the same people who helped get your disordered abode into its present state. Teamwork isn't just more efficient timewise. It's critical if you want to make permanent organizational changes.

Learn as a team to clean as you go. No one is too young or too old to help in some way. Children can learn to put away one toy before taking out another, and the whole family can help load the dishwasher by rinsing and placing their own used tableware in after each meal. Hang hooks for coats and clothes, collect boxes and bins for toys, file paperwork as you're finished with it, and easily find what is needed later.

Most of all, don't expect perfection at all times—the white glove test died with the 1950s. Ten minutes a day of family pick-up time, with everyone pitching in once a week for an hour to accomplish the big cleaning, and your house will stay comfortable for daily living and inviting when unexpected guests arrive.

· · · ·

BEING MARRIED TO A hockey pro may have meant bright lights and her husband's triumphs in the papers. But as the trash talk between players piled onto the gossiping and sniping of the more competitive hockey wives, Kate had often dreamed of "less glamorous" ways for Keith to make a living. So when the team doctor had called early the previous fall to tell her Keith was in the hospital and needed a surgery that would likely take him permanently out of the game, she'd had trouble working up a sorrowful face for her husband's bedside.

The phone call two nights after the surgery seemed a clear lifeline to both of them—the management at WHZE reported a newly changed format and wanted a local sports star to anchor the nightly Sports Talk. Keith accepted the general manager's offer, and in two weeks they'd moved in with his parents in Vermont. The next day the girls were enrolled in the local first grade, and a month later the couple's offer was accepted on the house next to the Bermans.

Kate smiled, happy about their new life, as she turned the van into the Hazelton East Elementary pick-up circle. The school looked like something out of a Norman Rockwell painting; prim and neat in red brick and white trim. Swings and slides on one side, and Old Glory waving proudly in the circular median. She took her place in line behind the already-waiting vehicles, then nosed forward as teachers distributed children like as many shapes in a FisherPrice sorter ball.

"Buckle up, girls," Kate called as the twins clamored into the back seats and a teacher slid the side door closed.

"Mommy, Daddy said—" they began together.

"Yes, we're going for ice cream."

Ten minutes later Kate sat in a cotton-candy-pink and white booth. Across the table, the girls' tongues battled in a sticky ice cream marathon to see who could devour the dripping cones before the chocolate scoops of Ben & Jerry's ended up on hands and shirts. Kate skipped a treat herself, choosing to spend the time developing her plan of attack on Tiffany. She had to find out how the box had arrived in their home.

"Suze, Sam. Did any strangers come by the house last night?"

"Na-uh." Blond curls shook in choreographed tandem.

"No one you didn't know?" She pressed to no avail. Both girls encored the head shaking routine. Playing the good mom, she reached over with a napkin to catch a huge drip before it hit

Samantha's sleeve. "And Tiffany or Meg was with you in the house the whole time?"

Suze nodded, as Sam said, "Except when we heard the firecrackers."

"Firecrackers!" It was far too early for Fourth of July shenanigans. Hazelton statutes forbade fireworks of any sort in the town limits, and the law was strictly enforced. "Where?"

"Behind the house," Suze said between licks. "In the bushes at the little park."

A line of trees and grass circled the McKenzies' cul-de-sac. This green crescent buffer bounded the end of theirs and the neighbors' backyards. Christened "the park" by the girls, the end rolled up to a high-fenced creek screened by evergreens. While initially apprehensive about the nearby water, Kate had been thoroughly charmed by the sleepy little development, cut out from Vermont's emerald wilderness. The more they looked, the sooner she'd shared her family's initial enthusiastic opinion that the blue Victorian house made the top pick. Besides, she'd told herself, if the seven-foot fence didn't deter Sam from the creek, Suze would run and tattle.

But with this fireworks incident, those trees obviously can hide more than just the fence.

"Did you see who shot off the fireworks?" she asked.

Sam cut a look her sister's way, then stared intently at her ice cream as she replied, "It was dark, and Tiffany told us to stay in the house while she went out back to check."

The dropped gaze, coupled with the other twin's shamefaced expression, nudged Kate to dig deeper. "But you followed. Right?"

Suze bit her lip, and Sam offered an ambiguous shake of the head.

"Girls—"

"I told her we should've stayed in the house!" Suze gave her sister a stony glare and turned to her mom. "But Sam ran out the door, and I thought I needed to make sure she found Tiffany okay."

Kate wanted to grab Suze before the tears started, to hug the guilt out of her little body, but the issue was too important. Adopting a quiet tone and mother-down-to-business attitude, she said, "You both know the rules. If you have a sitter, the sitter rules."

Blond heads nodded. The distinctive sound of a sniff came from Suze's direction, and Sam had the grace to look slightly sheepish.

"I don't want to be difficult about this, girls, but you should have obeyed Tiffany. No matter how exciting following her might seem—" Kate raised an eyebrow at Sam, then turned to Suze "—even if the goal was to keep your sister out of more trouble."

"Are we going to be punished?" Suze asked, her half-devoured scoop running muddy rivulets down the back of her hand.

Sam, always cool under pressure, took a big swipe of her ice cream and suggested, "We could have to clean our room for punishment. That would make us remember to obey the sitter next time."

As if Kate hadn't already mandated the chore be completed by the following afternoon. *Oh, well, at least one Saturday task can get struck off the list.*

"It's a deal," Kate said. "Hurry and finish up, then go to the bathroom and wash your faces and hands."

All stress vanished, and the twins finished their treat in record time. While they were cleaning up, Kate mentally amended the questions she needed to ask Tiffany and was startled when the teenager actually appeared before her eyes, apron and white ice cream hat in hand.

"Tiffany? Do you work here?"

"Hi, Mrs. McK. Yep, most Fridays and all-day Saturday and Sunday—for the past month now." Tiffany put the apron to her waist and turned her back to Kate, holding the cotton ties behind her. "Can you tie this into a cool bow? Try to make it kinda sexy, okay?"

"I've never really had a talent for sexy apron bows, Tiff."

The teen sighed. "No one does, but a girl can hope."

Kate pulled the loops taut and said, "I thought you needed to be sixteen."

"Mom decorated the owner's place." Tiffany twisted, using the silvery, solar glaze on the window to check out her backside. "If I want a car next year, I have to earn some money."

Surprise, surprise. Kate had expected Valerie to produce a shiny, red Porsche for her beloved offspring. "Good plan, Tiff. In fact, I wanted to talk to you about your job last night."

"I told the girls to stay in the house."

"You're not in trouble. My daughters share an impetuous nature," Kate assured. "But I wondered how long all of you were outside."

Tiffany scrunched her forehead. "Five, maybe ten minutes. We couldn't find whoever shot off the fireworks. More of your neighbors came, and a couple had flashlights. That's when we found the burned firecrackers under one of the bushes." The teen's brown eyes grew large as she retold the drama. "Someone said it was a good thing we'd had all the rain lately or your neighborhood might've been torched."

"And the house seemed exactly as you left it?" Kate pressed.

"I guess so." Tiffany raised her right hand and chewed a cuticle. "The back door was open and the light on, but I figured we did that. Did somebody steal something?"

"No, no problem with stolen articles." Kate wondered what direction to go next. The heavy bathroom door clunked, and the girls created a weaving, skipping pattern toward her through the tables. Her sleuthing moment was over. "I just thought someone might have dropped by."

"Nobody except the pizza kid."

Sam and Suze hit Tiffany from both sides, enfolding her hips in a giggling hug.

"What pizza kid? You mean Louie?" Kate asked. Louie was the neighborhood delivery person for Hazey Pie, the town's local, award-winning pizzeria.

"Sure. Louie had a pizza for us, but we didn't order it." Sam grinned up at Tiffany.

"But you told me no one came to the house last night," Kate said.

"No strangers!" the girls chorused.

When would she learn? Meg hadn't mentioned seeing Louie either, or the firecrackers.

"It was some mistake," Tiffany said, returning the girls' hug. "Louie's ticket said your address, and he got plenty miffed. He called the dispatcher and argued a lot but finally left after I kept telling him we wouldn't pay for something we didn't order. I'm not sure what made him madder, though, the messed up order or the fact his cell battery was dead and he had to look up the number to call from your phone." She pulled her hair into a ponytail and clipped it under her hat. "I gotta go, Mrs. McK. My shift starts in a minute."

"Okay, thanks, Tiffany."

The aproned teen slipped behind the counter. Kate contemplated whether to detour by Hazey Pie to see if the order taker remembered anything about the person who placed the pizza delivery request. Could Louie be in the paid service of whoever tried to frame Kate, using the pizza delivery ruse as a ploy to get more than pizza into the house? After all, he had used the phone. Did he use the one in the entry or the kitchen?

She asked the twins and received shrugs in reply.

How carefully would Tiffany have watched if he'd used the kitchen phone? Would he have an opportunity to hide the box in the utility room? The more she thought about it, the more her mouth watered for a hand-tossed pie, and her brain hungered for answers to her questions. Maybe Louie should make a delivery to the McKenzie household that evening. They could have cheeseburger potato casserole any old evening.

• • • •

SHE HEARD THE TELEPHONE pealing from inside, as she shoved her key into the front door lock. Kate scooped up the receiver and heard the dial tone. Caller ID offered an out of area message.

"Darn."

"What's wrong, Mom?" Suze dumped her backpack on the entry hall bench.

"Nothing, sweetie. Missed the call." Kate pointed a finger at the adolescent detritus that littered the area at the girls' return. "Go ahead and take your things upstairs, you two. We don't want to walk around this all weekend. Change clothes and bring those shirts back. I can get everything into a presoak. And start your homework, too. You can do it at the kitchen table."

"But it's Friday!" Sam wailed.

"You're right. Start cleaning your room instead."

Kate hid a grin when Suzanne punched Samantha's shoulder. The pair banged up the stairs, the rumbling reminiscent of a herd of cattle. The phone rang again.

"Hello."

"Hi, dear. Can you hear me?" It was Kate's mother-in-law, Jane, on a static-filled connection.

"Barely. Where are you?"

"Close enough to Florida to finally use my cell phone," Jane replied. "The satellite TV in the lounge had a report at noon saying Amelia Nethercutt died. Is that true?"

"I'm sorry, but yes, very true." She'd been afraid of this. "I tried calling earlier to tell you but got an out of range recording."

"I didn't catch the cause of death. Was it her heart? What day is the funeral?"

Kate took a deep breath. "I haven't heard when services will be held. I imagine early next week. But in regard to her death, Jane, Amelia was murdered."

"Murdered!" Jane gasped. "Oh, poor Thomas. He'll be lost without his mother. I hope Sophia keeps an eye on him."

"Right now, the only thing she seems to be keeping an eye on is her inheritance." Kate explained the morning's discovery that Sophia had already removed the glass chest of collectibles.

"Sounds about right," Jane said. "I'm certainly glad she didn't collect Keith that time he came home from college. Though it surprised me she would even let the radio station hire him after my smart son spurned her affections all those years ago. Carrying long grudges has always been one of her gifts."

"Keith and Sophia?"

"Yes, hard to imagine. Isn't it?" Jane's chuckle mixed with cell phone static. "I thought since her husband has controlling interest in the radio sta—" The line went dead.

CHAPTER SEVEN

NOTES FOR MY ORGANIZATION Connection at the Book Nook:

Five Gremlins That Combat Organization Efforts

Fear of Failure. *Staying positive fights this meanie. You must think you can, like the "Little Engine That Could." Small progress is still progress and leads to big finishes.*

You'd Rather Do Something Else. *Overcome this tyrant by scheduling an early hour each day to work on organization, leaving the rest of the day free for more enjoyable tasks. Or make doing a favorite activity contingent upon completing specific projects.*

Setting Goals and Priorities That Are Too Broad. *Masked as a life-coach, this baddie challenges you to do your best but ultimately guarantees failure. Instead, define exactly what the assignment is. List each clutter-task—then prioritize. Do big stress chores first, and break everything into mini goals that can be completed within small periods.*

Trying to Finish Too Quickly. *Pushy gremlins get beaten when you realize many organization projects can't get done in one sitting. On the other hand, waiting until you 'have time' often means projects never even get started.*

Hanging On To the Past. *Sentimental and thrifty, this organizational jinx hates saying goodbye to anything. Determine each item's real importance. Strive to discard 30%. Can't bring yourself to throw away something still good? Give to charity or hold a tag sale.*

• • • •

SOPHIA AND KEITH. SOPHIA and Keith. Sophia and Keith.

An icy sensation had settled in Kate's spine after hearing the names together in Jane's voice, and she shivered as the names looped continuously in her brain, twining through treasured memories like demented ivy. All the conversations she and Keith had shared over the Nethercutt job, both before and after the murder, and he had never once mentioned anything about knowing Sophia. Why hadn't he said something?

Her conscious mind told her he'd just been taking the husbandly, wimp-out approach to the situation. But, that cold sharp fear at the base of her brain scratched like a finger scraping off a scab, and made her wonder if he...

No. She hadn't listened as those few witchy hockey wives whispered their lies whenever the team played away from home, so why should she build up deceptions in her own mind now?

Still...

The obsessive frigid finger tapped again, leaving her numb with the next thought. Could Sophia be setting Kate up in order to make another run at her former beau? He didn't answer his cell. She speed-dialed Keith at the radio station, taking deep breaths as ringing began at the other end.

The bright voice of Eileen, the station's pert, nineteen-year-old receptionist, answered after four rings. "WHZE radio. All talk all the time."

"Hi Eileen, it's Kate McKenzie. Can I speak with Keith please?"

"Um, sorry Kate, but he's gone to the Big Apple. Didn't he leave you a message?"

"New York?"

"Uh, huh. He took off with Mrs. Nethercutt-White about an hour ago on the corporate jet.

He has some big sports interview lined up for tonight."

Pain shot through Kate's left temple. She dropped her head into her hand. "I haven't checked the messages...Sorry I bothered you."

"Oh, no trouble at all." Eileen's voice maintained its cheerful chirpiness, never realizing what she'd said set off an atom bomb in Kate's world.

Sophia and Keith. Sophia and Keith winging their way together to New York City. Numb, Kate replaced the telephone on its cradle. Sounds of a developing screaming match drifted down from upstairs. She experienced guilty relief knowing her daughters would stay in their room, prolonging the argument unless she intervened.

Which won't be anytime soon.

She didn't like taking advantage of a negative situation, but she needed time, alone, to work through all of this.

In the kitchen, the phone system light blinked to signal a missed call and message. She loved the money they saved running voice-over-internet-protocol instead of a landline or souping up their cell minutes, but at that moment she hated their Ooma system. The long gap between each red flash silently accused her of being a fool. After she hesitantly pushed the touchpad's pulsing triangle, Keith's voice penetrated her funk.

"Hi, honey. I get to interview Wayne Gretzky in New York tonight while he's in town for some benefit. Can you believe it? Buzz was supposed to, but the boss thought it'd be better if a former hockey player, namely yours truly, interviewed the hockey legend. Is that awesome, or what? WHZE has connections with a TV and sound crew to tape the interview, too. If I do this right my ugly mug may show up on ESPN!"

Tears spilled from Kate's eyes.

"Anyway, I won't be home tonight. I'm really sorry. I figure you're probably still a little stressed about last night, but hey," his voice turned gruff for a moment, and he cleared his throat. *"The cops seem to be focusing their attention away from you, right? I talked to Gil at lunch, and he told me the paper's police beat reporter said the state guy pulled in the family members again. Wish I could be home with you, though, but the boss has business in the City tomorrow morning, and I gotta wait until the corporate jet returns to Vermont. Tell the girls I'm sorry about missing their soccer game tomorrow, but I'll bring something back for them—for you too. Love you, babe."*

The click at the end of his words sounded to Kate like a steel door slamming shut on her marriage. If he loved her so much, why hadn't he tried to reach her on her cell phone?

• • • •

KATE WANDERED SIGHTLESSLY through the house. When her fingers twisted nubby fabric she realized she stood by the sofa in the living room and had no recollection of walking there. She sank into its comfy embrace, conscious thought slipping away. Minutes passed, maybe hours. She had no idea how much time elapsed, or what her jumbled ruminations were all about until two blond heads popped up in front of her.

"What's for supper?" Suzanne asked.

"We're hungry," Sam added.

Better than a clock, the lengthening shadows outside the window marked time long past the regular McKenzie dinnertime. Kate sighed, took a second to get her bearings, then forced her way back into mom-mode and asked, "Your room's all clean?"

"Perfect!" the girls chorused.

"Even under the bed and in the closet?"

Sam gave a calculated nod, as Suzanne's shoulders shifted infinitesimally.

What to do, what to do. Forget it.

"Terrific. Want to go for pizza at Hazey Pie?"

She took their screams as assent and ushered them toward the van, driving in silence while the twins chattered nonstop behind her.

The aroma of spicy sauces assaulted the senses even before the girls wrestled open the heavy oak door. Waiting to be seated, Kate scanned for Louie, and the twins played hopscotch on the tiled floor.

"Is Louie on duty tonight?" she asked the high school-aged hostess. Their booth sat near the front window. Sam and Suze were handed coloring menus and individual quad-packs of crayons. The pair attacked the pages, each wanting to be the first to complete her artistic masterpiece.

"Sorry, no. He had to go out of town for a few days." The teenager smiled and turned to leave.

"Just one second." Kate stopped her. "By any chance is the person working who took phone orders last night?"

The hostess wrinkled her forehead. "Let's see, that was Pete and Ellie. Ellie's here, but Pete called in sick."

"Could I talk to her?"

The girl took a step back and looked at the order area behind the counter. "She's super busy."

"Well, could you ask her a question for me?" Kate heard desperation creep into her voice. The hostess apparently detected the anxiety, too, because she nodded and said, "Sure. What do you need to know?"

"A mistaken pizza order came to our house last night. I just wondered who placed the order."

Smiling ruefully, the girl said, "Happens all the time. People give the wrong address or a bunch of teenagers playing pranks."

"I'd like to find out whatever I can, though," Kate prodded. "I live at 223 Chestnut Circle."

With a shrug, the girl said, "No problem. I'll ask. A server will be by to take your drink order in a minute."

The hostess returned just as they slipped straws in their sodas. Her look made it clear the answer wasn't the one Kate wanted.

"Sorry, but Ellie said it was Pete. They talked about it for a second with Louie. He came back steamed from going out on a no-sale. She remembers Pete saying he'd thought he remembered a woman placed the order, but it was busy so anything's possible."

"Mommy, can I have an ink pen?" Sam was already tired of her crayons.

"Me too," Suzanne mimicked.

"Thank you," Kate said to the hostess, and grabbed her purse to search for additional drawing options.

Their segregated pizza, half artichoke hearts and sun-dried tomatoes and half pepperoni, arrived perfect. The girls dug into their spicier end with such zeal they stayed oblivious to their mother's somber mood.

Why were the two people she needed unavailable? Coincidence, or calculated? She longed to drag out a pad and pencil and scratch her thoughts and concerns onto paper but didn't want to explain to the girls. When none of the pepperoni side was left, Kate requested a carryout box for her half, minus the one piece she'd taken a single bite from and paid the bill.

They saw the phone message light pulse frenetically as they arrived back home.

"Hi, hon," Keith's excited voice came through the speaker. *"Thought I'd catch you now, but here's the update. Everything went great! Met up with some New Jersey Devils I know, too, and we're all going to get together tonight. I'm staying at the Metropolitan, room 447. Tell the girls I love 'em. Love you, too. Bye."*

Kate called Directory Assistance for the number of the Metropolitan Hotel.

"Keith McKenzie's room, please," she said.

After four rings, the hotel's automated voice mail came on. She didn't leave a message.

"Don't even worry about this," she muttered to herself, "He's just spending some hockey catch-up time with his Devils friends—not some demon home-wrecker."

"What mommy?" Suze asked.

Kate started. "Oh, nothing, sweetie."

"Okay." Her daughter smiled, then grabbed her Barbie off one of the kitchen chairs and skipped from the room. Kate wished reassurance came as easily for adults.

• • • •

ONCE THE GIRLS WERE asleep and the house quiet, Kate documented the questions rolling around in her mind. Danny and Sophia were top of her list at the moment.

Consider:

1. *Why is Danny implicating everyone in the murder—is he really trying to be helpful, or diverting suspicion from himself?*
2. *Why didn't Sophia say something about knowing Keith when we met at Amelia's? For that matter, why didn't Keith tell me Sophia had the hots for him ten years ago?*

She stopped for a moment and thought over the last entry. Was her earlier doomsday outlook due to lack of sleep and not having either of her most supportive allies around to talk to? Normally she took her problems and concerns to Keith or Jane. Should she try to talk everything over with Meg?

Kate sighed. Their friendship was too new to have the heavyweight foundation needed to unload this kind of personal baggage, but she knew the relationship might never advance any further unless she forced herself to let down her guard and allow Meg to really come into her world. Her neighbor had certainly done her part these past few months, always inviting Kate to activities, introducing her to anyone and everyone in town, and being a generally great person. She sighed again.

It wasn't that she didn't want to be friends, but her history whenever she took the chance to open up to people made her more than a little wary. Keith always teased about her reserve, but after having moved constantly during childhood—and having found herself in much the same program after becoming Mrs. Keith McKenzie, pro NHL goalie-wife—an attitude of caution in regard to personal relationships had become standard operating procedure. Couple that with certain toxic hockey wives. *Well...trust is a precious commodity.* She'd always been a worrier, she had to be with the lackadaisical way her parents had approached life, and things had gotten worse after the girls were born. She'd ended up in various therapy programs, but the therapist in Pittsburgh was the best and had been the one to convince Kate to write as many detailed notes as she needed to get all of the never-ending tasks and troubling thoughts out of her brain.

Funny how hard it was to escape the patterns created in childhood. Sure, all the family moving had honed her organizational skills at an early age, but the practice made it more difficult to be flexible. Each change gave her new things to stay concerned about, problems she was often still too immature to worry over—but that hadn't stopped her.

Friendships were a wild card she finally decided to forgo almost completely. Just as she thought she'd made a real friend in her new school, found a confidant—whoosh! Another day, another protest to hook her parents, and Kate found herself in another new apartment in another new town where her mother and father heeded a new calling.

Wait a minute.

Enough anger coursed through her veins from the current circumstances, she didn't need to dredge up kid-years ire, too. Her parents had a mission, and she'd just been trapped in the jet stream they'd created.

That's all, and that's history. She snapped her rubber band. Nothing positive came by revisiting the past, especially to keep from dealing with the present.

The question on the table was could she, and should she, open up to Meg?

Letting fate provide the final vote, she walked into the darkened living room and peered through the curtains of the front window. All the lights were out next door. Okay, question answered. Kate suddenly felt six years old again—and very, very cold. Moving to the kitchen, she pulled the cocoa from the pantry.

Funny how nothing the hockey wives ever said shook her nearly as much as this lost phone connection with her mother-in-law. Well, that and her husband's unplanned business trip accompanying an old flame.

She took her cocoa to the table, then penned her next two questions. The first was more than a little scary, but abject fear of the second made her stomach roil.

3) Is Sophia setting me up for the murder to cover up her own crime, or to try another attempt at Keith?

4) Has Keith seen Sophia since we've moved to Hazelton? Is he having an

She stopped short of writing the last word. *Affair.* Okay, she'd let the word slip into her thoughts, but an affair? Had she missed any signs? Sure, Keith came home at erratic times, but Kate knew how social he was, and he always told her who'd held him up to talk. No pattern of missing hours or nights, or any inconsistencies to point toward infidelity. He never smelled of strange perfume, and his shirt collars always came home lipstick-free. Kate paid the credit card bills and tracked down any dubious charges, but should she expect a credit card trail if they met at Sophia's or put the expenses on a corporate card? After all, they were presumably staying in the same hotel that very night. Moreover, what about Sophia's husband?

Who was the man who gave her the "White" to tack on after the hyphen?

Kate chewed her lower lip. She'd let fatigue and paranoia take control tonight. Nothing more. No way was her husband cheating on her.

In a bold move, she crossed out question number four and scribbled five more, almost as if each addition further reduced the likelihood of the struck sentence.

4) ~~Has Keith seen Sophia since we've moved to Hazelton? Is he having an~~

4) *Who picked the lily of the valley for the vase in the kitchen? Amelia, Danny, or Mrs. Baxter?*

5) *If questioned, will the pizza order clerk remember anything about the person (or voice) who placed the order delivered to our house some time after 7:00 p.m. on Thurs. night? Probably a long shot.*

6) *Who can tell me what Thomas is up to? Does his business need a transfusion of cash? Does Meg know anything about him?*

7) *Mrs. Baxter was a childhood friend of Amelia's. How well did the transition work out when it became an employer/ employee relationship?*

8) *What are Danny's plans for the future? Does he see himself as heir apparent to the Nethercutt Empire? What is the Nethercutt Empire?*

Jane might be the best lead on the last question. Maybe number seven as well. While Kate was only at the Nethercutt mansion the one day with Amelia and Mrs. Baxter, the women's attitudes toward one another had seemed strictly professional. No word or deed between the two on the day of the murder even whispered of a childhood bond, which had probably included dolls and pretend tea parties. However, through a succession of marriages, Amelia had been gone a good many years. Any friendship that survived such an absence would have a tough time staying on steady terms. And Amelia liked being in charge, regardless of any adolescent adventures the pair might have shared.

As an adult mistress of the manor, Amelia's manner likely sent a "keeping you in your place" message to anyone in her employ. Besides, how nostalgic can one be with a former friend when their places shifted from girlhood confidants to servant and mistress?

Mrs. Baxter's house also puzzled Kate, the frou-frou front room in sharp contrast to the stainless-steel coffee carafe. Yet equally at odds were the woman's décor and design employed in the Nethercutt kitchen—all work, no frills. If the kitchen in her cottage resembled Amelia's, that could tell the tale. Or, had she taken the carafe from the Nethercutt's? Had she removed anything else from the mansion?

9) Sneak by Mrs. B.'s cottage and peek in the kitchen window.

Kate smiled. She'd need some kind of backup excuse in case she got caught, but another side trip to Mrs. Baxter's place was definitely in order.

She paused. Even as she wrote each letter, she wished the ink would disappear from the page.

10) What was the value of the items Sophia took with the display case? And if she'd assumed those items belonged to her, could she have been the one pilfering valuables before Amelia's death—using the justification they were hers anyway?

11) Has anyone entered our house through the back door since Tiffany unlocked it and ran outside last night?

12) Do I dare call the police and ask them to look for fingerprints in my laundry room?

She already knew the answer to the last question. There was no possible way of getting official help unless she gave the police everything, and she couldn't do that, so number eleven was a non-starter as well. Getting the police to help answer either question would not only get her further entangled as a possible suspect but likely implicate Meg.

Kate closed the casebook. It was late. Maybe if she went to sleep her mind would work out all the puzzles and have everything solved by the time she woke in the morning.

"Sure. And maybe I'll figure out a way to clone myself, too."

CHAPTER EIGHT

SATURDAY, APRIL 10TH – To-do

- *Girls' soccer game—home field (thank goodness)*
- *Plan what to say to Keith.*
- *Pick up Jane and George this evening.*
- *Work on Book Nook presentation. Don't worry—really.*

• • • •

LISTS OF TASKS AND worries woke Kate before the alarm went off Saturday morning. Dawn was just a promise in the sky when she plopped onto the rattan loveseat on her front porch, warm in her tightly wrapped robe and bunny slippers, and holding a cream-filled cup of coffee. The comforting weight of her casebook lay in her lap. The sun rose in golden ribbons over the Green Mountains, glittering light mixing with the peaks' blue-green swaths and eventually pulling the sky awake to a clear, crisp blue. White pine, sturdy hemlock, and balsam trees created a darkened, shadowy palette. This solitude was what she needed. Nothing beat a bright new morning to ignite a person's determination toward solving a problem, she decided. Or two, or twenty.

Even a few minutes of solitude is priceless.

It could be a game-changer, she knew, offering new solutions and possibilities to hold stress at bay. She had no revelations but felt better capable of tackling the day ahead.

An hour later, she had the girls up, fed, and bullied into soccer uniforms, getting them out the door earlier than usual. She marveled at the smiling faces of her twins, and knew the extra time that morning made all the difference. Those few precious minutes, not having to rush like most Saturdays, added calm to her troubled soul and kept the girls from arguing their way past teeth-brushing to van loading. She was nearly out the door when the telephone rang. It was Keith, no doubt in her mind, but she had no intention of talking to him until his return. This was too big to discuss over the phone. She turned off her cell before he tried that communication avenue.

At the curb in her housecoat, Meg slipped envelopes into the mailbox and raised the flag. She waved down the van. "Just wanted to tell you I put the *package* in the safe deposit box yesterday."

The girls were already immersed in an argument over which sister was better at imitating Rock Star Barbie. Kate didn't worry about being overheard. "I can't tell you how much I appreciate your help. I'll figure out a way to get the, uh, package back to...um...where it belongs as soon as possible."

"Don't be too quick. You may need to give the thing to the police if you find anything else. Any ideas about who put it in—" Meg glanced into the backseat, then held up a hand to shield her mouth from the twins and whispered "—in your house yet?"

Kate checked the mirror. The argument had moved on to who kicked a ball the farthest. From experience, she knew this exchange could last for hours with neither girl noticing anything going on around her. She turned back to Meg and briefly related her ideas about the firecracker incident and pizza delivery.

"I can't believe Louie would be involved. I've known the kid forever." Meg chewed her lower lip for a moment. "The boys must've been getting out of the bath when he stopped by. But I definitely wouldn't have been concerned."

"Yeah, I figure I'll be able to eliminate my suspicions as soon as I talk to him," Kate said. "It's just his out-of-town trip right after the incident that gives me reservations."

"Those firecrackers." Meg stared off toward Kate's house, as if she had laser vision through the Victorian's blue siding and into the wooded area beyond. "I figured they were set off by some teen with too much time on his hands, but you're right about a perfect distraction if someone wanted everyone away from your house."

"Mommmmeeee, can we get a slushie on the way?" Suze pleaded.

"Yeah, Mom, we're thirsty," Sam added.

"Not before the soccer game. Water bottles are in the back cooler," Kate called over her shoulder. "Gotta go," she said to her neighbor.

"Sure." Meg smiled. Then her green eyes took on a surprised look. "Hey, where's Keith?" Kate's backbone stiffened. "We'll talk later."

• • • •

"ARE YOU CRAZY?" MEG slammed both palms onto the McKenzie breakfast table, jostling the steaming cups of coffee. "What could possibly make you think Keith might be having an affair? Especially with Sophia."

Kate fought to hold back tears that threatened whenever she thought about this very question. Her mental turmoil had staged a continuing battle during less intense moments of the girls' soccer game—which they won—and throughout the drive home. The coach had whisked away all comers for a hotdog party in his backyard, and the twins had hardly noticed Kate beg off as they joined giggling teammates in the coach's huge Suburban.

Now, across the table from Meg, she finally voiced the worries she'd been vacillating over all day. Mounting circumstantial evidence pointed decisively, at least in her opinion, toward potential marital woes.

"Did I tell you how Keith and I met?"

"Yeah." Meg gave a sideways shake of her head, like she wasn't sure she understood the question. "You were coordinating a big shot corporate event at a Vancouver Canucks game for a group of

Portland executives. You each looked into the other's eyes, and bam! I love that story."

Kate smiled, in spite of herself. They had shaken hands and knew immediately from the first touch. Her right hand tingled even now at the thought. "Yes, I think we could've powered all of Vancouver."

Her love for hockey began in an instant, and their courtship was just as quick. Three months later she was Mrs. Keith McKenzie, her wedding a last extravaganza planned as an events coordinator, and she relocated to the Canadian Pacific.

"What I didn't tell you was the underhanded ways some of the hockey wives helped their husbands' careers by shoving a wedge into other players' families with gossip and innuendo. Most of the couples were really nice. But for a few...the competition extended past the ice." She stood and paced. "I know the same thing happens in the corporate world."

"At newspapers, too."

Kate stopped at the coffee counter to gather her thoughts before continuing. "There was always small clique of snippy wives who built tension between couples, saying things in whispers that just stayed in your mind. That's what happened to Keith and me, anyway. Nights we argued caused friction and little sleep. Travel days when I stayed behind heightened the tension and ultimately led to him not having his mind on the game during crucial plays. Any mistakes Keith made allowed other husbands to step in and increase their own worth with the team."

Meg scooped up the mugs and joined her at the coffeepot. "That would be ingenious if the plan wasn't pure evil."

"Got it in one, friend." Kate sighed and followed Meg back toward the table but only to set down her cup. "It's not an easy life. When other couples broke up, we vowed to double our efforts. After the girls were born things got better—then worse."

She walked over and replayed Keith's first phone message, where he'd repeatedly said "boss" instead of naming Sophia. Kate still hadn't listened to the message from that morning, the one she'd raced from the house to avoid, so the women heard it for the first time together.

"Hi, honey. Me again. I keep missing you all. Well, I'll be home tonight. Tell the girls I love 'em and hope they win today. I—"

Keith's conversation halted as a double knock came over the speaker.

"Oops, that's the door. Gotta go. Love you and the girls. Take care."

Tandem beeps signaled the message's end. Kate moaned, "That was probably Sophia," and burst into tears.

"Oh, honey," Meg wrapped arms around Kate, and rubbed her back as she sobbed. "Don't let this be the evil wives all over again. Keith loves you."

Kate pulled away and grabbed a napkin to dab the corners of her eyes. "Easy to say, but..." After a couple of deep breaths, she finished, "You have to admit the evidence looks pretty daunting."

"Girl, you are jumping to ludicrous conclusions." Meg wrapped an arm around Kate's shoulders. "I've known Sophia peripherally for years. Yes, she's a piranha, I'll give you that, but Keith loves you. The proof is in his eyes every time he's near you."

"Then why keep it secret he had a fling with Sophia before we were married?" Kate felt heat rise in her face. "And that she owns the radio station?"

"Well, technically, neither of those things is true," Meg said, not meeting Kate's eyes.

"What do you mean? What haven't you told me?"

Meg shrugged. "Only the little things I remember and a few conversations through the years." She looked at Kate and shrugged again. "Okay, gossip. Everyone loved seeing the witch get her comeuppance. Sophia was after Keith like Jane said. However, if the phone line hadn't gone dead your dear mother-in-law likely would have told you Sophia got nowhere. Keith was nice, took her out a couple of times, but their fling fizzled—it never sizzled."

"Which brings us back to my original question. Why did you and Keith and everyone but my mother-in-law keep this from me?"

"I didn't think about saying anything," Meg replied. Kate glared, and she rushed on, "Hey, it was ten years ago, for heaven's sake. I've had two kids and very little sleep in the meantime. As far as why your husband kept mum, you said it yourself—men are chicken. Keith is no different. Didn't you make a list of all this last night? That's how you work, right?"

"Yeah..." She sighed, pulling her notebook from the counter. "I'm jumping to conclusions, I'll admit it. Everything rational I've already told myself is true, and I'm letting my irrational side take control today."

"You're human. Cut yourself a break."

Kate smiled. Yes, this is what friends were for. She filed the thought away as a reminder to goad her the next time doubts kept her from searching out a friendly ear. Trust. "You're right. Thanks."

"My pleasure," Meg said, before her grin wavered a bit. "Besides, I know what husbands are like when they cheat. Keith doesn't show the real signs."

"You can't mean Gil?"

"Years ago." Meg nodded. "With a young hussy reporter who thought he'd hoist her up the success ladder." She offered a crooked smile. "And believe it or not, it actually made our marriage stronger."

"You're okay?" Kate reached out and took her neighbor's hand, but Meg pulled free and scooped up the notepad.

"Ancient history. I was tied up with babies and missed all the red flags. We'll talk about it some other day. In the meantime, we need to plan your next move. Where should we start?"

Her friend's brisk, no-nonsense attitude was the perfect tonic, and Kate smiled despite herself as she watched her neighbor's red corkscrew curls bend over the long list. For all her own organizational skills, Kate recognized her need for someone to give the old rah-rah during down times. And she'd certainly hit basement level lately. "Well, I'm not sure how to handle the first question, and I'll need to wait until Keith gets back for the second and fourth—"

"Which we now agree are moot." Meg raised an eyebrow and grinned.

"Definitely moot," she concurred, smiling. "The biggest concern is still whoever is setting me up. If we figure out that missing link, we can presume a good probability we've found a tie to the murder or the murderer."

"Whom we want to identify but carefully avoid."

"Hey, I'm not a girl waving a death wish," Kate said. "I only want to keep my hide out of jail."

Running a pink fingernail down the list, Meg divvied up the rest. "Okay, you need to maintain a handle on Danny. He might let something slip and tell whether Sophia is setting you up."

"But I thought we'd struck off the affair angle?"

"Don't confuse one issue with another." Meg looked up from the list. "Sophia is a mean, mean bitch. Always has been, always will be. If she killed Amelia, she'll find a fall guy, and what more perfect pawn than the wife of the guy who didn't fall for her charms years ago?"

"I am glad you know everyone around Hazelton." Kate took a sip of her cooled coffee, her earlier anxiety reaching an equally mild temperature.

Meg shot her a mischievous grin, those dancing freckles standing out more than usual. "Oh, not everyone, but experience tells me who to detour around and who fuels the gossip chains. Sophia meets both criteria. Which brings me to numbers six and seven regarding Thomas's current activities and Amelia's relationship with her domestic help. Mother can likely provide information in those areas. The bridge group is scheduled to play at her house this afternoon, and she asked me to come over to help serve refreshments. What Mother can't contribute, the other nosy biddies she plays with probably can."

"You're terrible."

"Ain't I though?" Meg's grin turned wicked.

Kate took the list and planned her own next move. "So, if I can connect with Danny, I might find out about the gardening procedures around the mansion. Discover who picked the deadly blooms."

"Try charming his father, too. William Nethercutt is a committed ladies' man."

"Really? I had him pegged as a staid tax attorney."

"You pegged right, as far as the tax attorney goes. Except that staid is far from a valid description. Married at least six times in the last twenty years, with no less than five times as many girlfriends during the same period. He also keeps a hand in his ex-wives' lives."

"Danny mentioned his parents still get together for dinner."

"And likely much, much more." Meg wiggled her eyebrows suggestively.

"You're kidding." Kate smiled and shook her head. "How does he have time to make a living?"

"His law partners wonder the same thing."

"How do you know all of this?" Kate asked, amazed at the breadth of small town gossip.

"No one ever tells me such intimate information."

Meg shrugged. "You haven't lived here your whole life. Mark is on a ball team with one of the partners' sons. The father never makes the games, but the mother does and has no ethical dilemma over spilling what should be confidential information. While our sons miss fly balls, we mothers get entertained by the law office soap opera."

"Remind me never to use his firm," Kate said.

"This is Hazelton. Very little remains secret."

"Except who killed Amelia Nethercutt—"

"The police are working on it."

"—and who's trying to set me up," Kate finished.

"Yeah." Meg took a final sip of coffee. "But we're going to get to the bottom of that. Mark my words. I need to get home and round up my men for some weekend chores, but I'll call if I learn anything. Don't forget to do the same."

"I promise. Thanks for all your help."

Meg crinkled her nose and waved her hand to imply indifference, as she headed for the back door.

"It's one thing to have a plan of action," Kate muttered as she shot the dead bolt home.

"It's quite another to actually have a clue about where to begin."

Facts, fantasies, options, and opinions cluttered her overworked mind. Employing the same methods as she would approach a disorganized room seemed the best answer. She needed to quantify the brain clutter.

It seemed logical to assume Amelia discovered her belongings in the antique store, as reported by the garden club, and the guilty party murdered her in an effort to keep from being unmasked as a thief and possibly disinherited. Yet, why use a stolen treasure box to incriminate Kate? According to what Meg gleaned from Hyacinth and the girls, Amelia already discovered the thefts before Kate was even hired. So, the murderer/thief either hadn't known Amelia knew, or decided to try pointing to Kate as a thief and peripherally tie her to the murder after the fact. Or, someone besides the murderer/thief killed Amelia and, afraid of being tarred for both crimes, roped Kate into the circle of guilt. Too many possibilities.

The big picture was clear. Time to state her needs. Unfortunately, the major ones simply mirrored her goals.

"But my minor needs definitely revolve around Danny," she said, marking a big star at his section of her pad. She tapped the pencil point on the page and let her mind relax to see if an inkling of an idea emerged. "Nothing that doesn't seem contrived or ridiculous." The business line rang.

"Stacked in Your Favor, this is Kate."

"Ms. McKenzie." A deep voice elegantly enunciated her name. "I am Charles Webster Walker, attorney to the late Amelia Nethercutt."

A sinking sensation hit Kate's stomach. Had they already discovered the box was missing? "Y-yes." She took a deep breath and tried again. "What can I d-do for you, Mr. Walker?"

"A sticky situation is developing, and I hope you can help us in the resolution," he continued.

He knows.

How could she prove she hadn't taken it? And Meg. Would they arrest Meg, too? Why had she let Meg take the damned thing?

Kate suddenly realized she'd missed the lawyer's words. "I'm sorry, but would you repeat what you just said?"

"An inventory, Ms. McKenzie. That's what we're looking for," Walker explained. "Until we get an accurate inventory of all the collections, Amelia Nethercutt's estate cannot be settled. A specified requirement of the will and making it imperative to have an inventory in hand within the next sixty days."

"Inventory the whole house?" Kate heard the incredulity in her voice.

Walker apparently heard it as well. "We realize this is a colossal undertaking. While we would prefer a complete price for the entire job, we understand if you must charge an hourly rate to accommodate your crew."

My crew? Kate hoped Meg had nothing to do for the next two months. Wait a minute. What was she thinking? After the last few days she would be crazy to actually consider this. Was she nuts?

"Look, Mr. Walker, the offer is flattering, but I—"

"Please, Ms. McKenzie, meet with us before you say no." The sound of papers rustled through the receiver. "You're already familiar with many of the collections." *That's an understatement!*

"The most efficient plan calls for you to supervise the cataloguing process."

"But, the short time frame and the sheer number of items—"

"We'll provide whatever you need," Walker promised. "I'll even send over one of my law clerks and a laptop computer to assist with the data processing."

It would be a great way to sneak the box back in the house.

"Come to the heir meeting today and let us discuss the situation, Ms. McKenzie." There was a new note of pleading in the lawyer's voice.

"I suppose I could," Kate replied. "But the police—"

"Have been dealt with, and I'm assured you are cleared of any suspicion." His voice rang with finality. "We're in agreement then. Wonderful. Does your schedule have any available openings this afternoon? Say two o'clock?"

"You don't want to give me any time to think about it, do you?"

Walker chuckled. "I confess that was part of my reasoning. Though, more importantly, we need to get the wheels turning to avoid a delayed settlement of the estate."

Did she dare dig for a little more information? "I assumed a Nethercutt Trust was created to minimize taxes."

"Yes, one would expect such an instrument to be in place," Walker mused. "The Nethercutts were nothing if not, shall we say, particular about their things and the future of those items."

Okay, no real information, but I didn't exactly voice it as a question... She reminded herself to try another approach at a later date.

Kate looked at the clock. She still needed to pick up the twins and get hold of Meg. "I'm not sure I can make it by two. Could we meet later today, or sometime Monday?"

"How about four this afternoon?"

The man was not going to give up.

"One more concern. I understand Sophia Nethercutt-White is out of town at the moment.

Shouldn't we wait for her to attend?"

"I spoke with her from the plane a half hour ago, just before the pilot landed," Walker replied briskly. "She's...she's *interested*, shall we say, in getting this situation rectified so the conditions of the will can be met."

Shall we say.

The front door opened, and Keith called, "Hey, honey, I'm home."

"Yes, I think I can handle four," she told Walker, and replaced the receiver as Keith's exuberant face lit up the kitchen. She crossed her arms, her pent-up anger surging once more to the surface.

"Did you get my message?" He rushed over and wrapped her in a hug, oblivious to his wife's body language. "ESPN! Can you believe it?"

She pushed out of her husband's embrace. "Why didn't you tell me about your history with Sophia Nethercutt-White?"

"How did you find out?" He tried to take her hand, but she slapped his away. "It really wasn't anything, Katie, and besides, we're talking years ago. We dated a couple of times. We parted friends."

"What kind of friends?" She crossed her arms again. "Sophia isn't known as a forgiving sort. She doesn't seem the type who readily hires ex-lovers to work at her radio station."

"First, we were never lovers." His eyebrows came dangerously close to meeting. "Second, I don't work for Sophia. Her husband signed my contract."

"Then explain why you told me you were going to New York with, I quote..." She raised her hands and crooked two pairs of fingers in the air for emphasis. "...'The boss,' and Eileen informed me you jetted off with Sophia? When I put two and two together, it adds up to Sophia being your boss."

"Well, technically—"

Kate slammed her hand on the counter. "Don't give me semantics, damn it! You tried to mislead me. Why?"

"I wasn't being intentionally misleading, I just, uh..." His gaze circled the room, as if rescue could come from thin air.

"Did you want to hurt me?" She took a deep breath and held it.

"Don't be ridiculous, honey." Keith stepped forward to hug her again, but she sidestepped out of reach. "I didn't mention any of this because I didn't want to hurt you."

"I don't think you even thought of me." She knew her words sounded childish, but the injury had been bottled up too long.

"Of course I did." He ran both hands through his hair. "That's what I've been trying to tell you."

"No, you said you didn't want to hurt me. But you did. You wounded me, Keith, and what makes the whole thing doubly worse is other people give me information I should have received from *my husband*. Your mom had no idea I didn't know."

"My mom?"

"Yes, she and your dad are flying in late tonight." Kate poked his chest. "But don't try to change the subject. Why was Sophia necessary for you to interview Wayne Gretzky?"

"She didn't go to the interview. She had business in Manhattan and took me along on the company jet to minimize travel expenses."

"Yes, fueling up a corporate jet is always cheaper than getting a Jet Blue ticket."

"The plan was to make everything expedient. We didn't need to drive into either Burlington or Boston and go through the security time drain."

"It was so expedient you had to stay overnight before you could return? I called your hotel room and only got voice mail."

Keith's face colored, and Kate bit her lip. Whatever he said next was going to be important to their marriage.

After a long minute, he shook his head. The tension in his body abruptly disappeared and made him seem to wilt before her eyes. "Look, I love you. I'm sorry." His voice held a note of pleading. "Okay, I didn't think. You're right, I never thought about what would happen if you found out and put everything together the wrong way. I really screwed up, babe."

"Oh, no, don't grovel." She dropped into a kitchen chair and put her head on the tabletop.

"Then what do you want?" Steel crept into his voice, and she recognized the question as one she needed to answer for herself, as well as for Keith. She couldn't explain why she held to this argumentative course. But he was her husband, dammit, and he should understand.

Kate kept her head down as chair legs scraped and Keith joined her at the table. The wall holding the stress of the past few days buckled and broke, and her tears came quiet and steady. A minute later, her husband's strong, familiar arms wrapped around her, and she was pulled onto his lap. She spoke into his shoulder, "I'm sorry."

His chuckle was deep and reassuring. "You goose. I'm the bad boy here, remember?"

She pulled back and shook her head. "I knew better, but I've had a lot to deal with. I couldn't keep everything in perspective. You walked in the door, and I...I...I think I had to punish you."

"Calm down. We're cool." Keith ran his hands in long strokes down her back. She felt the stress retreating. "Have the police hassled you anymore?"

"No, I haven't heard anything from them, but Amelia's attorney told me I'm cleared as a murder suspect. Well...for the time being anyway." She detailed the discovery of the box.

Keith grasped her shoulders and locked gazes with her. "Why didn't you wake me when you found it?"

"I couldn't see why both of us should lose sleep." She brushed at the tear-stained spot near the collar of his shirt. "I was going to tell you the next morning, but you and the girls left without waking me."

"And you called the radio station and talked to Eileen instead."

"Because you didn't answer your cell. Then I called your hotel last night, and you weren't in your room."

He kissed her forehead. "You've had a rough few days, honey. You were right to want to punish me. Where is it now?"

She frowned. "Meg's safe deposit box."

"Why?"

"We thought getting it out of our house and away from contact with me was a good idea."

"Yeah, makes sense, I guess."

She leaned over and kissed him. "Speaking of Meg, I need to call her. We're requested for a job which will allow us to slip the ebony box back into the mansion. That's why Amelia's lawyer called in the first place. He wants us to inventory the collections for the estate."

Keith's response was a slow whistle. "From what you've said that sounds like quite an undertaking."

"Yes, but I haven't agreed to do the job yet, just to meet everyone today at four." She jumped up and went to the phone. "And I still have to see if Meg can go with me."

"There's no 'if' about it," he warned. "You're not going without her."

"Yes, sir."

Looking around, he asked, "Where are the girls? I've got hockey sticks autographed by Gretzky."

"I'm sure they'll love them. The team won the soccer game, and coach opened up his backyard for a barbecue and weenie roast." She glanced at the oven's digital clock. "In fact, one of us needs to run pick-up duty."

He pulled the Jeep keys from his pocket. "I'll go. You call your partner in crime."

She was a digit away from completing Meg's mobile number when Keith returned.

"Forgot. I brought you a gift, too."

She accepted the shiny gold bag. Inside was a snow globe of the White Rabbit from *Alice in Wonderland*, the small pewter figurine giving the appearance of hurrying elsewhere, and an oversized pocket watch in his tiny hand. The Carroll novel had always been her favorite, but her stomach lurched at the thought of how life lately seemed a little too close to the through-the-looking-glass variety. She smiled anyway. "It's beautiful. Thank you."

"See, I always think of you."

Tears threatened a repeat performance. She gave a big sniff.

"Don't make me feel guilty again," he warned. She shook her head and moved forward to hug him.

A long kiss later, the Jeep roared out of the cul-de-sac as Meg's cell number rang.

"What's up?" Meg greeted.

Kate outlined the lawyer's phone call, and the prospective job ahead, before asking if she wanted to go along as an associate, Meg laughed. "Try stopping me."

CHAPTER NINE

HIDE YOUR FILES (Good tip to throw out during presentation)
No room for a filing cabinet? Create secret storage by converting an old footlocker into an ottoman. Add wheels, and pad sides and top before covering in a material that coordinates with living room furniture. You'll have a great ottoman, and after placing hanging file folders inside it'll be an "outta-sight" way to store files.

• • • •

"I WANT TO GO ON THE record as saying I'm against this." Sophia's eyebrows made a strong, shapely V, matching the plunging neckline of her black silk jumpsuit.

Kate and Meg felt the rest of the Nethercutt heirs' eyes, including Mrs. Baxter and the pinstripe-suited representatives from two foundations, pivot their way. The estate's silver-topped lawyer, Charles Webster Walker, kept his steely blues trained on the paperwork in front of him. Everyone was gathered in the Nethercutt mansion's expansive dining room, seated around a massive seventeenth century carved table, and benevolently watched over by a shaggy, Alaskan moose head jutting out from the wall behind the attorney. Kate laced her fingers tightly together under the tabletop and wondered for the hundredth time if there wasn't some less lunatic way to sneak the box back into the house. Meg, on the other hand, grinned like Miss America.

"With all due respect, Sophia," Walker reminded, "that is not your call. As Amelia's designated heirs, it is in everyone's best interest to get an accurate inventory of the estate."

"The bequests of which we still aren't privy to," Bill Nethercutt grumbled. "Mother was signing a new will the day she died, and as a beneficiary, I—"

"In due time, William. In due time," Walker said. "I can't, of course tell, you specifics of the will, either the one in effect or the one she would have signed had her death not preceded the opportunity, but we must follow Amelia's wishes. I can state the new will carried no significant monetary changes. A few small shifts in bequests, nothing much more." He shuffled papers for a moment. "A different timetable was to be implemented, but such will not cause undue hardship to anyone. Under the circumstances the old will must stand."

"All well and good to know." Bill grabbed the water pitcher and refilled his glass. "But when do we hear the terms of the will and the benefits of its ramifications firsthand for ourselves?"

"The funeral is scheduled for Tuesday afternoon and, per the terms of the will, the reading must take place no sooner than forty-eight hours later." Walker cocked an eyebrow warningly. "To provide a proper period of mourning."

Tension built in Kate's neck and shoulders. Just listening to the stilted speech between everyone was enough to make an already edgy situation worse. She realized her two-day meltdown was part of the problem, too, but she wanted to shout, "Loosen up, people. Hug each other. Your mother just died." Everyone seemed to be playing a character in some secret tableau, and she wondered if her role was to play the fool.

The attorney flipped over the top page of his notes, and Bill and Sophia glared at each other. Danny took a pen from his pocket and wrote something on his left palm. Mrs. Baxter rubbed her temples. Amelia's son, Thomas Lane, scratched an ear and squirmed in his chair, and the two foundation men were visibly uncomfortable.

Upon meeting Thomas for the first time, Kate truly understood the term "a study in contrasts." Amelia's only child was a stocky man who still looked like the chunky boy he had likely been thirty years ago. His soft voice alluded to prep school studies and the suit he wore shouted Armani, but his fingernails and demeanor more closely matched the weed-whacker haircut he wore that emphasized early gray. She also wondered over the perplexing fact his surname matched Amelia's maiden name.

"We cannot proceed without proper inventory. It is paramount." Walker sighed. "Unlike the late Mr. Nethercutt's will, Miss Amelia's was anything but straightforward. To each of you, specific collections have been bequeathed, but the pieces are not named individually. We must ascertain what exactly is in the house to determine who gets wh—"

"Like the curio in the entry," Bill Nethercutt broke in, glowering at his sister.

Sophia could have chilled a glacier with her tone. "Father always said those pieces were mine, brother dear."

"See here, Sophia—"

"Then there are the other collections," Walker interrupted the quarrel, "which are bequeathed to charities and museums. As our two esteemed guests are here to represent." He nodded to the ill at ease, pinstriped clones. "Without an accurate inventory, we cannot file correct tax records either."

"But why must we rush and take any cottage-industry organizational..." Sophia fluttered a hand. "...Joanie-come-lately to do this? What does organizing have to do with inventorying?

Why can't we itemize everything ourselves?"

"I'd be happy to help," Thomas offered.

Danny raised an eyebrow and then spoke for the first time. "I could probably—"

"Oh, come on." Bill shook his head. "None of us has experience in this. Ms. McKenzie's company can perform the service much faster. The longer we take, the longer we wait until the will is dispersed."

"Exactly what experience does she have?" Sophia turned a laser-like glare in Kate and Meg's direction. "Or should I say, they? Again, as I asked a moment ago—"

"Ms. McKenzie's qualifications are more than adequate, and as both your stepmother's attorney and the executor of her will, I repeat that the decision is not yours to make," Walker broke in with measured tones. "She is already familiar with the collections."

Sophia pursed crimson lips. "How do we know she isn't a thief? Things are missing from all over the house."

"She isn't the one who has already walked off with items of value," Bill Nethercutt snapped.

"She was questioned by the police for the murder," Sophia returned.

"As were the rest of us," Bill said.

The lawyer tried to resume order. "The police have ascertained she is no longer a suspect."

"Unlike the rest of us," Thomas Lane added.

"She is bonded for any mishap or misappropriated item which can be shown to have been in the house at the start of the job," Walker finished. He looked at Kate. "That is correct?"

Kate nodded, swallowing hard before she acknowledged, "Yes, Mr. Walker."

"A puzzle box is already missing. One of Daddy's favorites," Sophia said. "And I certainly didn't take it. The entire collection was intact last week when I followed Mummy into Daddy's upstairs study to search for her reading glasses. It was on the display table, and now there is nothing but bare space to mark its place. You mark my words, I'll find out what's happened to it."

Kate gasped and Meg scooted a Waterford crystal glass closer, saying, "Oh dear, you have those silly hiccups again. Try a little water."

"Thanks." Kate smiled her relief, faking a hiccup as she took a big swallow.

Bill continued on as if no break had occurred. "We don't know if it was stolen, any more than if the other things that seem to be missing are truly gone. Each item could have simply been misplaced in this chaotic depository of a house."

"Mother was complaining last week how several of her ivory fans had disappeared."

Thomas said. "And she was saying something about pincushions or thimbles, too."

"It was thimbles, Uncle Thomas," Danny said.

"Precisely the point," Bill continued. "From a tax standpoint Charles is exactly correct. Inventorying everything is crucial to getting the will executed, an obviously massive endeavor, and I believe we should be supportive of Ms. McKenzie and her partner." He smiled their way. Kate would have felt better if the smile had reached his eyes. "Let's not find fault before they even begin."

Sophia stalked over to the sideboard, an immense piece Kate remembered Amelia saying was wrestled out of a German schloss. As the heiress poured herself a cup of coffee from a stainless-steel carafe, the viper pounded her point home one more time. "As I've already stated for the record, I'm categorically against this and feel we should search farther afield."

"Why? So you can hire your own crew and pay them off for hiding the fact you've been pilfering treasures?" Bill accused.

"I never—"

"Don't give me that—"

"Well, we wouldn't be in such a hurry, Bill, if you weren't in desperate need of funds."

"I have no power over the speed with which—"

"Everyone, please!" Walker slammed his file folder on the table, successfully gaining the group's attention. He continued, "If we haven't yet scared off Ms. McKenzie, she will be doing the job. Unless anyone has any other *relevant* business, this meeting is adjourned. We should all tour the house and discuss fees with Ms. McKenzie and Ms. Berman."

Kate found herself following Mrs. Baxter and Sophia, the men trailing behind. Time to extend the olive branch. "Sophia, I can't tell you how exciting it was for Keith to get the opportunity to interview Wayne Gretzky yesterday. I wanted to—"

"Keith?" Sophia revolved on her stiletto heel. Mrs. Baxter paused in the hall. "Ah, yes. McKenzie. You're married to Keith McKenzie." Sophia pursed her lips. "It's often quite surprising to find who men choose as their mates."

"Miss Sophia!" Mrs. Baxter brought a hand to her shocked face.

Kate willed her own expression to stay blank. "You must hear that often about your own marriage."

Anger darkened Sophia's ivory complexion. She pivoted and stalked away. Kate heard chortles from the group behind her, the laughter increasing to full volume at the thunderous slam of the front door.

"Way to go, Kate." Danny patted her shoulder. "Wish I'd known that was the easiest way to get her to leave."

Kate stumbled a little on weak knees.

Meg smiled at her. "I'm proud of you. You're learning, Katie. You're really learning."

"May we continue?" Walker asked, the only person not exhibiting or trying to hide a smile. It was unclear whether he was afraid to show his feelings about a woman whose business affected his own, or if he simply had no sense of humor.

The tour left Kate exhausted and Meg wide-eyed. The adventure began in the library crowded with medieval weapons and nineteenth century medical equipment. The group worked its way through guest bedrooms that housed such disparate furnishings as board games and train paraphernalia, past a sewing room storing geological specimens, and a computer room doubling as an antique Venetian mask cache. On and on they walked, finally arriving in the conservatory/ wildlife sanctuary near the entrance to the greenhouse.

"We don't need an inventory of the plants, but I believe the rest of the rooms will more than keep you busy," Walker remarked as everyone formed a semi-circle in the conservatory. A brilliant assortment of tropical birds, housed in a Victorian-styled aviary, screeched their displeasure at having company. "Perhaps we could retire to the parlor."

"Good idea, Charles," Bill replied.

Kate found Danny at her side and decided to try striking another task off her list. "I'd seen the greenhouse, of course, but didn't realize Amelia had birds. Who'll take care of them?"

"The fowl will go to the zoo in Boston most likely." He scowled over his shoulder. "No one liked the damn things except Gramma. I hope I get the orchids, though."

"Amelia grew orchids?" Kate prodded.

"No, I did. But she paid for fitting out their area of the greenhouse," Danny explained. "They're very fragile. The plants need special heaters and meticulous care."

"You helped with all the plants?"

"Me and Uncle Thomas."

They passed a tall vase of tiger lilies on a table in the hall and Kate asked, "Did you grow those?"

"Yeah, sure." Danny stopped and ran his left index finger along one of the orange blooms. Kate saw "Natalie 2K" scrawled in blue ink on his palm, then turned her attention back to catch the wistful expression on his face. He said, "Gramma liked forcing bulbs to keep flowers in the house year-round."

With a clear view through the doorway, she noticed nearly everyone had taken seats in the parlor, the same place she'd last spent with Amelia. White roses graced the coffee table. "Is someone still picking flowers for the house?"

Danny nodded. "Uncle Thomas. He's kind of a creature of habit, and it was his job to keep fresh flowers throughout the place. He's done it for years. Goes around, checks which bouquets need changed, brings in newly cut ones."

"That's nice," Kate said. "Sort of a continuing tribute to his mother."

His face darkened and he shrugged. "Yeah, I guess."

As the teen shifted from foot to foot, Kate wished she had more time to pump him. He seemed almost ready to say something, just as Walker called from the parlor. "Ms. McKenzie... Oh, there you are."

"We're coming, Mr. Walker." Kate stepped across the wide, marbled hall. "Danny was telling me about the plants that are grown here."

"Yes, Miss Amelia was a renowned horticulturalist," Walker said. "The greenhouse and its contents are already taken care of separately in a codicil she recently added to the old will. The greenhouse is self-contained, so there is no need for an inventory before everything goes to the Hazelton Garden Club."

Kate heard a gasp. Thomas, sitting on a chair by the window, turned pale. "A new codicil?"

Danny spoke up in a strangled voice, "You...you mean the plants...they'll all go outside the family?"

"The structure as well," Walker said, before turning officious again. "That's a bit of letting the cat out of the bag at this point, though there shouldn't be much concern. The monetary value will be small compared to everything else. Once she made that small change, however, Amelia decided to make more, which led to my drawing up the new will. In the meantime, Ms. McKenzie, what kind of hourly fee do you require, or would you prefer to provide a price on the entire job?"

"I don't think—"

"We cannot possibly give you a price at this time," Meg cut in, pulling Kate down onto the settee beside her. "We need to regroup at the office, plan what resources are required. Why don't we send you a complete proposal on Monday morning?"

"Yes, yes," Walker nodded. "A proposal early Monday would be most efficient. Then you can begin in the afternoon. We can't get this project started soon enough."

"Uh—" Kate began.

"Absolutely," Meg spoke over her.

• • • •

KATE FOLLOWED THE ACTION out her kitchen's bay window as her husband and children competed one-on-one with Meg's all-male bunch on the Berman's improvised back patio/basketball court. Gathering dusk settled over the group and automatic lights came on around the neighborhood. She wondered about people and relationships. Gil had the trustworthy, fair good looks of a television news anchor that seemed wasted with a print news career. Meg always appeared an auburn willow beside him, completing the picture of a golden couple. Now knowing about the affair, Kate marveled at her friend's steadfastness, wishing for more information but not comfortable enough to ask. Across the table, a pencil to her smiling lips, the redhead watched her three men join forces to take the lead. Kate sighed.

Meg turned an emerald gaze her direction. "What's wrong?"

"Oh, nothing, just...everything..."

"Don't get your stomach all knotted up over this job." Meg's smile grew as she tapped her pencil eraser on the paper before her.

"How many times will you be able to work with big-moneyed lawyers who say 'Damn the cost'?"

"That's not exactly what he said."

"Pretty much. Anytime they offer you their employees as help, say they need something big done in the next sixty days, and are ready to accept any price, they're basically saying money is no object."

"When did he say he would accept any price?"

"When we said 'the cost proposal would be sent Monday morning,' and he said 'good,' we could start the same afternoon."

"I don't think he meant—"

Meg raised a hand. "Trust me, he did."

Kate shook her head. "You're probably right, but we can't do this job. The more I think over everything, the more I realize we need to use our bid to get us into the house one more time, then leave and never go back."

"Think of the college money you can set aside for the girls," Meg coaxed. "The vacation you can take to, say, Disney World. Would you be able to swing a summer trip if you don't do the job?"

"We'll be lucky to finish the inventory before school starts in fall. The only way we can accomplish the job in sixty days is if we spend the following six months recuperating. Forget leaving town this summer."

"Okay, a winter vacation instead. Christmas in San Diego. Think of escaping the cold and snow."

"As pleasant as that sounds," Kate said wistfully, "my family wouldn't buy it. They're diehard snow bunnies." She sighed. "And to be honest, I kind of like the *Ye Olde Christmas Card* look of Vermont during the holidays."

Meg threw her hands in the air. "You're going to argue with everything I say, aren't you?"

"It's simply too much for two people. The money would be wonderful, yes, but we'll be working twelve-hour days. Are you ready for that?"

"Even with Walker's law clerk?"

"We need more help than just data entry. We could probably use a museum curator on staff, too, but one who specializes in *everything*." Kate poured herself another cup of coffee. "Besides, I'm not comfortable having a law professional with us on a job we're taking as a means to return stolen property. Even if we didn't steal anything."

"I hate when you're realistic."

"I'm always realistic. Does that mean you always hate me?"

"You know what I mean."

They were startled by the doorbell chime.

"Who could that be?" Kate headed for the front, checking as she did to be sure the fathers' and kids' basketball game was still casualty free.

"You're obviously more in tune with doing the job than you want to believe," Meg called. "And itching to get back to this bid without any interruptions."

Her friend's optimism made her grin as she opened the door, but the happiness faded instantly as she recognized the visitor. Lean as a leopard and just as deadly, Valerie James, local decorating diva and Kate's ascribed business enemy, stood tall in leather boots and a jacket that cost more than Keith's last paycheck.

"Hello, Valerie." She forced a nice tone. As much as Kate disliked the woman, she appreciated having a steady babysitter in Tiffany. "I didn't see you walk up."

"My little Miata was swallowed behind your behemoth on wheels." Valerie pointed toward the driveway. "Since your van was outside, I knew you were home. Though, how you can stand driving such a clumsy thing—"

It seemed best to ignore the remark. "What can I do for you?"

"You can start, darling, by inviting me in," Valerie replied, the bored drawl adding a silent "of course" to her words.

Kate stepped aside. "Meg and I were just having coffee in the kitchen."

"Going over your bid, I suppose." Valerie's heels rang on the entry's parquet floor.

Shocked to silence, Kate followed. They were in the kitchen before she could ask, "How did you learn about our Nethercutt bid?"

"I told you there are no secrets in Hazelton," Meg said, frowning. "What business is it of yours, Valerie?"

With an elegant shrug, the designer replied, "I came to offer my services. During a phone call this evening with Sophia, I discovered, Kate, that you might be in over your head." She gave a half-grin. "I'm redoing the White mansion's master suite while Sophia's husband is convalescing in the hospital due to some geriatric malady." Then she waved her hand, much the way Sophia had done earlier that day. "The room's going to be truly stunning. Anyway, we were discussing the finishing touches, and she suggested I get with you and offer my services in inventorying the Nethercutt collections. I might be interested in some pieces for my more wealthy clients. I'm getting new referrals every day. Working on the inventory will put me right in the thick of it, you might say."

"You might say." Kate echoed.

"Great idea, Valerie. What would you want for an hourly rate?" A tiny wink from the redhead warned Kate to play along.

The decorator quoted a rate several levels higher than the pair had previously discussed. Meg nodded and jotted the number down on her pad. A few small details later Valerie swept out of the door, reminding Kate for all the world of a fur-less Cruella De Vil on her way to view Dalmatian hides.

"Okay." She confronted Meg. "I didn't ask while she was here, but now I have to. Have you lost your mind?"

A smug expression filled her friend's face. "Think about it. Sophia doesn't want us. For help she suggests someone who anyone in town knows you would say no to. I agree with your reasoning about the proffered law clerk, but we do need at least one more body. Accepting Valerie may first seem like lunacy, but think for a minute, and those crazy pieces fit perfectly in our favor. Best of all, we'll be calling Sophia's bluff."

"As in keep your enemy near so she can't attack without warning?"

"Exactly. We get the assistance we need, and Sophia's scheme loses its momentum. Valerie will likely show up late every day and give us time to slip anything that shows up, like the box, back into the mansion. She can't help herself from dropping information she thinks makes her look important. We'll gain valuable 'intel' we wouldn't learn otherwise. Plus, we know what to charge for an hourly rate that would be the absolute top limit."

"No kidding. But we aren't going to really bid her figure are we?"

"Yes, we are." Meg's nod was decisive. "If Walker wants us to do the job as badly as I think he does, he'll pay. And I absolutely will not work for a penny less than Valerie."

Kate pulled her ear, thoughtful. "At least with her help we'll be able to work six or eight-hour days."

"And she'll be able to tell us the real names of some of that stuff. During our little excursion today, I had no idea what a lot of those things were called."

"Yes. It's hard to record an inventory when you keep writing 'funny looking whatsit.'"

"Glad you agree."

"Still," Kate said, moving back to take her seat to finish compiling the bid page. "Recognizing an enemy spy is all well and good, but I hope we don't soon find ourselves with knives in our backs."

CHAPTER TEN

SUNDAY, APRIL 11 – First Tasks

- *Meet George and Jane for breakfast.*
- *Make sure twins have activities for church service.*
- *Turn on chicken cassoulet in crock pot before leaving*

• • • •

"AND THEN GEORGE CHA-cha'd right into the table with the punch bowl, knocking kiwi-strawberry-passion fruit all over us and everyone else within ten feet!" Jane McKenzie said, joining with the entire table as they laughed at the unexpected antics of Keith's usually sedate, pipe-smoking father. George, unlit pipe to his lips, chuckled right along, a granddaughter at each side.

The McKenzie clan circled around a huge corner table at The Maple Inn, a favorite local B&B known for Vermont country breakfasts. Kate almost moaned with her first bite of blueberry pancakes. *Forget commercial air-fresheners, this place could make a mint bottling the syrup fragrance.*

Despite arriving back late the night before, the elder McKenzies appeared relaxed and refreshed. George looked patrician-comfortable in his Sunday suit and tie, his salt-and-pepper mustache twitching in a half-smile with every remark. Jane, twinkling cornflower blue eyes adding sparkle to her words, seemed fresh as ever, not one un-dyed brunette hair out of place. The plane's night-time landing, coupled with the long round trip to Burlington International Airport, came too late for the girls. Keith ran solo the previous evening to pick up his parents, leaving with instructions from Kate to ask if the group could get together before church for breakfast. Agreement was unanimous.

Everyone seemed as relaxed as the cruise couple. While stories unfolded of warm Caribbean waves and bright island sun, a bevy of packages made a steady entrance out of Jane's capacious handbag, and now both girls wore rainbow-hued coral necklaces around their collars. Kate fingered the pretty, batik-print notebook her mother-in-law chose especially for her, wondering how she'd gotten so lucky. Most women didn't count their in-laws as friends and supporters. She looked at the shark-tooth key ring they'd given Keith and the stack of matching tie-dyed T-shirts beside her own purse and sighed, content. No useless trinkets for Jane McKenzie—she bought souvenirs worth carting home.

Kate hoped to find some time after church to get Jane alone to discuss Amelia's murder and the later developments. The big question was what to ask first. Coming out of her reverie, she noticed her tomboy twin's once pristine white shirt bore evidence of pancakes. "Oh, Sam, you have maple syrup on your sleeve."

Jane whipped the napkin off her lap and dipped it in a water glass, reaching out to her granddaughter. "Here, dear, give me your hand."

"Well, if I eat one more bite I'm going to burst." Keith signaled for the bill. "I love this place, but I'll be running off this breakfast all week."

Margaret Newton, owner and expert meal-planner for the B&B, caught Keith's gesture and worked her way through the crowded room of satisfied customers. "Everything all right at this table?"

"Wonderful, Margaret," Keith replied, his words seconded by everyone's nodding heads. "We need to pay our check, though. Reverend Parker does like his congregation to show up on time."

"I hope this member can stay awake during the sermon." George held out a hand as Margaret withdrew her pad.

"Dad, I'll get it." Keith rose from his chair.

"Nonsense." George snatched the paper from the inn owner's hand and smiled to cover the bad manners. "I haven't had to pay for a meal all week."

"That's not exactly right," Keith argued.

"Sure it is. The cruise ship had tables ready for us twenty-four hours a day." George counted money from his wallet and pushed a handful Margaret's way, then turned to Jane. "You about ready to go, Mother?"

"Yes, dear."

Kate smiled as Keith gave up after the usual fight. She turned to the girls. "Go wash your sticky fingers and meet us at the van."

"We want to ride with Grandpa and Grandma," Suzanne said. Samantha backed her up with a long, "Please."

"We'd love to drive these darlings in our car," Jane assured. "We've missed having the little gigglers around."

The girls responded in typical giggly fashion, getting their sticky fingers all over Jane's red wool suit as they hugged her before racing to the bathroom.

"I'm sorry—" Kate started.

"Pshaw." Jane waved a hand. "Not every grandmother has tangible evidence of her granddaughters' love. I'll be the envy of the senior's class this morning."

After gathering jackets and belongings, the adults made their way to the front, chatting with acquaintances along the way. The girls met them at the door, their reflections haloed in the windows by the brisk Vermont sunshine.

"That was the best idea," Jane said. George handed his key ring to Sam, and the girls raced to the La Sabre.

"Well, thanks again, Dad," Keith said. Kate nodded and smiled.

George fingered his pipe. "Need to do this more often. Girls will be grown up and driving before we know it. Won't have time to sit down and eat with us old geezers."

"Oh, don't remind me." Kate used a hand to shield the sun from her eyes as she watched her daughters unlock the Buick and climb into the backseat. "Some days I wish they were older. Maybe they would listen to what I say. Then I think about them driving and going off on their own, and I just cringe."

"That's natural," Jane said. "But don't go getting your hopes up. I think teenagers are worse at listening than first-graders."

"Gee, thanks."

Kate relished the quiet ride to church with her husband. Neither had anything to say, but the silence remained comfortable, not strained. Given her silly worries of the previous few days, she chastised herself again over her fears. She took Keith's right hand, and he shot her a grin as the van entered the church parking lot.

Somehow everyone stayed awake through the sermon, though Jane had to give George a couple of nudges. A full stomach seemed to agree with the twins, too, and they sat quietly in the pew sharing a coloring book and crayons.

All seemed suddenly right in the world, at least for the moment. Kate closed her eyes for the final prayer.

On the drive home the van resumed its regular twin-tone noise level, and Kate contemplated what vegetable dish to add to the chicken cassoulet that should be nearing completion in the crock pot. Until the fight broke out in the back.

"I found it." Sam said.

"You gotta share," Suze returned hotly. When Kate turned around, she added, "Right, Mommy?"

"Share what?" Kate worried Suze had already broken her necklace and wanted to wrangle her sister's as a replacement. But no, both girls still sported the coral chokers. She looked down at Sam's hands. Her heart sank. She saw the piece of highly carved ivory. "Sam, give that to me."

"Can't I keep it, Mommy? See, it's a pretty fan." The child opened the ivory ends to release a hand-painted silk scene.

Kate had already intuited what the item was and where it belonged, but this absolutely confirmed her fears. The fragile piece, part of an expensive collection, belonged in the bamboo case on the back wall of Amelia Nethercutt's lavender guestroom.

• • • •

"KEITH, WHAT ARE WE going to do?" Kate asked, after sending the girls to wash for lunch. She no longer had the imagination to think about complementary side dishes and just lifted the crock server, placing the cassoulet in the middle of the table.

"Want me to heat up these rolls?" He held up a package from the counter.

"Huh? That's not what I meant."

"I know. You were talking about the fan." Without waiting for a decision on the bread, he filled a baking sheet and started the toaster oven. "Let's get through lunch. We can decide later what to do about everything else."

Kate distributed the plates and handed the necessary silverware to the girls as they bounced into the room. "I don't think I have an appetite anymore."

"Why, Mom?" Sam asked, peering over the tabletop to see the crock's creamy contents.

"Did lunch burn?"

"Your mother's a wonderful cook, Sam," Keith replied, lowering his voice to phony, authoritative mode. "She would never *burn our food*."

The twins giggled. "Yes, she has," they chorused.

"Never!" He moved in a menacing, Frankenstein style. "Treasonous words cannot be said in this house. You must be punished."

Both girls ran from the room, screaming in excitement.

"Oh, stop, please." Kate dropped into a chair.

The grin disappeared from her husband's face. "I'm sorry, hon. I'll go get them calmed down and ready to eat. I wasn't thinking."

"No, I'm sorry. You lightened the mood, and I do appreciate it." She propped her head on one hand and straightened scattered silverware with the other.

"You'll feel better after you eat."

She nodded but didn't believe him. The only thing that would make her feel better was to find an end to this nightmare and stop looking over her shoulder all the time.

Who had the opportunity to slip the fan into her van, and when? While they were at church? Yesterday at the meeting in Amelia's mansion? Kate thought back to how the heirs all left on Saturday. Of course, Sophia had stormed out ahead of everyone. Danny, still upset, had been the first of the remaining group to depart, his dad trailing after him. Thomas stayed with the lawyer while Kate and Meg left, but she remembered him dropping out of sight a few times before and after the tour—ostensibly to smoke. That gave him the opportunity to break into her van. The lock didn't show tamper marks, but she and Meg dropped their purses and jackets on the buffet as they had entered the meeting. Had Thomas been brazen enough to lift her keys as they all sat around the huge table? Was there a time no one would have noticed? Yes, at the time the lawyer talked about the will. Every eye stayed trained on him. Or, when Bill and Sophia argued.

Thinking of Sophia reminded Kate how the step-daughter diva had been a late arrival herself. A mental picture flashed in her mind, replaying the sweeping grand entrance Sophia employed, plopping her fur wrap atop everyone else's belongings, then lingering to pick through her vintage alligator bag for a compact. "I must remove this shine from my nose," Sophia had said. Kate now wondered whether the shine was the only thing the viper removed.

Everyone wove in and out during the tour and had ample opportunity to steal the key and hide the fan. After church would have been harder. None of her suspects attended the McKenzies' church, so no one had a chance of stealing her key and putting it back today unless one of her fellow parishioners was a confederate. Though, that didn't count the possibility the key could have been surreptitiously borrowed Saturday by one of the heirs to make a wax mold, and a duplicate key used this morning.

She moved to the oven as the timer pinged to signal the bread was done. Standing did more than physically straighten her backbone. Kate realized she was truly angry. She filled the breadbasket, vowing not to let this mental hustler win. "No way."

"What, Mommy?" Sam asked, the girls almost tiptoeing back into the room, Keith at their heels.

Poor things. As long as she let herself get frightened over every new setback, her family remained as much victims of this fiend as she was. "Just...um...telling myself not to let a headache ruin a wonderful Sunday afternoon with my family." She smiled at each girl, then up at Keith, adding, "I think I've found the cure I need, and I'm not letting this get to me anymore."

"You sure?" He held the chair out for her.

"Absolutely. Now, who wants bread?" she asked. As everyone filled their plates, happy, and often silly, conversation reigned once more. Kate stayed a little quieter than usual, but no one seemed to notice. She had plans to make. Her fingers itched to get hold of her casebook.

First, she needed to talk to Meg. They needed to send a bid in the next day, but not as a ruse to get into the house one more time.

Stacked in Your Favor was going to accept the job, and not simply to make enough to take their families to Disney World. She'd show whoever pulled these nasty acts she was no convenient scapegoat. Until the unmasking of Amelia's murderer, Kate would enter the Nethercutt mansion at least five days a week, keeping her eyes and ears open.

There was no substitute for prudence, however. She needed to mandate some rules to protect herself and Meg, and she couldn't wait to tell Valerie how "for security reasons" they would do a group search of each other's belongings every day before leaving.

• • • •

"OH, YES, THOMAS IS a rather sad story," Jane said over the phone that evening.

Kate had been unable to get with her mother-in-law for a private conversation all afternoon and fell back on a telephone call after Keith and the girls left for an after-dinner ice cream run. "He seemed rather short on confidence."

She could almost hear her mother-in-law nod through the phone lines, as the response came, "Very low self-esteem. Amelia loved him without reservation, but she was never good at building confidence in others, her son included. She spent too much time polishing her own ego. It's all been such a sad situation."

"When we were introduced I noticed he had the same surname as Amelia's maiden name," Kate said. "Didn't she marry his father?"

"Oh, yes. Though of all her marriages and divorces that likely was the only one Amelia considered a failure. Dear, dear Joey."

The name of the husband Amelia said she always forgot about. "Miss Amelia mentioned him. From what she told me, I assumed the marriage was quite short."

"No, no." Through the phone Kate heard Jane take a deep breath, followed by a long moment of silence. "Until Amelia's marriage to

Daniel Nethercutt, hers and Joey's was her longest. Six years. I doubt she forgot a single day."

"This doesn't jell with what she said to me. She spoke as if he was inconsequential. Like she could barely remember him."

Jane's voice took on a quieter tone as she continued. "Amelia and Joey grew up together. I think Amelia always loved him, but he wouldn't get married right out of college, and she got angry and found someone who would. James Harper. The marriage was doomed from the start. After all, its foundation was built on nothing more than spite, hurt feelings, and attempted jealousy."

Imagining a young headstrong Amelia, determined to either get her way or make the man pay, came easily to Kate. Jane's next words confirmed these impressions.

"The marriage lasted little more than a year. Her second, to Charles Walker mere months—"

"Charles *Webster* Walker? The attorney?" Kate cried.

"Why yes," Jane replied. "Have you met him?"

"He's the one who hired Meg and me to inventory the collections. He's the executor of the will." This was getting way too complicated. "Isn't it a conflict of interest for Miss Amelia's ex-husband to be handling her estate?"

"I don't see why, unless he's an heir. I can't imagine Amelia leaving him any kind of inheritance. That wouldn't be her way. Of course, with the rumors of their affair—"

"A recent affair?"

"Again, this is all rumor, Kate, but it is why George and I moved all of our legal work to the lawyer in Bennington. We don't have a lot, but this is a small town and—"

"Did he know why you left?"

"We didn't say in so many words, but...still...I always liked Mr. Daniel."

"Well, given that Mr. Walker gave me the inventorying job he doesn't seem to be one to hold grudges against the McKenzie name."

"Oh, no, Charles might be a bit stiff, but he's a politician at heart and stays on pleasant terms with everyone. Never forgets a face and is always the first to offer help. Even after he and Amelia divorced, she relied heavily on him for keeping her financial affairs in order. Which was probably some basis for the rumors."

And could lead people to wonder whether Amelia killed her husband. Kate knew that angle was not something her mother-in-law would discuss and took the conversation back to its original path. "I can't connect the dots on what Miss Amelia said about her husband Joey to what you've told me. She acted like the marriage slipped her mind, yet none of it explains why her son doesn't use his father's last name. How did she finally get Joey to marry her? And what was his last name, by the way?"

"Oh, Cavannah," Jane said. "Sorry, more local trivia. Anyway, Joey Cavannah was eventually worn down and agreed to be Amelia's third husband."

"You make it sound like a bit of arm-twisting. I realize she had a strong personality, but was Joey so weak-natured?"

"No, no. I'm going about this all wrong. Let me start over. Well, not completely from the beginning, but back a little." Jane was silent again, apparently to collect her thoughts. "Joey hated hurting people. Actually, he avoided hurting anything. He was very much like Thomas, always attempting to be helpful, never wanting to make waves. Joey had an artistic temperament. He wanted to be an actor. Unfortunately, his family, and even Amelia, were determined he would go into politics."

"So, Amelia wanted to go to Washington for more than the cherry blossoms," Kate mused.

"What, dear?"

"Nothing. Go on."

"Anyway, like I said, Joey was an artistic sort and had no desire for the rigors and competitions of politics. But he couldn't fight everyone, and he had no champions for his dream. He went to law school to please his parents. But the longer he played the role of trying to be the good son, the easier it came for everyone to bully him into doing whatever they wanted. His will shattered as his dream died. Eventually even Amelia got her way and they married, though such a battle won is never a sweet victory, especially as she never kept her ambitions of his political potential and her social goals a secret. She should have just stayed married to Charles. Her marriage to Joey never materialized the way she envisioned, but Amelia was too stubborn to accept anything less than the powerful fairy tale she'd imagined."

"And Thomas?"

"The couple may have had their ups and downs, but he's definitely Joey's. The pressure the poor soul lived under from both his parents...and then Amelia..."

She could tell her mother-in-law was feeling uncomfortable about the turn of the conversation, how it smacked quietly of gossip. Jane kept an open mind but tried to keep her mouth closed on other people's private affairs. This information could be important. Kate pressed on, even if it meant smaller steps. "How long until he left his family, or did Amelia divorce him?"

"Oh, no, Joey couldn't leave. That wasn't his way, and besides, Amelia wouldn't let him go. Also, like I already mentioned, he had been systematically beaten into submission throughout his life. We would call it emotional abuse today, but back then people accepted it as bowing to family pressure. I guess we still do, actually. He did rebel a bit. Joined a community theater group, but his father heard about it and ended that. No Cavannah would humiliate the family by appearing on stage."

Jane stopped for a moment. After a pause, her mother-in-law spoke up again, either understanding Kate's need to know or else wanting to make sure everything was understood. "People talked, of course, wondering if Joey would finally decide enough was enough, and, well, poor Amelia had to have heard at least some of it. But she steadfastly refused to believe the marriage doomed. By the time she gave birth to Thomas, she and Joey had been married nearly four years. She looked ready to walk on air, and I know she thought the baby would make all the difference. In my heart, though, I never doubted her fall back to earth would be a painful one, and I was right."

"You said he didn't leave—"

"No, I said he couldn't." Silence reigned again briefly, then Jane added, almost in a whisper, "He killed himself. Joey drove his car into Hunter's Pond. He'd mailed letters to his parents and to Amelia, saying goodbye, and that he was very sorry. Joey's parents died within the year, his father from a heart attack and his mother from an accidental fall down the stairs."

"Oh, that's sad." Kate gripped the receiver. "At least Thomas was a baby, but poor Amelia."

Jane sighed. "She took the baby and left for Europe immediately after the funeral. I never even had a chance to speak to her. A few months later, I think it was while she lived in Italy, her parents died in a small plane crash. She came home to close up their house, listed it with a realtor, and disappeared once more. I followed her subsequent marriages and divorces in the paper, as surprised as everyone else in town when she returned to Hazelton after marrying Daniel Nethercutt. They bought that huge mansion, and, finally, Amelia seemed happy. Truly happy."

"And Thomas?"

A tsking sound came over the receiver ahead of Jane's words. "Of course, I have nothing to gauge anything on. I didn't see the boy grow up. I suppose Amelia had him use the Lane name to protect him from anyone who knew about his father. But Thomas always seemed a shadow person to me. Like someone who's perpetually waiting to be told what to do next."

The front door slam announced her family's return. "I have to go, Jane. Thanks for talking about this with me."

"I hope I helped, dear."

As she replaced the receiver, Kate wondered what real help would look like at this point.

CHAPTER ELEVEN

• • • •

<u>*MONDAY, APRIL 12TH*</u> *Memo to Self:*
   I will not get discouraged.

• • • •

KATE SAT ACROSS THE kitchen table from Meg, with Valerie James at one end. They silently watched as Valerie, stunning in jeans and a faux zebra fur vest, perused the contract they'd finetuned and printed an hour earlier. Everything hinged on the diva's decision. Would she sign or wouldn't she? The Stacked in Your Favor bid sheet was ready to send to Charles Webster Walker's office as soon as the contract carried her signature. Without a third person, Kate and Meg already acknowledged over morning coffee they couldn't undertake the job, money or no money, access to return items to the mansion or no access. They'd again tossed around the idea of using the proffered legal assistant but decided their first instincts were still best. It was Valerie or nothing.

"No matter how annoying she is," Meg had quipped.

In addition to the workers-searching clause, Kate added a requirement that no persons outside of employees or agents of Stack in Your Favor enter the premises during the weeks of inventory. She even left a place in the contract for Charles Webster Walker to countersign to the conditions. Not that she completely believed said limitations would keep out the mysterious thief, but their inclusion in the contract might make things more dicey for anyone caught inside the mansion who couldn't explain his or her authorized entry.

The interior decorator scanned the first page, nodding as her gaze hit the area of work hours and per hour salary. Then, as expected, her face darkened when she read the final clause.

"You're requiring I do *what?*" Valerie shrieked, giving each a glare hot enough to melt steel.

"I thought the wording was clear," Kate forced herself to breathe evenly and keep her voice calm, leaning a little sideways to pretend to read the contract, "Let me see if I can expand on it a bit. We're requiring all regular and contract employees of Stacked in Your Favor do hereby agree to—"

"I can read, damn it!" Valerie slammed one hand on the contract, making the pen jump. "I just don't understand why you added such a stupid condition."

"Oh, I see," Kate replied. She heard a muffled snort from Meg's direction. "Well, this is simply a formality to keep everything on the up and up for our bonding company. After all, we'll be around countless rare and valuable objects, and if anything turns up missing, my carrier will be on the hook for the appraised amount."

"Sophia is not going to like this."

"I beg to differ. Any good businesswoman understands the value of insurance—and its restrictions. Plus, she's already expressed concerns about certain items vanishing in the last few weeks. This contract clause keeps everything clear and defendable. It's not that I don't trust you or Meg, but if all of us can firmly back up each other—"

"Given the fact as how signing is, as you say, only a formality, we won't actually be searching one another."

Kate shook her head. "On the contrary. We will definitely conduct the group searches at the end of each business day. I didn't mean to imply we were only giving lip service to what the contract stated."

Unbelievably, the decorator's face turned a shade darker. "I'm uncomfortable with this clause."

"In that case, I'm afraid you can't work on the Nethercutt job."

Kate extended a hand toward the contract. In the same instant, Valerie snatched it out of her reach. "Just a minute. Let me think." She looked at her cell phone for a second, then dropped it into her designer bag. "I really must consider my own company's liability."

"Of course." Kate sat back and contemplated whom Valerie almost called—the insurance company for the design firm or Sophia. It didn't matter, they knew Sophia was up to something, and Valerie was likely a player in the plan, but knowing for sure could be helpful. She looked at Meg, who was still unable to speak but whose bright eyes telegraphed *Valerie's hooked. We've got her.*

And got her they had. She winked back.

"Okay." Valerie ripped the pen off the tabletop and, with huge, angry, flourishing strokes, signed her name on the line beneath Kate's and Meg's countersignatures.

"Terrific." Kate scooped up the contract. "I'll go make each of you a copy and send the bid to the lawyer." She headed for her office. "Be back in a sec."

Ten minutes later, after copies were distributed and a call from Walker confirmed receipt and acceptance of the bid, Valerie steamed out the front door. Still obviously controlling the urge to scream, she called over her shoulder, "I'll meet the two of you at the mansion at one o'clock. I have to go see...a client."

Kate held her breath as the door slammed, but it was too much for Meg. The redhead exploded, dancing in leaps, lunges, and giddy quick steps after the hysterics took control. They looked at each other and simultaneously collapsed in jubilant laughter. As they shared a dishtowel to wipe away tears, Kate asked, "Do you think she heard us?"

"Who cares?" Meg waved the towel. "It'll give her more to whine about when she sees Sophia."

Already on her feet, Kate moved over to the coffeepot. "So, you think she was heading for lunch with her mentor?"

"Absolutely." Meg found a chair at the table and wrapped a hand around her refilled cup. "Thanks. Releasing that much energy at one time is draining. I need this. By the way, did you talk to Jane about what's been going on?"

"I asked for the historical scoop, but I didn't tell her someone's trying to paint me as a thief and murderer."

Meg smiled. "Good thinking. Saying something along those lines worries most mothers-in-law. Even if the idea is just to label you as a kleptomaniac."

"You don't suppose this is nothing more than a case of pinning the blame on the outsider, do you?"

"You're not the only non-Nethercutt-relation involved. Think of Mrs. Baxt—"

"But I am the only Hazelton outsider," she stressed, waving away the rebuttal Meg started. "I know, I know. Being married to a McKenzie gives me status, but face it, folks in Hazelton don't just sweep you into the fold. Even with Keith or his parents always around to make introductions, I've felt the restraint. I'm not complaining. Everyone's been welcoming to me, but it's still something to consider. If I stood before a Hazelton jury, they couldn't say for sure what I 'could or would do.' I'm an unknown quantity."

Meg shrugged. "True, the other players in Saturday's meeting are either native to Hazelton or have been associated with the town a decade or more. It doesn't explain Danny, though. He seems to want to implicate everyone indiscriminately. Did you ask Jane about him?"

"No, I'm going to try to squeeze what I need from Tiffany instead." Kate took a cautious sip. "She ought to be able to more readily describe his behavior away from the family. Nothing like the school setting to reveal a person's real character."

"But Tiffany goes to Hazelton High," Meg replied. "Surely Danny is in one of the nearby prep schools."

Kate shook her head. "He wore a class ring the first time I met him. It was Hazelton's."

"Interesting." Meg picked up the pen. "It was already a shock when I found out Tiffany wasn't in private school, but there's no way I would presume Danny a public high student."

"Unless his dad's financial straits are too stretched to accommodate expensive tuition rates," Kate suggested.

"Or the kid's been kicked out of the better ones already," Meg returned.

Something to consider. Kate bit her lip as she speculated on what transgressions warranted expulsion. "Mrs. Baxter did say she and Amelia thought Danny used drugs."

"A tried and true way to receive the scholastic heave-ho. Most of the elite schools boast such a long waiting list that without legacy status or a big donation they don't have to tolerate negative activity from students. And from what Sophia said, we can assume Bill lacks the cash to provide a cushion for bad behavior on his son's part." Meg stood and grabbed the cookie jar from the counter. "Got any chocolate in here?"

Kate retrieved a couple of Milky Ways from the back of the refrigerator. "You're in luck. The girls didn't find these."

Her all-time favorite, Kate savored the sharp crunch as the first bite snapped the cold chocolate coating, the creamier center waking her taste buds. As they munched, she related what she'd learned from

Jane, while savoring the rich caramel that clung to her teeth. Her mouth watered each time a word made her tongue brush a cache of rich goodness. "Call me crazy." She licked a chocolaty fingertip. "But, I'm more paranoid after learning Miss Amelia and Charles Webster Walker were once married. He seemed kind of pushy about us taking the inventory job."

"There's no 'seemed' about it," Meg said. "He definitely wanted you working on those collections. But he's long been known for taking care of his clients, and I'm sure your very outsider-status was a lure."

"I guess I see your point. No one in the Nethercutt clan acts like they can be trusted."

"Once he'd set his mind to hiring you, and given the limiting condition of the will, he pretty much had to take any bid you offered," Meg continued. "I understand your creeped-out feelings, but time is truly the relevant issue here, and you're qualified and already on the spot. It's hard to put old Charlie-boy, Esquire and young Amelia together, but it makes sense. I remember he ran for mayor years ago, and the papers said he was once married to a socialite."

"Didn't he ever marry again?"

"Nope." Meg popped the last bite of candy into her mouth. "He's such a strange duck, always pleasant to everyone but different. I never could see him married at all."

"Did he win the race?"

Meg shook her head. "He got beat by an ordinary housewife, Myra Robbins, whose only claim to previous office was PTA president."

"I've met her," Kate said. "She's Eileen the receptionist's mom. She was at the station one day when I met Keith for lunch."

"Yeah, nice lady. Once people found out she was running, she had no trouble getting the votes to win. Served two very successful terms. Unexpectedly got pregnant with Eileen and retired. Her other kids are much older, both boys. They graduated ahead of me."

"Did he ever run again?"

"Nope. The closest thing he came to political life afterward was when the community theater did a revival of 'Mr. Smith Goes to Washington' and he played understudy to the Jimmy Stewart role."

"Funny how Amelia married two men who liked theatre."

"Just goes to show we all have our types."

Kate pulled out the pad she'd scribbled her notes on. "Speaking of types, I keep coming back to something Jane said. How Thomas seems to always want someone else to tell him what to do. If Jane felt this way, wouldn't his family tweak on that, too? Could someone coerce Thomas into killing his mother?"

"And then plant the stolen objects on you?"

"You might think I'm crazy, but no," Kate said. "I don't understand the motive, other than to keep me as a reserve suspect. I mean, if someone really wanted the items to get me into trouble, the police would have received an anonymous tip or something. But I'm being set up now to use if needed later..."

"Mmm...I hadn't thought about that. Yes, you should have heard something from them by now." Meg twisted the pad her way. "Don't forget to transfer these notes into your casebook. I'd hate for one of us to misplace information at this point."

"I will. My conversation with Jane ended in a hurry last night when my family came home, and with getting the girls off to school and all I haven't had time this morning to transcribe everything."

"Plus, you needed to add those embellishments to the contract." Meg giggled.

"Don't start laughing again," Kate warned, smiling. "We still have lots to do before we meet Valerie." She took the empty cups to the sink then headed upstairs for the attic. By the time she found the correct storage box, Meg had joined her.

"It's too neat up here," her neighbor complained. "I'm never letting you into our attic."

Smiling, Kate withdrew a set of blue and gray baby monitors. "Don't be hard on yourself. I've only been here six months. You've lived in your house nine years. Besides, it's my job to keep things organized. People watch gleefully, waiting to catch me in a slip up. It can be exhausting."

"Makes absolutely no difference, but thanks for trying to make me feel better. What are those for?"

As Kate held up one of the plastic monitors, the plug at the end of the cord swung out and slapped her knee, destroying an idea she'd had only moments before. "Nothing. I forgot the source unit needs electricity. Darn. I thought they'd make a good audio alarm for the van."

"Oh, I get it." Meg grabbed up the plug. "Leave the microphoned-end in the van and use the receiver in the house to hear if anyone breaks in and leaves treasure behind."

"Yes, but there's no DC adapter. I'll have to think of something else."

"We have walkie-talkies at my house," Meg offered. "They probably need batteries, but the boys were using them a couple of days ago so they aren't broken yet."

"But the mike needs to be keyed—"

"Duct tape or rubber bands."

"You're a genius!"

Meg grinned. "Ain't I though? But it isn't any fresh epiphany. Don't you dare tell the boys, but I've used the trick before when they were up to something and I needed to find out what. Everything comes through loud and clear."

"I guess I'm lucky I have girls."

Meg's grin turned wicked. "Wait a few years. There'll be plenty of secrets to ferret out in the not too distant future, my friend."

"Don't remind me. Just help me rig the camcorder."

· · · ·

THEY ARRIVED AT THE mansion ahead of Valerie, despite having to go by the lawyer's office for a front door key. Meg stayed back to set the walkie-talkie alarm, while Kate grabbed the laptop computer and video case and headed inside.

The house felt decidedly empty. It seemed too unreal to think the inhabitants, a rich eccentric couple scouting out Georgetown antiquities less than a month ago, were both dead. With death and murder hanging in the air, Kate had the constant urge to check over her shoulder.

She made her way into the parlor, where they'd decided the night before to start the inventorying. By the time Meg joined her, Kate narrowed down one corner as having the best overall scope for the cinematic enterprise.

"Are you going to camouflage the camera, or let Valerie know we're taping each day?"

Kate set the video camera on a tabletop and punched the red button to start recording. "I doubt we have a choice. It uses tape and only records for a couple of hours, not like the newer digital machines. Even if we hide it, I don't think I can possibly change out the cassette three or four times a day and not get caught."

"You're right." Meg pivoted to take in the room. "But truthfully, I can't see it doing much good. With just one stationary camera there are too many places to get out of the lens' sight and scoop something into a pocket."

"Very true," Kate plopped into a tall Queen Anne chair. "Besides, Valerie isn't the one framing me. She's merely Sophia's spy. But what can we do? Even with another camera, we'll never catch our culprit unless we tape twenty-four hours a day."

"I've got an idea. Where's your cell? Ben tried to use mine as a tub toy last night, so it's still covered in rice to try to save it."

"Yikes." Kate grimaced and passed her phone. "Who are you going to call?"

Meg punched in the numbers and held up a finger. "Yes, Gil Berman, please. This is his wife." During the wait, she explained, "My dear hubby has a friend in the surveillance trade. Don't ask any questions, because I have no answers, but he may be able to help us with this little dilemma."

As she greeted Gil over the phone, the front door opened. "Hi, honey, hang on a second while I go to another room." Meg passed Valerie in the doorway.

"Where's she going?" The decorator arrived dressed exactly as before, looking more ready for a shopping safari than an afternoon picking through musty collectibles.

"Needs to talk to her husband." Kate pulled the computer case onto the coffee table and removed the laptop.

"I hope you don't expect me to do any typing." Valerie anchored a scarlet-taloned hand on one hip.

She smiled and shook her head. "No, I'd planned on bribing Meg for that."

"She types?"

"Yes, and quite quickly, I understand. It's how she and Gil met, through her typing for the newspaper. Even if she's a little rusty she should do much better than you or me."

"I didn't mean I can't type."

"I knew exactly what you meant." Kate plugged in the power cord and booted up the machine, then innocently asked, "And how was Sophia?"

"Fine, she—" Valerie glared. "How did you know I was meeting with her?"

This woman is Sophia's secret weapon? Kate wanted to laugh but kept her smile steady. "I'm really not sure. Guess I just assumed, what with you decorating her house and all."

The explanation was apparently rational enough for "the mole."

"Yes." Valerie seated herself regally on the Chinese silk settee. "Their master suite is turning out superb. Sophia said I'll be getting scads more referrals once all her friends tour the rooms."

"That's nice."

"What is?" Meg asked, reentering and sliding the cell phone back into the open pocket of Kate's purse.

"My design work for Sophia," Valerie answered.

Kate wasn't sure how long she could take this conversation and decided to rein it in. "Well, we have work to do, ladies. Meg, would you do the typing honors, or should we write everything on pads and take turns adding the inventory into the computer?"

Meg shrugged. "Typing is fine with me. You want it in word processing or a spreadsheet?"

Unable to resist, Kate turned to Valerie. "Which do you think would be best?"

The decorator's red lips opened and closed several times, until she finally said, "Whatever the two of you prefer. I'm the hired help, after all."

"Nonsense." Kate watched Meg's shoulders wiggle in silent laughter as she bent over the keyboard. "We value your input."

"Honestly, it's up to you," Valerie said.

"Okay, I guess a spreadsheet might give us more sorting options. And Meg, if you could code on of the columns to put in each of our names as you add items, we'll be able to track later who inspected and inventoried what objects in case the insurance company needs confirmation. We need to add dates, too."

"Will do," Meg answered, face hidden by her curls. She hit a couple of keys. "Pick your posts, and we can start."

They started, all right, Kate almost jumping out of her shoes when a back door slammed shut.

CHAPTER TWELVE

ORGANIZATION WHEN THINGS Don't Go As Planned

- **Stay Calm.** *Anger creates negativity and wastes resources. Focus on something you can accomplish.*
- **Don't Complain.** *Regroup to see what can be salvaged or modified. Time is precious—don't waste it griping.*
- **Have a Back-up Plan.** *Sometimes, patience is the only option. Consider alternatives, like people and resources not normally used.*
- **Schedule in Some Extra Time for Unplanned Emergencies.** *Pad your schedule with small blocks of minutes to accommodate unexpected disasters.*
- **Determine What CAN Get Done.** *Don't let a schedule paralyze you. When something cannot be completed as planned, skip that task and move on—don't let the day be a total washout.*

• • • •

MEG, VALERIE AND KATE raced across the marbled hall floor and almost slid when they reached the ceramic kitchen tile. They picked up speed as they exited the back door. One carriage-styled garage door stood ajar, the dark depths taunting them to enter. Meg and Valerie headed that way at a full run.

Kate snatched desperately, fingers catching Meg's sleeve and plucking the soft back of

Valerie's vest. "Wait! We don't know what's in there!"

The pair slowed then stopped, exchanging embarrassed looks.

"I guess that was kind of dumb," Meg said, her color high.

"Fools rush in." Valerie shrugged, before throwing a furtive glance over her shoulder.

This could be dangerous. Kate raised an eyebrow. "I'm glad you said it. Would hate to think I'm the only one thinking this through. Let's return to the parlor and get a cell phone before we traipse around places that could be hiding someone. And can we please all stay together?" Valerie pulled an iPhone from a hidden vest pocket. "I have mine right here."

"Good. Keep it handy." Meg set off again toward the garage, waving them to join her.

"We aren't really going inside." Kate kept her feet planted on the flagstone walk. No way was she walking into a potential ambush. "The fact we don't see anyone suggests that if someone did slam that door it was to escape our sight."

"We're not going inside." Meg turned, hands on hips. "We'll just open one of the doors wide to allow enough light for us to peek through the windows."

Jeez! It's like we're in the middle of a Lucy and Ethel escapade. Pointing toward the two forested acres behind the estate, Kate said, "By now, any intruder with half a brain is already across those woods and cutting through the nearest neighbor's place. We can't even be sure there was an intruder at all, but that doesn't mean I'm ready to play Batgirl to your Wonder Woman either."

"Who am I?" Valerie asked.

"What?" Kate and Meg asked together.

"Who am I?" Valerie repeated. She pointed at Kate. "If you're Batgirl..." She turned her finger on Meg. "...and you're Wonder Woman, then who am I?"

"Very annoying," Meg snapped. "I can't believe you. Of all the juven—"

"Wait a minute, I—" Valerie started

Kate held up a hand. "Stop, both of you! I was being sarcastic, not giving out complimentary nicknames. I was just—"

"Demonstrating yet again how you two band together," Valerie cut her off. "I understand. Let's move on. They're likely long gone, like you said." She turned on her heel and headed for the garage, radiating her irritation like an aura.

Replicating turn-of-the-century design, each bay to the three-car garage was side-hinged and latched in the middle. After Valerie heaved the ajar door fully open, the trio took positions at the sides, peering into the cavernous interior. Kate wiped damp palms down her slacks and shifted a step to better see inside. Automotive tools hung from a pegboard along the back wall, but nothing was labeled to point up anything missing or being readied by some mysterious marauder to strike one or more of the women. A dark blue MG, likely Danny's, was the only car in view, but the vehicle stood on a hydraulic lift, leaving little means for hiding anyone. A couple of large multi-drawer tool chests could have shielded a person from view, but by looking in various windows the women determined no one crouched behind either one.

"So, did someone run in here or not?" Meg asked.

"I'd guess not." Kate's heart pounded in her ears.

Waving at a walk-through door in the east wall, Valerie said, "Or the person shot out that side door and is long gone, hidden by the trees."

"Well, we've already gone this far." Meg took off walking around the building. "I say we check out the rest of the area as best we can."

The backyard resembled a still life in green, although none of the flowers had yet bloomed, a set of filigreed steel furniture and one whimsically-sculptured cupid fountain added interest to the scene. Everyone stayed well away from the forest. The thick glass of the greenhouse, like individual viewfinders to the unique beauty inside, offered a careful scrutiny through the windows. The sudden fall of a rake made the women leap in surprise, then freeze, waiting for a new danger. Nothing else happened. No one was there.

"We must have scared 'em off." Meg picked up the rake. "Or it was nothing more than one of the mansion's doors closing in a draft."

"Don't be ridiculous," Valerie strode ahead. "We heard the back door slam, and it wasn't a draft. It was someone. Someone who wasn't supposed to be here. I'm not saying anyone dangerous, but definitely a person or persons unknown who wanted his or her identity kept that way."

"I'm still for calling the police," Kate mused, as she and Meg followed Valerie back to the parlor. "After all, we picked up the key today, and the lawyer said, except for his own key, we had the only copy."

"Like he has a clue how many keys are in circulation." Valerie sniffed, planting herself in the middle of the sofa, and laying her arms possessively along the back. "I'll bet any number of people has access to this mansion."

Thinking of anyone in particular? Kate knew her face mirrored the look on Meg's, and that they shared the feeling Sophia could, and would, enter anytime she wanted. Who else might have a similar agenda?

"Good point, Valerie." Meg closed the laptop and shoved it back into the case. "We have nothing to offer the police if we called. We can't even narrow down suspects. After all, the alarm wasn't set when we arrived."

"You're right." Kate retrieved her cell phone. "However, Mr. Walker should be notified, for our own protection."

Valerie jumped up from the sofa. "I need to find a ladies' room. My nerves are too sensitive for this kind of stress."

If she met Meg's eyes, Kate knew they would both burst into laughter. A deep breath later she dialed the attorney's number.

"I think you should leave immediately," Walker said, after his secretary left Kate on hold for more than five minutes. "The slammed door may have been a ruse to get you outside, leaving the intruder to hide inside. I'll send out a security team, but I don't want you to take any chances with safety, Ms. McKenzie."

"I quite agree, Mr. Walker. Security looking around is a good idea, but activating the alarm system already in place is useful as well."

"Generally, the alarm is on," Walker explained. "But knowing your group was coming this afternoon, I went by at lunch and deactivated it. I'm not authorized to release the code to anyone. Insurance you understand."

Kate did understand. Her first job out of high school was interning at one of the nation's largest insurance companies, and she found many of the rules arcane and illogical. Besides, if the intruder was a family member Amelia had likely given out the alarm code herself.

"Have you reset the code following Miss Amelia's death?"

"Not yet. But I'll have the security team take care of it this evening."

The answer did nothing to reassure her Walker was on top of the situation. "When you came by to deactivate the alarm, did you open the back door?"

"No, I entered and exited through the front." The lawyer coughed. "Listen, Ms. McKenzie, in case someone is in the house, I want you to—"

"Don't worry, sir," Kate interrupted. "We're leaving."

"Well, one day down," Valerie remarked, coming in at the end of the conversation. "Even if we haven't gotten anything inventoried, time to close shop for today." The laptop case hung from Meg's shoulder.

Kate nodded. "Let's clear out and meet back here in the morning, after I get the green light from security."

Valerie scooped up her tiny, faux alligator bag and headed for the door. "Well, if I don't hear anything different in the early a.m., I'll assume I should report at nine."

"Whoa, missy." Meg dropped the bag gently to the floor and ran after the departing decorator.

"What?"

"We still have to search each other."

"But we didn't get any work done."

"But we've all been in the house." Meg walked back into the parlor and scooped up the video camera, the red light signaling it was resolutely recording everything within view. She pointed the lens at the other women. "Katie, you and Valerie search each other then one of you can hold this camera while the other searches me."

"I'm not removing any clothes—" Valerie protested.

"Don't be absurd," Kate snapped. "We're not making an Internet porno flick for crying out loud." She shoved her tote-sized purse into Valerie's grasp and held out a hand until the diminutive reptile bag was released to her.

Nothing out of the ordinary surfaced, as expected, and the tension diminished slightly by the time she finished Meg's search and Valerie turned off the camcorder. Once outside, Kate credited her careful planning for another job success and pulled out her van keys as Valerie's Miata tore down the drive.

"She is more agreeable than I'd expected." Meg slid the side door open. "I think this may work out, despite the odds. She simmers pretty high but never boils over."

"I agree." Kate opened the driver's door, then froze as her eye fell on an item propped in the bucket seat. An African death mask, one she knew normally hung with the collection displayed in the conservatory, sat angled comfortably against the upholstery and stared sightlessly out the windshield.

Kate's hand shot to her chest. "Omigod! Meg, look!"

"Now we know why we were lured to the back of the house," Meg said as she stepped closer.

"Yes, to taunt us with something else that should be in the house." Kate took a cleansing breath and snapped the rubber band on her wrist. She leaned in and used a two-handed grip to extricate the mask from the seat and shoulder belt. All she needed now was to mar some priceless artifact. "At least we can get this returned before Sophia or anyone else can miss it."

Meg took a long look around, her gaze sweeping every direction. "You don't think someone is taking pictures of us with this mask, do you?"

"Stop." Kate used her hip to close the driver side door, and laughed shakily. "I'm the worrier in our group. Your job is to always minimize my reactions. If you turn paranoid now, I'll have to find a new best friend."

Meg hurried up the porch steps to unlock the front door. "You're right. This is where I should have said, 'Don't worry, Katie, even if we do get arrested we can testify in the defense of each other and share a cell while we await the verdict.'"

"Thanks. I needed that."

Kate and Meg re-hung the mask, then rushed home and scanned the video at super-fast speed. Since the walkie-talkies hadn't squeaked a bit of evidence, they were desperate to spot any sign of the mask thief. Nothing and no one came to light.

"But the conservatory is on the opposite end of the house from the parlor. It would be a fluke if the video caught anyone." Kate sighed.

Meg nodded. "The intruder probably went out the back door with the mask, and headed for the front while we were investigating the back."

"Some sleuths we are."

"One misstep, Batgirl, nothing more."

Kate held up her purse and key ring. "Even more scary, though. These stayed safely in the parlor's video range the entire time."

• • • •

KEITH HAD A RARE EVENING off thanks to the radio station replaying his interview with Wayne Gretzky. Kate would have normally lined up a babysitter for a night out, but circumstances remained far from normal. Instead, she, Keith, Meg, and Gil all sat around the McKenzie kitchen table and discussed the growing seriousness of the situation. Thumps and bangs echoed from upstairs to indicate the kids were taking full advantage of their parents' preoccupation and enjoying the usually forbidden game of indoor dodge ball.

Meg had already filled Gil in on past days' events, and his thick blond hair showed the evidence of having run frustrated fingers through repeatedly. True to their natures, the husbands telegraphed their feelings in open expressions. Keith's showed relaxed interest, while Gil's fair complexion turned stormy.

"I think you need to go to the police," Gil said, tilting his head ceiling-ward as an unusually loud *whomp* reverberated from the upper floor. "Maybe I should go—"

Kate touched the top of his left hand, halting his rise from the chair. "Wait. See if anyone screams." When nothing more than another round of bumps and thumps followed, she finished, "They're obviously okay, and as long as they're focused on the game we can talk out our options."

Keith raised an eyebrow. She knew he probably wondered who this strange blond woman was not racing upstairs to assess the damage, but she ignored the questioning brow and seconded Gil's recommendation. "I agree we should probably take this to the authorities. The mask was too blatant. Almost a dare."

"No, Kate—" Meg began.

"The police may not see things our way," Keith cut in.

Gil shook his head. "Whoever this is, the level of potential threat is escalating."

"But what if setting me up does have something to do with Amelia's murder?" Kate bit her lip.

"You're right. Exactly," Gil said. "One more point for going to the authorities."

"Handing Kate over to the police as a potential thief isn't the answer either." Meg's thin brows made a jagged line above angry eyes. She turned to Kate. "Think hard before you do this, honey. You can't control what conclusions they may draw in order to close a high-profile murder case." She clasped her friend's hand. Kate's fingers felt cold next to Meg's warm ones.

"Right." Keith moved to the back of his wife's chair, and wrapped his arms around her, bending to rest his chin on the top her head. "You've already been interrogated once and cleared, but who knows what may happen if you go in again. The state police are under pressure to find her killer, and you don't want to be accused of concealing evidence in a murder investigation."

She twisted to look up at him. "One more reason to go. If they're aware someone is trying to frame me—"

"They might think you're doing it to yourself to cast suspicion elsewhere," Keith added.

"That's ridiculous, I've been cleared."

"And we want you to stay that way." Meg squeezed her hand. "Don't jeopardize your freedom."

Overwhelmed, Kate looked at Gil, who appeared thoughtful. She asked, "What's your take on this?"

He stared at her a moment, then shrugged. "Actually, I'm beginning to think our spouses make a number of good points." He checked at his watch. "My surveillance guy should be here any minute. Let's find out what help he can offer for your work time in the mansion and get his opinion on everything else."

The doorbell chimed.

Jefferson Meeks was a former all-state tackle, and he looked like he could still pull down a six-pack of halfbacks. His huge left hand dwarfed a leather portfolio, and at Gil's introductions, he used the other to shake all around.

"This guy's the best in the business," Gil said, smiling. "No matter what the situation, if I need to find out anything on anybody, I call Jeff."

The big guy ducked his head modestly, then grinned, his smile bright as moonlight on snow against his dark skin. His voice rumbled. "Gil's one of my biggest fans."

"Well, hopefully we'll all be fans after tonight," Keith said. Once confidentiality assurances were obtained, Keith laid out the situation and addressed everyone's fears.

Meeks's answer was a long whistle. "If anyone needs my help, you ladies do. How 'bout I meet you on-site in the morning around seven and get more cameras set up to monitor who goes where and why?"

"Sounds great," Gil said.

Practical as always, Kate had to ask, "How much will this cost?"

"Doesn't matter." Meg turned to Meeks and said, "You can send the bill to Charles Webster Walker."

CHAPTER THIRTEEN

Motivation:
STACKED IN YOUR FAVOR, LLC
KATE MCKENZIE, PRES.

• • • •

Tuesday, April 13ᵗʰ

• • • •

WORDS TO STAY ON-TRACK:
"Organizing is what you do before you do something, so that when you do it, it's not all mixed up."
— Christopher Robin —
GOAL(S) FOR THE DAY:

- *Meet with Meeks.*
- *Get "you-know-what" put back.*
- *Go by Mrs. B's and check out kitchen.*
- *Attend Amelia's funeral this afternoon.*

• • • •

TRUE TO HIS WORD, JEFFERSON Meeks waited in front of the Nethercutt mansion the next morning as Kate and Meg arrived a little before seven. He climbed out of his nondescript white van as Kate and Meg debarked from their blue one. Mrs. Baxter's place showed closed curtains and no lights, but Kate couldn't tell if the house was uninhabited or the woman chose to sleep late since she didn't have to report to a job. Regardless, she wanted to see inside the cottage again.

"I've worried about not first getting approval of your expenses," Kate said to Meeks.

"No problem." His voice sounded even gruffer in the early morning. "Spoke to Mr. Walker myself late yesterday evening. Told him your concerns and what surveillance I thought necessary. Like was said last night," he nodded toward Meg, "the man told me to just send a bill to his office."

"I have the key, but not the security code." Kate trailed the other two to the front door, everyone's arms laden with notebooks and cases holding the paraphernalia of their respective professions. "Did he happen to mention that as well?"

"Nope, but it doesn't matter," Meeks replied. "I got here about ten minutes ago and did a reconnaissance through the windows. The security system isn't activated."

Sure enough, when Kate opened the door the alarm remained silent, and everything appeared exactly as the previous afternoon.

"You think Walker's security team really came by?" Meg asked, waving a hand at the panel. "Or were his promises yesterday all talk?"

"Doesn't matter." Kate smiled at Meeks, "We came prepared."

He grinned. "I'll do some inside recon. See if anybody's been up to any foolishness in the nighttime hours." He pulled a clipboard and pen from his heavy briefcase before leaving it by the door. "A few diagrams will help the process, too. Gotta note where cameras can do the most good."

Meg removed her backpack and withdrew a thermos and cups. "Want coffee before you start?"

"Naw." He shook his head. "In surveillance you learn to begin the day with at least a pot, and my morning punched in a couple of hours ago."

"Remind me never to join his profession," Meg said to Kate, as she handed over a full cup.

"You and me, both." She led the way back into the parlor, and added, "Enter my web, the spider said."

"Huh?" Meg joined her on the settee, their knees inches from the carved rosewood coffee table.

Kate waved a hand. "I'm beginning to get superstitious about this room."

Meg was quiet for a moment and sipped her coffee. "The action does all seem to start whenever you're in here. From the tea with Amelia where you unwittingly became a suspect, to the heir gathering where we witnessed Thomas's and Danny's devastation over not getting the flowers, to yesterday and the ominous door slam and eventual death mask in the van."

Kate laughed shakily. "Glad to know I'm not the only one seeing patterns."

Leaning to pat her friend's knee, Meg reassured, "We're going to get to the bottom of this, Katie. Come on, let's think. I decided on a few things last night to ask Valerie, like exactly what she did do on the way to and from her bathroom trip yesterday."

"Yes, after finding the mask every action seems suspect, but there's no proof she did anything. Besides, why leave the mask where we could easily replace it right after discovery?"

"Beats me, but I'll certainly be tagging along anytime Miss V. takes a future potty break."

"I'm sure she'll have something to say about that."

Meg grinned. "Don'tcha just bet."

They heard Meeks make his way across the floor over their heads. *At least I hope it's him.*

An irrational sensation struck Kate. "This is going to seem silly, but I feel like the parlor is laughing at me."

"At this point you're right to feel paranoid."

"Something else." Kate stood still, waiting for her jumbled thoughts to clarify, and an image of the cursed death mask hit in a strong and worrisome way. "What if the mask was left on the seat so we *would* immediately bring the thing back into the house?"

"What do you mean?"

Kate pulled white cotton gloves from her pocket. "We're using these while we work to keep from damaging anything we touch, but we took them off yesterday as we left."

"I don't follow."

"I wasn't wearing gloves to take the mask back inside." An icy chill slithered along her backbone. "The death mask and my fingerprints are hanging on the conservatory wall right now.

At least I hope they are."

Without another word, the two jumped and raced to the rear of the house. At the entrance to the conservatory, the horror was apparent even before the women skidded to a stop. A large empty spot, highlighted by a silver hanging hook, revealed the worst.

"Gone!" Kate wailed. "You know what this means don't you?"

Meg nodded, "Someone wanted one of us to touch the mask."

"No. The blasted thing was left in my seat. He or she wanted my prints on the mask, and I delivered everything exactly as ordered. How could I be such an idiot?"

"You're no idiot, Katie, just conscientious." Meg wrapped an arm around her shoulders. "We were caught up in the moment and wanted to quickly minimize the damage."

"And made everything worse." A lump grew in Kate's throat.

"Made what worse?" Meeks's rumble startled them from behind.

Kate blinked back angry tears and filled him in on the latest situation. His expression hardened. "You need to call the police, little lady." He offered a clean handkerchief to Kate. "You're right to worry about what folks will think, but this isn't anything to mess around with here. Someone's setting you up for some serious shit."

"What could be more serious than murder? They've already set me up for that."

"Uh-huh, but getting tagged again is going to make the suspicions much harder to get away from," Meeks replied.

Kate glared at the empty spot on the wall. *I've had just about enough. It's time to kick butt and take names.* "What do you suggest for a next step? Other than me wearing gloves all the time?"

Meeks crossed his arms and looked like a huge god of thunder. "Soon as I get through today, think I'll mosey back over to your house and set up some more cameras."

Ever pragmatic, Kate asked, "How much will they cost?"

He shook his head. "Pay me whenever you can. This isn't any time to be quibbling about what you can afford to have installed. The way I see it, you can't afford not to have as many eyes as possible watching your back. Be they human or electronic."

• • • •

BEFORE THE POLICE ARRIVED, Meeks and the women went over exactly how much of the tale needed retelling.

"Say you recognized the mask was gone because you had to straighten it yesterday," Meeks told Kate. "They'll assume then it was crooked on the wall, and you won't need to go into any more detail."

"That really is the truth," Meg assured Kate. "It was hanging a little off-center yesterday before you straightened it."

"Yeah, but only after I'd re-hung the cursed thing."

Meeks frowned. "Exactly what the police do not need to hear. You were in the house. You were commissioned to do a job. You touched things. Nothing more, nothing less. That way if a crime is committed later and something else you've touched is found on the scene, there's a logical explanation for your fingerprints. Are we clear?"

"Absolutely," Meg said.

Kate nodded.

"Okay, fine." He pulled out his cell phone. "I'll call this in." He frowned. "One last thing, Kate. Don't look so damned guilty."

This time Lieutenant Johnson used the spotless kitchen for an interrogation room. Upon arrival, he separated the three of them, leaving Kate's interview for last. As she finished, Johnson tapped the notebook page with his pen and nodded. "Your statement matches the others, Mrs. McKenzie. We'll call the insurance company about a photograph, and, if none is available, use the description you've provided to check local pawnshops, antique vendors, and all the online auctions."

"The mask wasn't the first thing stolen." Kate crossed her fingers under the table as she held back the items currently in hers and Meg's possession. "Amelia's step-daughter—"

"Yes, yes." He sighed. "I've spoken at great length to various members of the deceased's family about missing items. Everyone seems ready to offer a favorite suspect to blame for the disappearances."

"Well, seeing as you already know—"

"Thanks for mentioning it." Johnson's response came as automatic, and his attention returned to the notepad.

She rose from her chair. "If that's all—"

"One more question, Mrs. McKenzie." Johnson leveled his gaze her way. "Do you have any idea why someone wanted to steal that particular mask?"

Kate remembered Meeks's earlier warning—"don't look so damned guilty." She stood straighter and forced her breathing to remain steady and calm. "No, sir, not a clue."

The kitchen door flew open. Valerie, angry and loud, cried, "I'm the last to find out something was stolen, huh? Goes to prove your compulsory search yesterday was less than worthless."

The expression that flashed across Johnson's face seemed both sly and interested. "I'm Lieutenant Johnson of the Vermont State Police. And you are?"

"Valerie James." Glowering, she shook his hand.

"Please tell me everything that happened yesterday, Ms. James."

Valerie's ire immediately changed to a smile.

Turning to Kate, he added. "Thank you, Mrs. McKenzie. That's all for now." *What kind of fresh hell will she get me into? Damn!*

At least Valerie had taken off in the Miata yesterday before they'd found the mask in the van. Lost in thought, Kate didn't realize she'd stopped right outside the kitchen, obviously within eavesdropping distance, until Johnson walked over and swung the door closed. Heat rose to her face as the officer in the front foyer stared at her. Another uniform stood guard at the top of the stairs. She was almost to the parlor when Johnson delivered his final shot, opening the door to call, "One last thing, Mrs. McKenzie."

Kate turned.

"Don't even think about leaving town."

CHAPTER FOURTEEN

HOW BUSY PEOPLE SAVE Time (Cover during presentation at Book Nook)

   1) _Budget time just like money:_

   a) _Buy monthly items (diapers, pet food, razor blades, etc.) through subscription for automatic ship and money savings._

   b) _Sign up to have payroll checks directly deposited._

   c) _Use automatic and online bill paying options._

   d) _Don't wait in line—buy stamps from USPS web site or many grocery stores._

   2) _Plan menus:_

   a) _A month of planned menus allows more efficient shopping and storing._

   b) _Sign-up for online coupon sites, and check saving strategy sites like www.couponmom.com._

   c) _Buy on-sale items ahead, but don't overbuy for items you won't soon need._

   d) _Post preprinted grocery list on refrigerator, checking items as you run out._

   3) _Other monthly shopping:_

a) Buy supplies and staples for your home on a monthly basis—weekly sale ads can save money, but also entice more shopping and spending.

b) Plan wardrobe needs and homework project supplies ahead, then make a big trip to shop early in the month to avoid costly and time-consuming Eleventh Hour maniac runs.

c) Use online shopping, especially when shipping is free—but don't let S&H charges discourage purchases, as they eliminate travel costs and parking problems.

d) Send gifts and flowers over the Internet.

e) Look to future needs—buy a bit ahead each month to save time and money.

f) Organize the year's receipts together, by store, in one big envelope or file, and have no difficulty finding one if a purchase must be returned.

4) <u>Regular administration tasks</u>:

a) Keep a bill-paying station stocked with checkbook, envelopes, pens, and stamps.

b) Use preprinted return address labels or purchase a customized self-inking stamp.

c) Set up regular timeframes to pay bills and mark each on a master calendar—if all are due at the same time, call and get due dates modified to accommodate your payday budget.

• • • •

IMPOSSIBLE AS IT SEEMED, the morning's events had a high probability toward getting even worse. Beyond their contract to babysit and bluff Sophia's stooge, with Johnson interviewing Valerie there was no telling how she might turn the tables to incriminate Kate and Meg— inadvertently or otherwise. Even the strongest reason for taking the job, to return incriminating items, backfired spectacularly, possibly disastrously, with the vanished mask carrying her fingerprints.

Worst of all, the crew's inventorying duties hadn't moved to the second floor, so she hadn't yet been able to unobtrusively return the ebony box and ivory fan to their rightful spots. Nothing offered a good reason for Kate to slip up there when Valerie and Meeks were around. She had gotten the items into the house, however, and hidden them under the dusty potted fern in the parlor, rearranging the frolicking gnomes for added camouflage. But until the pilfered items regained their true places upstairs they pointed a guilty finger her way. The surveillance cameras added another layer of concern, despite their obvious good.

What really irritated her was the missed opportunity to return the purloined items with the death mask the previous afternoon, after Valerie left and before the video monitors moved in. Should have. But twenty-twenty hindsight was useless in the face of the resulting panic to get the mask back into place on the wall. The ebony box and ivory-silk fan had flittered out of Kate's mind as quickly as New Years' diet resolutions.

Sheesh, talk about the perfect patsy. I'm helping the bad guy do his job. Or her job, she corrected herself.

With police traipsing everywhere, Kate remained jumpy most of the morning. Would they do a more thorough search in case the mask was secreted somewhere in the house, and discover her own cache before the two items could be replaced? Icing on the cake, added to the lieutenant's recent comments.

Telling herself to quit worrying was a useless endeavor, and the day provided little else to do as the team waited for the police to complete their duties and eventually release them. By ten o'clock, officers moved the threesome into the dining room, once the room attained "clean" status, to wait and watch as different law enforcement personnel crisscrossed the hall.

"Could we please go ahead with our inventory job?" Kate asked Lieutenant Johnson. She could feel a headache coming on, and though not crazy about working the day either, if they got anything done it would have to be soon. Amelia's funeral started at three, and she needed to go home and change.

"Where do you want to work?" Johnson stood in the middle of the hall and turned to get the floor plan's full effect.

Kate joined him on the oriental runner and pointed toward the front of the house. "We've been working on the parlor."

"You done in the southeast parlor?" he barked at a nearby technician.

"Didn't see any reason to go in there," the tech answered. "Want me to do it next?"

The women groaned. The lieutenant shrugged and grinned. "No, I guess not. The only thing positively missing is the mask. No need to create any more headaches." Kate's headache subsided a bit.

As they made their way into the parlor, Meeks came down the stairs. "I think I have things scouted out all right, and I've placed a few pivoting cameras on each floor, but I'll be over with my guys to set more later."

Meeks seemed to take up the entire parlor doorway. He pointed to a camera mounted high in one corner, across the room and a good distance from the windows. "They're all like that little one. Tiny but mighty. Uses wireless technology to send everything to our computers." The camera pivoted in a slow, continuous arc, keeping the room in scope.

"It'll spot anyone coming in and tell us whatever's taken, unless the item is right under the lens. That's kind of a dead zone. But you're more interested in 'whom' than 'what,' and this system should do the job." He hefted his two black leather cases. "You ladies need anything else before I go?"

"No, but thank you," Kate said. Meg nodded and smiled. Valerie looked bored.

"Well, guess I'll be g—"

"Just a minute, Meeks," Lieutenant Johnson called him back. "We'll want any evidence you collect on those tapes."

"You mean files. Everything's digital. And I'm afraid you'll need to get permission from my client."

"We've already spoken with Charles Webster Walker. He said we have his full cooperation."

"On the burglary of the mask?" Meeks questioned.

"Yes."

"But I wasn't hired because of the mask. My contracted duty predates that discovery. I'll be happy to turn over anything my client releases, but I can't agree to do so without his direct instruction." Meeks walked to the door and left without another word, leaving a red-faced Johnson in his wake.

Feeling a little cowardly, Kate moved further into the parlor, out of the lieutenant's line of sight. Meg and Valerie followed suit.

Law enforcement completed their tasks and vacated the premises within another hour. Kate's official workday had started at seven. It was past noontime, and she was shouldering the effects of a nearly full day and unrelenting stress. The idea of leaving for a restaurant meal made her giddy, but simply eating sounded wonderful, too. She was about to suggest a call-in pizza order, hoping maybe Louie would be delivering for Hazey Pie and she could follow up another lead, when the front bell rang.

"I'll get it. I need to get up anyway." Meg scooted the computer off her lap and went to the door, rolling her head as she walked to loosen neck muscles.

Seconds later Mrs. Baxter appeared, a worried frown covering her dumpling face. "Oh, you poor dears. Wading through all these dusty things."

Kate glanced down at the gray-brown streaks overlaying the print of her shirt and the blue in her jeans, and noticed Valerie equally and dustily decorated, including forehead stripes where she'd swiped her sweaty brow.

"If I told Miss Amelia once, I told her a hundred times we had to get someone in to take care of these things," Mrs. Baxter continued. A tear slipped down one powdered cheek as she faced Kate. "But, of course, that's why you were here to begin with, wasn't it dear?"

Kate quickly rose from where she'd been kneeling by the sheet music to hug the older woman. "In case you need me, I'll be at the funeral today, Mrs. Baxter. Don't forget that."

The cotton-haired cook pulled back and nodded, wiping her eyes with a lacey handkerchief. "I know you will, dear." She reached up and squeezed Kate's shoulder, then briskly blew her nose. "There. That's better." She took a deep breath. "I'm sorry I fell apart. Those spells hit when I least expect."

"Well, I'm glad you came today," Kate said. "I was going to go by your cottage on the way out to check on you."

Valerie loudly sniffed, drawing attention to herself. The smug look she shot Kate implied she had information but wasn't ready to spill.

Kate turned her attention back to Mrs. Baxter. "Did you come to say hello, or can we help you with anything?"

The cook took a final swipe at her reddened nose and shook her head. "Came to clean out the refrigerator and freezers. Stuff's going to ruin if I don't. No one in that selfish family ever thinks about such mundane things. Got an okay from Mr. Walker to donate the whole kit and caboodle to the homeless shelter. They'll be by in about an hour to pick up the donation."

"We were about to order lunch—"

"Order lunch?" Mrs. Baxter shook her head. "Not while I'm here you won't. You ladies come into the kitchen, and I'll make you a meal to remember. Nothing planned from scratch, mind you, but well worth every bite."

They had barely sat down before the cook swept a companionable plate of cheeses along with a basket of bread rounds and crackers for them to nibble on while they waited. Kate tried the Camembert first. Meg dived into the Vermont Shepherd and Valerie chose Maytag Blue. Cucumber and red onion salad followed, and Kate loved the cool, fresh taste, marveling over the black sesame seeds on top.

"I've never seen black sesames before."

"Just one of my secrets," Mrs. Baxter returned, beaming. "Now, for the main course," she stood on tiptoe in front of the open freezer, "would you like Korean beef bok choy, chicken grilled with peach salsa, or mushroom Bolognese?"

"You want us to choose?" Meg cried.

Valerie whined, "I can't."

Mrs. Baxter's smile shone bigger. "I'll put everything out and you can serve yourselves a bit of each."

The woman was true to her word. From freezer to microwave to table in less than a quarter of an hour, and Kate knew precisely why Amelia made her first task after returning to Hazelton to hire back Mrs. Baxter.

They passed on black-and-white parfaits for dessert, but all dove into the cherry turnover midgees and chocolate-dipped coconut macaroons.

"Oh, Mrs. Baxter, I've died and gone to heaven," Meg said, stacking her dessert dish on top of her spotless salad and dinner plate.

"Me too." Kate added her dishes to the stack and rose to bus the table. Meg grabbed the used silverware.

"And me," Valerie chimed in, remaining steadfast in her chair.

Mrs. Baxter beamed as she wiped her hands on a dishtowel.

A knock sounded at the back door, and Kate expected the homeless shelter personnel. The cook dropped the towel on the counter and bustled over to open the door. Bill Nethercutt entered instead.

"I had to pick up something in the garage and thought I heard voices," he said. "Figured I'd stop and say hello, but it looks like I might be in time for lunch."

"Yes, sir." Mrs. Baxter scooted to a cabinet, returning with another plate and silverware.

"I was feeding the ladies leftovers, but we've plenty more. Sit down and make yourself at home." Bill started with the beef bok choy. Another knock sounded at the door.

Mrs. Baxter admitted two husky individuals sporting crew cuts and flannel shirts, as Kate filled Bill in on the food plans.

"Oh, excellent idea," he said, but a line formed between his eyebrows. "Wish I'd thought of it myself."

He remained silent the rest of the time he was there, eating and staring as box after box of packaged frozen food disappeared into the homeless shelter's van. Kate wondered at this strange behavior from such a normally gregarious man. Was it the idea of Mrs. Baxter's exquisite edibles going to charity that silenced his tongue, or a dislike of the two individuals who came to get the food? With her last bite, Kate recalled his rumored money woes and decided it was likely the idea he couldn't take the delicious meals home himself.

"Did you find what you needed in the garage?" Meg asked.

He seemed caught off-guard by the question and stared blankly at her for several seconds. "Oh, yes," he said at last. "We'd left the keys to the MG in the glove box. I wanted to pick them up to keep Danny from getting any ideas about driving the car."

"But it's up on the rack," Kate said.

"How would you know that?" Bill asked, suspicion showing on his face.

Valerie jumped in to explain. "There was a prowler yesterday. We checked the garage and backyard."

"A prowler?" His fork slipped from his hand and clattered onto the plate.

"Yes, and one of your father's death masks was stolen," Kate added, "Charles Webster Walker is aware of everything. The police were here all morning."

"Here?" He pushed his chair away from the table. "Gotta talk to—" Then he stopped. Kate wondered who Bill wanted to speak with, and what he wanted to talk about.

He pulled keys from his pocket, and for a moment returned to a semblance of his former gracious self. "Ladies, it's been a pleasure, but I just remembered an appointment." He looked at his watch. "I'm sorry, but I really have to run."

I'll bet you do. But where are you running, Billy-boy? Kate wished she had time to follow, now anxious to witness how he would appear during Amelia's service in the afternoon.

• • • •

THE FUNERAL WAS HELD at the Episcopal Church in Hazelton, the small sanctuary overflowing with friends, family, and the out-and-out curious. The mingled scents from the floral displays that filled the front and lined the walls almost overwhelmed Kate's senses.

Local florists are probably making more on this funeral than they will for Mother's Day next month.

The family sat separated from the rest of the mourners, each member dressed in stalwart black. Handkerchiefs were the favored accessory, but she noticed Bill no longer appeared upset. In fact, from the distance he seemed almost giddy, having to wipe a huge smile from his face whenever his head turned Sophia's way. She, in turn, tried to wither him with a glare. Danny and Thomas, on the other hand, stayed absorbed by the sprays and stands of flowers, and Mrs. Baxter cried nonstop. Kate was glad the cook had been invited to sit with the others, though a little surprised Sophia would condescend to let "the help" fraternize in such a manner.

Most of all, she couldn't shake the feeling the next shoe was about to drop.

• • • •

THE NEXT MORNING, KATE ran fingers through her hair and noted her 'do getting too long again. She made a mental memo to call Dixie about a hair appointment. The twins looked cute in curls, but she liked to keep her blond waves at bay, and the most efficient way meant keeping her cut at chin length.

Just another expense.

She wondered how soon Charles Webster Walker paid invoices. Of course, she and her crew hadn't even worked a full day yet. With a sigh, she turned off the light and headed downstairs.

In the kitchen, she pulled out the pre-made French toast she'd frozen the previous week and made a cappuccino. She'd gotten hooked on Starbucks while Keith had played for Vancouver and they'd lived near Seattle. This single serving variety didn't meet professional standards, but it was cheaper and served her purposes to fight residual addiction attacks. And today's hit hard.

The cappuccino's rich smell tickled her nose and jolted her mind and stomach alive, its steam rising cloud-like in the chill air. Her ears tingled. Kate's pulse slowed, waves of comfort riding in the light's verve. Yes, this was what she needed.

She thought about Amelia's service and reflected on what she'd seen of the family. Bill stayed at one side of the first pew. Sophia sat a row back and at the other end, with Thomas midway down and Danny behind his father. Likely Bill's glee was due to putting something over on his sister, but the whole group seemed contentious. Only Mrs. Baxter shared Bill's pew, with the other relatives keeping a vast distance between one another, as if no one had wanted to sit near anyone else. Or trusted each other.

Everyone else, friends and community leaders, had whispered and cried quietly into tissues. She'd recognized the garden club all sitting together in the pews to her right, every member wearing a white orchid in Amelia's memory. Within the family pews only Mrs. Baxter showed great emotion, breaking down during a turn at the podium to speak about her late employer. Bill helped her back to her seat, her speech forever unfinished. Which led to Kate's next question. She wrote in the casebook:

1) Was Mrs. Baxter invited to sit with the family? Or did she just assume her place?

Again, Kate contemplated the relationship, or lack of relationship, between the wealthy matriarch and the cook. Two women who grew up together, shared space and conversation, but remained endless rungs apart on the social ladder. Mrs. Baxter's place at the funeral must have been by invitation, or Sophia would surely have opposed such familiarity between an employee and the employer's family. Then again, maybe she had. Maybe Bill invited the cook to push his sibling's buttons, and that explained his seeming delight and his sister's sourness. The more Kate thought about it, the more this scenario sounded like a sure bet. Those two were nothing if not consistently adolescent toward one another.

The questions and impressions were something to later talk over with Meg. Her neighbor and Valerie hadn't wanted to attend the funeral, choosing instead to stay behind and work. But they had already left by the time Kate arrived at the mansion at about five to make sure the place was locked up tight. The Berman house had stood dark as she'd arrived home, reminding Kate it was the nineteenth anniversary of Meg's mother's thirty-ninth birthday. She'd intended to watch out for the Bermans' return, but instead fell asleep, jarred awake at midnight with Keith's return. Obviously, her talents did not include surveillance work.

This morning, the mechanical surveillance pros stayed alert and professional. The small, camera Meeks had placed under the house's eaves at front and back doors identified, clocked, and categorized all visitors. Four more cameras hid around the perimeter of the house and yards. Meeks had called the previous night and explained that each camera operated under a live feed, loading directly into a computer in his shop. According to him, even an invisible man would find it difficult to enter her house without one or more of the cameras catching evidence of the intruder.

"Not even if the creep drops by parachute and onto your roof," he'd assured. "You'd be amazed at the peripheral range of these lenses."

Au contraire. Everything amazed her. Never in her wildest dreams could she imagine being involved in anything resembling her current predicament, let alone get interviewed by police twice in one week and hear the infamous imperative, "don't leave town."

There's nothing Valerie can say that can't be explained away. I've done nothing wrong.

Except hide and withhold evidence, that tiny voice of a guilty conscience whispered from behind her right ear. *Manufactured evidence*, countered the voice of justice and fair play. Evidence that would have done nothing but make the police focus erroneously on Kate. After all, no pertinent fingerprints remained on the box after she'd dropped it into the washer. But the police could have dusted her house and van for prints if they knew the stolen items had been hidden by person or persons unknown. "Wonder what the penalty is in Vermont for withholding information?"

Where had that line of thought come from? She shook her head. Obviously she was picking up a bit more lingo from the police, Meeks, and Meg than she'd realized, or she was getting more interested than she ever believed possible. Kate wondered what this new revelation said about her personality.

It was just self-preservation. Her mouth curled in frustration. And it came from continually getting set up as a dupe. She needed to stay focused. No telling what might happen next, and she still had to worry about where the mask might pop up and redirect attention her way. Lieutenant Johnson hadn't told Meg or Valerie they couldn't leave town, as he had Kate. Not that she wanted to go anywhere, but she didn't like the cloud of suspicion hanging over her head. She didn't blame Johnson. If the tables and jobs were reversed she would probably say and do the same as he. But still...

Which reminded her of another question. *What did Valerie tell Lieutenant Johnson?*

After the police left the mansion, she and Meg tried repeatedly to pull this information from Valerie but to no avail. Regardless of how they worded the request, the diva decorator ducked the issue and shot the squint-eyed, self-satisfied look a cat assumes after appropriating a dish of cream. Kate suddenly remembered the telling sniff and expression Valerie wore the previous afternoon when she mentioned wanting to again visit Mrs. Baxter at the cottage. The look was one of those "I'm in the know" kind that too often meant trouble. She fumed.

Not only was she clueless about what the look meant, but she forgot to go peek through the cottage's curtains.

Some investigator I am.

CHAPTER FIFTEEN

LITTLE TIMEFRAMES MAKE Big Differences
(Talk about this idea at presentation)

Like a television exec, use half-hour scheduling to get tasks completed. Divide the day into thirty-minute segments, first blocking out time for regular routine duties, then identifying any available half-hours for to-do list chores. While some jobs always require more than thirty minutes, short spurts are perfect for a surprising number of organized tasks. For example:

- *Plan weekly dinner menus or clip coupons.*
- *Bill paying and envelope addressing.*
- *Groom the pooch.*
- *Sew a button or repair a seam.*
- *Start a craft.*
- *Jot down Christmas and birthday gift ideas.*

Stay ahead with the thirty-minute rule, no matter how tight a schedule. Accomplish more without working harder. For big seasonal tasks, divide individual parts into half-hour zones and complete one zone per day. Handle large chores like heavy cleaning and clothing rotation the same way. Can't split up a large chore, such as painting a room? Employ half-hours to ready supplies and complete prep work like taping. Allocate a few minutes of every timeframe for gathering tools and supplies. Or designate the day's first half-hour to gather up needed materials for all tasks.

• • • •

"I GUESS I'M GETTING ghoulish," Kate said to Meg as she drove her van the route to the mansion. "Instead of thinking about Amelia during the service, I spent most of the time noting what each of our suspects did and their interactions with one another. Guess I'm converting to the dark side."

"Yes," Meg took on a deep, sinister voice. "You're one of us now." Kate grinned and slapped her shoulder.

As they glided down Main Street, Meg shouted, "Stop!" Pointing the Dazelight Donuts shop she asked, "Isn't that Danny getting off the tattooed guy's motorcycle?"

Kate nosed the van into a parking spot, and with several vehicles shielding them the women watched. Danny hung a helmet onto the back of the bike and waved, apparently thanking the driver for the lift. The bike roared off in a gargling crescendo, and the teen made his way into the donut shop.

"Okay, before we go in, what do we need to know?" Kate asked.

"You mean besides who killed Amelia?"

"Going for the obvious today, are we?" Kate grabbed her purse, withdrew the casebook, ticked off points with her finger. "Let's see. Get a handle on his dad's finances and find out why he goes to public school instead of private—"

"Which begs the question—why he's even here?" Meg interrupted. "By my calculations the first period bell rang ten minutes ago."

"Maybe he's out the whole week because of Amelia's death?"

Meg cocked an eyebrow. "When did donuts become part of the mourning process?" She groaned. "Sorry, no pun intended. Besides, he doesn't look very broken up to me."

"Emotional eating?"

A glance into the shop's plate glass window showed the teen ordering at the counter, accepting a tray with a Styrofoam cup and glazed donut, then settling into an empty booth. His gaze stayed fixed on the road as he sat, and he never touched his food.

"Who do you think he's waiting on?" Meg asked, coming to the same conclusion about his actions that Kate did.

"Might be interesting to find out."

A few minutes later, a gleaming white Mercedes purred into the parking lot and tucked itself into a distant, perimeter slot. Danny perked up.

"Looks like the eagle has landed," Kate said, as a silver-haired, very precise sixtyish woman got out. "Any idea who she is?"

"Uh-huh." Meg nodded. "Gabriella Cavannah-Wicker."

"You mean *the Gabriella Cavannah*?" Kate had never seen her, but had heard much about this woman whose family had stepped off the Mayflower and headed straight for Vermont. Plaques with the Cavannah name festooned Hazelton's more public locations. The first such marker Kate had noticed upon moving into town was the one prominently displayed above the arch leading to the children's section of the library. And the day of Amelia's death she'd said something about her in relationship to Mrs. Baxter's errands, but Kate couldn't recall exactly what except its connection to a budget issue. "How is she related to the Joey Cavannah who was Thomas's father?"

"Gabriella was Joey's sister, and she and Amelia have been in competition to see who would be unofficially crowned Hazelton's greatest *grand dame* for decades. Both families have been here since the dawn of time, but Gabriella believes she deserves extra points for having lived here all of her life. Even if she's never associated with the mere peasants. Amelia always trumped those points at parties when she held court and recounted her years living on the European Continent."

"And you know this how?"

"Mother." Meg grinned. "Due to her decades as garden club royalty, my dear mamma is guaranteed an invitation to any party where one-upmanship is the cocktail hour entertainment. Mother revels in such festivities and always exploits the events as opportunities to get hefty cash donations for Hazelton's beautification."

"But why would Amelia's and Gabriella's feud mean anything to the garden club?"

Meg waved a hand in the air. "Oh, my dear, Kate, you don't understand. Both women not only belong to the club, but each vie, or in Amelia's case I guess I should say vied, for top honors in whipping the other's butt each year and becoming president. With Amelia's death, Gabriella, as this year's V.P., will assume the mantle as club leader and probably run unopposed into the next century."

That's what it was. Some budget feud Amelia wanted to give Gabriella time to come to terms about.

Kate flipped to the first empty page in her casebook and noted the time, date, and location of this rendezvous, then turned back to her list of questions for Danny. "So, why would she meet Danny at the donut shop?" Kate looked into the window again. "Sure, she has a cup of coffee, but she made a face and pushed it aside. And I cannot even imagine her biting into any food served here."

"No, nothing could possibly be up to her standards."

Danny suddenly got red-faced at whatever Gabriella told him and shook his head. He jumped up and hooked an arm through the camouflage-print backpack he'd tossed beside him in the booth. Before he could stalk off, Gabriella grabbed his arm.

Kate and Meg studied the fascinating pantomime as Danny turned, his face shifting in an instant from scarlet to ghostly white at whatever Gabriella said, before resuming his seat.

Minutes later, the incongruous pair walked out together and climbed into the Mercedes. "Follow that car, Wonder Woman," Meg cried.

"No, I'm Batgirl—"

"Drive!"

Kate reversed out of the space, letting two cars pass before slipping back onto Main to tail the Mercedes. Traffic in Hazelton was never heavy until tour bus season, and she hoped they wouldn't be spotted. Gabriella didn't know her or what she drove, but Danny did and might recognize the van.

"Looks like they're turning onto the school road," Meg observed. And indeed, the Mercedes' left turn signal winked. "Drive on by. No point in following them into the high school's drop-off circle. We could follow Gabriella, but I don't even want to think about what kind of trouble we'd be in if we got caught."

"We're getting used to it. Getting pulled in as a public nuisance for running surveillance on Hazelton royalty might be more interesting, too."

"Likely, more boring." Meg removed the casebook from Kate's lap. "I would love intel on what made Danny angry, though. What could the old bat have on him?"

"Maybe he was trying to negotiate for the orchids," Kate suggested, her eyes scanning the road ahead. "You said she was a head honcho, after all. Given the animosity she and Amelia shared, Danny might believe Gabriella would go for a deal that went against his grandmother's wishes."

"Step-grandmother," Meg mused, turning a page to continue scanning the casebook's notes.

"Huh?"

"Nothing," Meg replied. "Wait a minute. What's this note about? Natalie 2K?"

Kate shrugged and hit the blinker to merge onto the road to the mansion. "Danny wrote it in ink on his hand. I saw it when we were talking about who kept up the mansion's fresh flowers, but Walker called us into the parlor to finish up with the heir meeting, and I never got the chance to ask him what the words meant. Any ideas?"

"I have my suspicions," Meg said. "But I have one fact. Gabriella's granddaughter is named Natalie, and rumor has it her recent Paris vacation was actually a cover story for time spent in a Swiss clinic specializing in drug dependency cases."

• • • •

VALERIE PACED THE MANSION'S front porch as they arrived, arms crossed tightly around her body. Which, given the morning's brisk temperatures, signaled both chill and irritation on her part. Kate opened the driver's door, and the decorator stomped over, boot heels ringing on the cobblestones.

"Where have you been? I'm freezing."

Kate looked across at Meg and walked around to the back of the van before answering. "We have more to do than just show up each morning. We have young children, husbands, and," she opened the rear doors and pulled out two collapsed boxes, "have to load supplies. Here, you can carry these so I'll have a free hand to unlock the door."

Valerie scooped up the huge cardboard squares, all the while muttering unintelligible remarks under her breath. Meg carried the laptop, and Kate grabbed her purse and the thermal bag she'd packed with snacks and drink containers. Now that Mrs. Baxter cleaned out the kitchen, water was the only on-site refreshment. And Kate was determined they were going to put in an entire day's work—without leaving for snacks. She also hoped the reading of the will, scheduled for the following day, wouldn't be at the mansion as well. Any intrusion seemed to wreak havoc on their work schedule.

Meeks had gotten Walker's permission to override the original alarm number and reset the system. Kate punched in the new code he'd given her the previous evening, and the red lights flashed off to show deactivation. When everyone and everything was inside for the day, she keyed it once again, comforted that no one could enter unobtrusively. Meg and Valerie followed her into the kitchen.

"Okay, Meg said you both finished the parlor after I left for the funeral yesterday." Kate placed bottles of juice and tea in the refrigerator. She watched Valerie lean the cardboard against the counter. "How about we move across the hall and work up the dining room next?"

Meg shook her head as she pulled a thermos from the bag and poured herself a cup of black coffee. "I understand your organizational mind wants to work the floor plan in some order, Katie, but why don't we do the study first? It's as chaotic as the parlor, and once we get the room inventoried the rest of the first floor will almost be a breeze."

"I think 'a breeze' might be a bit of a stretch." Valerie laughed.

"Hey! I added the 'almost' qualifier. The real challenge, of course, will be those upstairs rooms."

Kate felt a tickle of apprehension at the mention of the upstairs but hid her trepidation. "I guess your plan sounds workable. Okay with you, Valerie?"

Valerie produced a perfect, disdainful shoulder roll shrug. "Like it really matters what I think."

Meg cocked an eyebrow and planted a hand on her hip. Kate recognized a zinger was coming but letting a war of words erupt offered little productivity. Valerie acted offended at not being included in Kate and Meg's friendship, like a teenager left out of the in-crowd.

When Meg opened her mouth to respond, Kate cut her off with, "We all agree. Great. We'll move on to the study."

True to the description, the study was every bit as disastrous as the parlor. Kate assembled one of the boxes, placing it near the desk. On the wall behind were almost life-sized framed portraits of Amelia and Daniel. Hers seemed extra illuminated by all the diamonds she wore against her robin's egg blue gown. Daniel's captured a mischievous twinkle in his eyes, belying the staid three-piece dark suit, and traditional gold and onyx signet ring on his right hand.

"What are you doing?" Valerie asked.

"Preparing to store any papers. I don't want to be responsible for losing anything important. This afternoon I'll take everything to the lawyer's office for safe keeping."

"You and Meg already planned to work in here." Valerie's tone was accusatory. "That's why you brought those boxes today. I guess the whole question thing in the kitchen was one big charade, huh? Another joke on Valerie."

Kate felt her blood pressure rising. "No. I brought the extra boxes in case I needed them.

Just as I'll bring more boxes tomorrow, and the next day, and each subsequent day until we're done with this job. One last time, do you want to continue working with us, or do you want to act like an adolescent?"

"I want to know where I stand." Valerie crossed her arms and tapped a foot.

"You're a contract employee of Stacked in Your Favor," Kate replied, wondering if Valerie's fit of pique was a new ruse she and Sophia had cooked up to aid in the spying activities, possibly engineered to divide and conquer. "You're working per the contract you signed. Nothing more, nothing less. I'm only going to ask one more time, what is it going to be?"

Valerie picked up her purse and stalked out the door.

· · · ·

WITH THEIR LEAST PRODUCTIVE employee gone, Kate and Meg settled into a quiet partnership. Kate wasn't sure how they could get the whole job done, and she and could tell by the crease between Meg's eyebrows that her friend was worrying along the same lines, but there was no reason to stop working on the study. There wasn't anything in the room they couldn't identify, which had been one of the key attractions to hiring Sophia's little mole.

"Of course, Valerie must renew her regular connection with the dark one," Meg snarked.

"As a last resort we can accept Charles Webster Walker's offer for loan of his law clerk."

"Or quit, and forget access to the mansion," Kate replied. "If we're bound by the contract, that means Valerie is, too. Right?"

"Let's wait and see if we want her to be. Litigation may be less stressful than her working with us."

The cameras were in place and recording every movement. Meg had taken the opportunity while Kate was at the funeral to 'inventory' the box and the fan as if they were simply items found in the parlor. Kate planned to mention them to Walker later, implying Amelia brought the items downstairs instead of them going missing, and let him deal with Sophia.

In the study, bookshelves towered along one wall, and the mahogany desk called to Kate like a siren's song. She couldn't wait to open its deep drawers. First, however, they studied the scattered collections of children's toys, some strewn and others meticulously displayed along the room's perimeter. This included dollhouses depicting various countries and decades, all quite old and valuable.

"Dollhouses, die-cast trucks, and half-sized, non-working stringed musical instruments." Meg surveyed the widespread assortment. "Now what?"

Where to start? Kate stood in the middle of the room, on the muted rose-patterned carpet, and did a complete three-sixty. "Beats me."

"Well, you're the expert." Meg flashed a grin.

"Don't even go there." She pointed at the computer. "Get that laptop up and running. Pronto."

"Yes, boss." Meg's grin grew bigger. She placed the computer in the middle of the desk and took a seat in the green leather chair.

"We'll start with the dollhouses." Something about the structures seemed wrong to Kate, but she couldn't decide what. She stared for several seconds at a trio beneath one of the leaded windows before the incongruity came to her. To be sure, she leaned over to get a better view through the back of each before speaking. "How strange. There aren't any dolls. Just...well... stuff."

"Huh?" Meg got up and walked over. "There aren't any figures, are there?" She twisted around the pagoda and the country house, rattling their contents. "Whoever heard of a dollhouse without a doll family?"

"Definitely weird," Kate replied. "Kind of like this place now." That's when they heard the front door open and close.

"I thought you locked up again after Valerie left," Meg whispered.

"I did and reset the alarm." Kate pulled a cell phone from her purse to call 9-1-1. Then she smelled Chanel No. 5, and dropped the phone into her pocket. "Don't worry, it's Sophia. But how did she get the new code?"

"Valerie either read the note Meeks gave you or watched you key the number in this morning," Meg replied. "Shows she reports regularly."

Kate nodded. "We must be high on Sophia's priority list. Valerie was beside me last night when he gave me the number. But it was so quick. She could only have caught a flash of the code."

"Some spies are highly trained." Meg chuckled. "But I think in her case we can chalk the unprecedented success rate up to a highly developed nosiness gene."

A moment later, Sophia stood in the doorway. "What are you doing in here?"

"Our job," Meg replied, oozing sarcasm.

"Aren't we the clever one today?" Sophia took two steps closer, reaching out to tap Meg's cheek. "I meant this room. I expected you to start *organizing* all the clutter upstairs."

"We'll be *inventorying* the upstairs next," Kate clarified.

Sophia sighed and pulled a vintage-styled alligator bag up to rest in the crook of her elbow. "Well, I'd love to trade little witticisms with you, my darlings, but I have far too many things to accomplish this beautiful day. I'm here to pick up Daddy's coin collection. He always said the coins come to me, you know."

A wave of perfume followed as she crossed to the desk and opened a lower drawer.

"Hey, missy, you can't take that!" Meg stomped across the room and snatched away the large metal case that appeared out from the depths.

The action took Sophia aback for only a moment. She grabbed one end and tried to wrestle the collection from Meg. Through clenched teeth, she said, "You will let go."

"Not a chance." Meg's face was redder than her hair. "Kate, call the police."

"Police?" Sophia's expression mixed complete disbelief with the effort of the struggle. The next instant she caught a foot around Meg's ankle and the redhead went down in a heap, allowing Sophia to gain complete possession of the heavy case. "Don't be ridiculous."

"Why you—" Meg grabbed a harmonica from a nearby lamp table and aimed for Sophia's head.

"Stop," Kate cried. The two adversaries turned toward the sound of her voice. "Sophia, Meg is right. I can't let you take anything—"

"I *can* extract whatever is mine from this house, and you *will* end all of this silly discussion about telephoning the authorities." Sophia circled around the far side of the desk, to avoid further contact with Meg.

Kate closed the door and blocked the brass knob with her body. "Okay, but you have to sign a receipt stating you took the coin collection. I must have proof. I won't be held responsible."

"What makes you think I would even consider doing such a thing?"

Meg joined Kate at the door. "Because the surveillance camera is recording this entire incident, and you'll look like you're trying to pull a fast one otherwise."

The smirk disappeared. "What surveillance camera?"

Kate pointed to the corner where Meeks' little mechanical wonder arced back and forth, documenting every action the shiny lens witnessed. Sophia's jaw dropped. "Daddy never put a camera in here."

"No, we did," Kate said.

"On whose authority?"

"Your family's attorney," Meg replied, leaning casually against the wooden door, as if to emphasize the shift in power.

"So, are you going to sign a receipt for the coin collection?" Kate asked. "Or do you want to chance looking like a thief, and give your siblings a video record to use against you in court?"

"But they're mine." Sophia hugged the silver case. Her words held pain and bitterness. "If that damned Amelia hadn't decided she had to take her stupid Washington trip and tire Daddy out with her last party, these coins would still be his. Now, though, they're mine. He promised."

"And I'm sure you'll hear Mr. Walker confirm that when the will is read tomorrow," Kate said. "Until then, however, I need a receipt for any item removed from this house."

Sophia worried her lower lip with her teeth, and the alligator bag slipped back down her arm. While Valerie's bag was good faux, Kate had no doubt Sophia's was the real deal.

Probably wrestled the beast to its end by herself.

Deepening the frown on her face, Sophia shoved the coin case toward them. "Oh, here, just take them back. But if Mummy forgot and gives the coins to one of the men, I'll hold the two of you responsible."

"How—" Meg started.

Kate held up a hand to interrupt her, while accepting the case with the other. "Fine, I'll put the case with the papers from the desk. I'm taking everything to the attorney's office later today for safekeeping."

"Okay, I—" Suddenly, Sophia's hazel eyes grew wide, and she pivoted on her three-inch heels. "Where's Ms. James?"

"Valerie..." Kate paused, trying to decide how to word what had occurred earlier. "Let's just say she no longer wanted to work with us."

"Preposterous. She's supposed to—" Sophia stopped, her jaw snapping shut.

"Valerie's probably been trying to reach you," Meg drawled, crossing her arms. "To see what she should do next."

A flash of alarm crossed Sophia's face, but she recovered quickly. "Why would she do that?"

"Because she's your—" Meg began.

"Your design expert," Kate finished. "If Valerie's decided not to work here anymore, we thought she would want to spend more time working on the job she's doing for you."

Sophia glared at them. "I've been in meetings all morning." She pulled a phone from her purse. "I haven't had a chance to check my messages, but perhaps I should see if Ms. James wanted to meet with me about...about the work at my home."

She put the cell phone to her ear, then immediately returned it to her bag. "On second thought, talking to her in person might be more expedient. Make for a more fruitful discussion when we discuss the...project...if we are face-to-face."

"Or two-faced to two-faced," Meg muttered. She stepped away so Kate could open the door.

"What did you say?" Sophia demanded.

Before Meg could reply, Kate said, "Nothing. She simply offered a lunch option."

Turning to Meg, she added, "Yes, tuna fish sandwiches at the Book Nook is a wonderful idea."

Sophia's eyes narrowed as she swooshed out in another perfumed haze, but the final look she shot their way said she wasn't buying Kate's lunch story.

CHAPTER SIXTEEN

'Day before' To-Do List:

PROJECT ASSIGNMENT FOR <u>Wed. Evening, April 14th</u>

• • • •

GET MATERIALS READY for tomorrow's presentation. Saree expects a lot of working women juggling kids and jobs. Make up tip sheet on how to find time, something like:

- *Sign up with news sources for email reports & get all news in one place or via a home page.*
- *Order prescriptions online or ahead by phone, and avoid pharmacy wait times at pickup.*
- *For any shopping, call ahead to check stock and order groceries online then pick up at store.*
- *Screen calls. Don't be afraid to nicely tell people you're too busy to talk.*
- *Sign up for automatic bill payment.*

***Or maybe call this "Top 5 Ways to Make Time in the Day." Or add two more for "Seven Ways to Save Time & Sanity," adding ways to energize as well as save time. Like—

- *Combine exercise with errands, wear pedometer & walk to stores & appointments.*
- *Avoid clock-watching stress. Set a timer when there's limited time to do a task.*

• • • •

"THIS IS MUCH BETTER than those cold sandwiches we stashed in the cooler," Meg said, attacking her Book Nook Cobb salad with gusto. "You don't suppose Sophia killed Miss Amelia because she thinks step-mummy caused Mr. Daniel's death, do you?"

"I wondered the same thing. The suspicion is even stronger if she learned about the uncomfortable comment Amelia made to me the day she died." Kate blew on a spoonful of soup.

The aroma alone was nirvana.

They sat tucked away in a corner table, reveling in the warmth and cheerful views of the surrounding windows. The sun, beaming down from the day's gorgeous blue sky, offered a solar massage across Kate's back. Between the radiating heat and Saree's *soup d' jour,* perfect beef-barley comfort food in a bowl, Kate's taut muscles released the morning's tension.

Book-buying patrons swamped the store during the noon hour, and the women were nearly finished before Saree could break free to stop at the table. Dressed in a vibrant magenta sheath, with a necklace of hammered gold medallions draped around her neck, the bookseller could almost compete with the day's outdoor brilliance. When she smiled, on the other hand, there was no contest.

"Well, chickies, my food is good today, no?" Saree planted fists on her narrow hips, gold bangles cascading down each arm in chime-like tones.

"The food is wonderful." Meg loaded her fork with egg and avocado. "Exactly what we needed."

Saree lifted a suspicious eyebrow at Kate's order, pointing with a graceful. "This soup..." She wiggled a scarlet-nailed forefinger. "...most unlike you, chickie. You are adventurous eater, always. Do you have troubles this beautiful mornin'?"

Kate shook her head, smiling. "No one can hide anything from you, can they, Saree?"

"Ah, but masters teach me." Saree half-closed her dark eyes. "For this shop I buy Sherlock Holmes, Agatha Christie. I read very close and follow their methods. Human behavior. Spot sameness in people, note differences to individuals."

"Excellent observation." Meg sipped her iced plum tea. "If this job gets any crazier, we might need to hire you as a consultant."

A crease formed between Saree's eyebrows, and she turned back to Kate. "Job? Another job givin' you worries?"

Kate shook her head. "No, actually this is an offshoot of the original Nethercutt commission. Meg and I are inventorying the contents of the mansion to fulfill the terms of the will. Well, Meg and I and Valerie James that is."

"Valerie James? You work with her? She is..." Saree looked wildly around, as if hoping the right word would come to her through the air. "She is, she is *conceited*, and, and..." Throwing her hands in the air with an elegant gesture, she signaled defeat.

"You understand why I needed comfort food today." Kate grinned. "Things should be looking up, though. Valerie stormed off the job this morning."

"That is good, chickies." Saree walked to the counter and removed two snicker doodles from the cookie display. She returned to their table and set a cookie-laden napkin beside each of the partners. "Here, eat. Rejoice that witchy woman gone."

Meg touched the top of her cookie with one finger and licked off the sugar and cinnamon, adding, "Well, one anyway. We still have Sophia."

Saree tsk-tsked and placed a hand on Kate's shoulder. "But you will still speak here on spring organizin' tomorrow night, yes? The books, they are stacked in back, the ones we discussed. And I have brand new line, too, sent from good publisher. You are not too busy—"

"Don't worry, I'm all ready. I've even put together a little takeaway paper to give people ideas and reading lists after they leave tomorrow night."

"What about the newsletter thing you've been tossing around?" Meg asked.

"Newsletter?" Saree echoed.

Kate waved the idea away. "Oh, just an idea I dreamed up to attract a little business. I thought about doing a quarterly newsletter, using the seasons to keep people on track. Maybe get them to consider hiring me to help organize their homes or businesses. Just to keep my name in front of the public. But I'd have to find some place to put the newsletters—"

"Why not here? My counter is wide, and stack should not take big space." The shop owner's face lit up again as a new idea came to her. "Oh, the home center. They should leap for your excellent information."

"I don't know about excellent—"

Meg made a pshaw sound. "Don't be modest, Katie. Your newsletter would be great. Plus, Saree's right, home centers would be a perfect complement to your ideas and offer all the organizing shelves and storage options people need."

A book-laden line of customers formed at the cash register. Saree excused herself with a quick smile and wave. "*A demain,*" she called over her shoulder.

Kate smiled. "Until tomorrow."

• • • •

VALERIE RETURNED ABOUT three, again wearing her cat-and-the-cream smirk.

"Nice of you to rejoin the party," Meg said, looking up from her book cataloguing. "Do you intend to work or just make sure the knives in our backs are buried to the hilt?"

"Listen, Meg Berman, I don't have to take any of your—"

"Stop it you two," Kate said. No way she wanted to lose the part-time babysitter she and Meg counted on the most. "I assume you've spoken with Sophia and she's pushed you back into this project, offering *carte blanche* to keep us in our places. Start cataloguing the bookshelves with Meg."

The files seemed to multiply in the drawers, and Kate stacked another load into the box. Beyond the coin collection Sophia withdrew earlier, the desk held a treasure trove of items. The most interesting discovery lay tucked in the far back of the middle drawer. A satin-covered journal. Kate smiled as she opened the cover and recognized Amelia's distinctive handwriting.

She set it on the blotter to go in on top of the box and left that drawer for last as well.

By the time the desk was nearly empty and the box equally full, the only task left was the center drawer. All of the toys and the rest of the room's floor inventory was documented in the computer file. Meg and Valerie were on the final bookcase. Kate pulled out the wide mahogany middle drawer.

"When we're finished in here, I'd like to move on to the living room next." Kate kept her head down, her attention focused on the jumbled contents. A bit of white caught her eye, back where the journal had been, and she withdrew a scrap of paper that said, "G. Cay." and listed a long string of numbers. It may have been a note Amelia kept in the journal or just a scrap hidden under the book, but to Kate it looked suspiciously like reference to some kind of account.

Regardless, it's up to Walker to figure out whether the note is important or trash.

She slipped it into the journal for safekeeping. Out of habit, she made a mental list as she worked, but she itched to grab one of the cloisonné pens from the big middle drawer and jot thoughts down on one of the desk's many stylized notepads. An upward glance revealed Meg and Valerie working in a simmering cease-fire manner. All afternoon, Meg had listed book titles on a pad, rather than having to constantly stop and start to enter them into the laptop. Valerie followed her example with another pad. Balanced at the top of the library ladder, the redhead recorded book titles and edition information from the shelf near the ceiling. The truant decorator did likewise at the bottom, her cell phone on the floor beside her. But by the set of their shoulders, Kate knew another outburst could come at any moment.

Taking advantage of the opportunity, her hand hovered over a jewel-like pen for one instant then grabbed a pink toned one and a pad of scratch paper. She tamped down her guilt by reminding herself she wasn't stealing the pen, simply making notes to solve Amelia's murder. The late woman would not only approve but would applaud Kate. She scribbled quickly as the pair's backs were turned.

> *1) What is Sophia's true purpose for wedging Valerie into this inventory job, and what did she say to convince Valerie (or order her) to come back after this morning's temper tantrum?*

Messing with Kate's business and being a thorn in Meg and her respective sides would tickle Ms. James to no end, but the big question was still what did Sophia hope to accomplish? Kate resented the fact Sophia excelled at pushing her buttons and had insinuated Valerie into her daily life. Not to mention the whole lingering jealousy thing about Sophia and Keith she couldn't get out of her mind.

But most of all, the woman's a bitch.

Kate moved on to the next sibling and scribbled out her next thought.

2) Who did Bill decide he needed to go see when the shelter guys came, or was there even an appointment at all? Was he really trying to catch up with the shelter guys? If so, why?

She wrote Thomas's name, then added "father?" beside it, wondering if he was privy to the tragic family history and whether he blamed Amelia for any part of his dad's suicide. But she didn't want to write the question, and not just because it all seemed too sordid and soap opera-y. No, Thomas, somehow, seemed as much a victim in this family of vipers as was the murdered Amelia, and Kate wanted to minimize his place in her free-writing, suspect-musing exercise. Danny was a different story.

3) What did Danny discuss with Gabriella Cavannah-Wicker, and did the Natalie 2K he had scrawled on his hand refer to Gabriella's granddaughter?

"Are you goofing off?" Valerie's voice cracked like a shot, and Kate guiltily stuffed the page into the pocket of her jacket.

"Of course not," she said. When Meg raised an eyebrow, Kate didn't doubt the blush she felt was much too apparent. She turned to brisk action and pulled out the center drawer to dump the rest of the contents into the box, then grabbed Amelia's journal from the desktop and placed it atop everything before she closed the flaps. Hefting the bulky cardboard container, she shuffled to the door, saying, "I was just making a list of what I need to bring tomorrow. After I take this out to the van, I'll come back and help you finish, and we can leave."

"What's in the box?" Valerie stood and blocked her way.

"You watched what I was doing. It's all papers and files from the desk. I'm taking them to the lawyer's office." Promising herself not to let Valerie rattle her again, she countered with, "If you'd stuck around earlier you would have heard me say so."

"I'm not sure Sophia would want you to—"

That did it. The box fell to the floor in a resounding thump, and Kate felt her face grow red again but this time with anger. "I don't give a *damn* what Sophia wants. And I don't care—"

Meg climbed down from the ladder as Valerie said, "Don't go fooling yourself about being the boss here, Kate McKenzie. I'll have you know Sophia—"

"Sophia, Sophia, Sophia," Kate cried. "If you want to be her little puppet—"

"Puppet! I am n—"

"Ladies!" Meg got their attention and held up the cell phone that had been lying on the floor. "Speaking of Sophia, I believe this text message is from her."

"Give me my phone." Valerie snatched it out of Meg's hand and smiled as she read the small screen. "Anything you have to say to Sophia, I guess you can tell her yourself. She wants to see you immediately."

Valerie scrolled the text back to the top of the screen and handed the phone to Kate, who read, "TELL THAT IDIOT MCKENZIE WOMAN TO GET OVER HERE NOW, OR SHE AND HER HUSBAND WILL BE JOB HUNTING TOGETHER."

• • • •

KATE SLAMMED THE BOX into the back of the van. How dare that witch order her around. And threaten Keith's job to boot. She had half a mind not to go, let Sophia simmer in her own juices, but that really wasn't an option. Ms. Hoity-Toity needed to be shown what happened when she sent word through her minion for Kate McKenzie to come at once and stand court.

"Wait, Katie, calm down," Meg continued the placating routine she'd begun back in the study.

"This is too much. I'm having it out with witchy-woman." She pulled the keys from her tote bag.

"At least let me drive."

"Oh, no." Kate climbed into the driver's seat. "I'm getting there of my own volition. I don't want her to think I'm so upset I need someone to drive me."

"But you are too upset." Meg piled in on the passenger side. "You might—"

"Wait for me." Valerie ran up and slid open the side door, climbing into the backseat.

"Get out." Kate turned in her seat. "You can get the blow-by-blow from Sophia later."

Rolling her eyes, Valerie said, "I'm not coming along to see you publicly humiliated. I'm coming to help."

"Help what? Put me in my place?"

"No." Valerie's voice took on an overly patient tone. "To help you put your world back together when you shoot your mouth off at Sophia. The best thing you could do is not go. You're going to blow everything. But since that doesn't seem to be an option, someone needs to be there to work on Sophia in your favor after all is said and done."

Kate felt her head spinning. "You want me to believe your only aim in tagging along is to help me?"

"Come on," Meg said. "I've heard a lot of crap in my life, but this—"

"Of course, I'm going to help," Valerie interrupted, glaring. "We haven't finished inventorying this house yet, and it's important to my business to know everything inside."

"Oh, well," Meg replied wryly. "As long as your intentions are pure."

The exchange was enough to cut some of the strain for Kate, and she drove off at a normal speed. The closer they got to the White residence, the tighter the tension coiled between her shoulder blades. They pulled up at the curb of the Georgian mansion, and she jumped out, almost as if ejected from a rocket seat, and left the keys in the ignition.

"Kate, aren't you going to lock up?" Meg called.

"This won't take long."

"I'll do it," Meg said. "Wait for me. Please, Katie."

Kate never slowed her step. A split second later, she heard the back-door slide as Valerie climbed out, followed by a crash and "Damn," and she recognized the sound of a dumped purse, the contents pinging and rolling on the asphalt.

Valerie's purse spill worked in Kate's favor. She had little need for an entourage when confronting Sophia.

At the heavy oaken door, she pressed the doorbell again and again. No answer.

"Okay, this rips it, Sophia!" It wasn't enough the harpy ordered her there—but ignoring her at the door and making sure her domestic help followed suit simply ramped things up to a level Kate could not ignore. She fisted her left hand and pounded on the heavy wooden door. To her surprise it slowly swung open.

Still mad, but puzzled, Kate stepped into the dark foyer. "Sophia!" Again, no answer.

She stomped into the first room on the left, the formal living room. Her blood hit max pressure at the sight of Sophia, distinctive as ever in red lounge wear and glittering gold jewelry, stretched languidly along the couch, the missing African death mask covering her face and neck.

"If this is some kind of threat, I—" Her words died in her throat when she took a better look.

More than expensive rings and bracelets accessorized the scarlet outfit. An antique gold dagger stood tall in the middle of Sophia's chest.

CHAPTER SEVENTEEN

NOTE TO SELF – DON'T panic!

••••

"SO, AGAIN, YOU JUST happened to be in the same house where the occupant comes up dead." Lieutenant Johnson stared at Kate across Sophia's polished, inlaid gilt and ivory French desk. She wondered whether Valerie had "tweaked" the room but thought not. This office spoke of the same taste and elegance—and money—Sophia's alligator bag implied. Here was a space the late woman had created for herself and quite possibly by herself. Well, at least Kate assumed the desk was for Sophia's use. The exuberant ormolu style didn't appear at all masculine, and anyway, wasn't the elderly Mr. White off in some health facility somewhere, and— "Mrs. McKenzie!"

Kate jumped in the chair, startled. "I'm sorry, Lieutenant. This has really been a stressful time for me...but...You want my statement, and I want to help, but I...don't have clue about... murder..." She sank back into the chair, feeling a sudden chill.

Meg had been the one who'd finally dialed 9-1-1. Kate had wanted to make the call herself, but she couldn't. The impact of Sophia lying there stayed burned in her memory, and the lethargy of such a profound shock left her body incapable of movement.

However, after the call had been placed, it seemed mere seconds before lights and sirens filled the air, twirling red strobes playing peek-a-boo in the softly curtained front window. Lieutenant Johnson had burst through the door, and tossed out orders like a trail boss, quickly dividing the women much as a cowboy would cut a herd of cattle, penning each in separate rooms to interview individually. Kate had been sequestered in the kitchen, with

Constable Banks standing guard over her as he had in the interrogation room after Amelia's murder. It was more than an hour before Johnson called for her. He had obviously interviewed Meg and Valerie first, making her worry further about whatever spin the interior designer put on the day's events.

She closed her eyes and saw everything again in sharp, Technicolor 3D, the red outfit with a darker red stain around the heart, not noticeable until the image of the knife registered. The knife. Had she touched it? She didn't think so. No, she hadn't moved. Yes, she was sure about that. She remembered dimly hearing footsteps race across the tiled foyer and into the room from behind, but she hadn't thought about moving, didn't think about the possibility of the killer coming back to hurt her, too. Then Valerie had screamed, "What have you done?"

The pressure built again inside, and she fought for control. Somehow, she had to tell the lieutenant something to make him believe she hadn't done this terrible thing, but words stuck in her throat. Sophia was dead! She'd ordered Kate over there, had sent the horribly nasty text message. They'd all seen the words, scrolled through the text to read the entire thing, and Valerie had taken such delight in Kate's immediate anger. She felt heat surge at the thought, countering her chills. She raised a hand to her throbbing temple.

"I understand your anxiety, Ms. McKenzie, but please understand mine." Johnson twisted the golden-brown leather chair around to grab a tissue from the box atop the bulbish-shaped chest even Kate recognized as a being French Rococo. He handed the tissue to her. "Everything you've told me is corroborated by your, for lack of a better term, partners. But we have procedures and—"

A knock interrupted his perfectly honed speech.

"What?" Johnson barked.

"Sir?" A crime scene technician poked his head inside the room, one latex-gloved hand maintaining a stronghold on an evidence bag hanging beside his visible leg. "We're done, sir. Everyone's loading up to leave."

"Got anything, Edwards?" Johnson asked.

The younger CSI guy gave a restless shrug. "Not sure yet, sir. Some fingerprints, but not a lot. Looks like the cleaning people are good at their jobs." As Johnson opened his mouth to speak, Edwards added, "One set around the edges of the mask, but no prints on the knife. We have to hope the mask prints are enough for a match. Knife handle was wiped clean. Definitely wiped clean. There were smears, like it'd all been done in a hurry, and the body was repositioned post-death. Probably not a long time following, but the victim was definitely posed on the couch after the attack that killed her."

"Very good. Let me know as soon as you have any results I can use," Johnson said as Edwards withdrew.

"Why reposition the body?" Kate asked, almost whispering. "And the prints on the mask are likely mine from the other day." Breathing didn't help. Her lungs weren't working right anymore. The organs took in air but forgot to send it up to her brain, so she felt light-headed. "Who's playing these horrible, horrible games?"

"Who indeed?" Johnson closed the large leather portfolio he'd been using to take notes and clasped his hands on top. "If you didn't kill her—"

"I didn't." Kate leapt to her feet. "Valerie's phone—the text message said to come here! You know that's what it said. She showed it to you when you arrived. I watched her show you."

He calmly extended a hand, a heavy gold watch lying across the wrist. "Let me have your phone, Mrs. McKenzie."

Perplexed, Kate searched the area around her feet until she saw her purse at one end of the desk. She removed the cell and handed it to the lieutenant.

After only a moment's observation he handed back the phone. "Okay."

"What?" Suddenly his purpose dawned on her. "You wanted to see if I sent the message.

Didn't you?"

"That is a part of my investigation," Johnson replied.

"I didn't do this. Any of it. But someone is determined to make you think I have." Kate cried into the tissue. A few seconds later she felt several more pressed into her hands.

Johnson said, "I'm going to have to ask you to stop working at the Nethercutt mansion. I'm resealing the estate as a crime scene. I will do the same with this house. That's standard procedure to allow the technicians to go back over any new evidence discovered. I'm sorry, but—"

"Don't. I understand." Kate waved her right hand, while she used her left to pinch her nose with the tissues. She felt sorry for him. He was grasping at straws like everyone else, hoping something had been overlooked in previous searches. "There's no way I want to go back to the Nethercutt mansion."

Johnson nodded. "It looks like everything is in order as far as this part of the investigation goes, but as before, Ms. McKenzie, please do not leave this jurisdiction."

"I have no plans for travel," Kate said, forcing a smile as she suddenly felt overwhelmingly tired. "Can I go?"

"Yes. I'll have someone drive you if you want."

She shook her head. "I brought Meg and Valerie. We need to take Valerie back to get her car before Meg and I can go on home. I'll let Meg drive. We'll be fine."

"Let me have one of the uniforms take Ms. James back for you," Johnson offered.

Kate felt the anger rise again in her face. "I meant what I said, Lieutenant." She shoved her purse under an arm. "I don't intend to go inside the Nethercutt house ever again."

"I don't doubt you, Mrs. McKenzie." Johnson spoke gently as he rose and circled the desk. "But I am concerned about you. I want you to go straight home to your family. Let someone else take Ms. James to her car."

She tried to swallow the huge lump in her throat. This man who'd seemed overtly threatening had become kindness personified. She wanted to trust him, believe he believed her, feel reassured this solicitous act was strictly from compassion over her welfare. But she couldn't. Her trust was gone, destroyed with the belief she would never feel safe. "That text message. Those horrible words..."

"Yes?" he prompted when she didn't say anything else.

She hung her purse on her shoulder and gave her nose one last vicious swipe. "Sophia didn't send that message, did she? Her killer did. Right?"

Johnson shrugged. "I won't know until the body is autopsied for time of death and we can obtain her cellular information. Even then the time frames may be too close to be sure."

This was all too much. He didn't have to tell her—Kate knew. And she worried the information offered only a double-edged sword at best. He was either trying to reassure and still keep her on her guard by revealing what he legally could tell, or working a sting to make her let down her guard. Regardless, she knew her unseen nemesis was at it once more and determined to get her imprisoned for something she hadn't done. If this villain couldn't get her accused of Amelia's murder, the next try was for theft. If not for theft, why not pull out all the stops and commit a second murder? Her anger renewed, she slammed the tissue into the gold-toned wastebasket beside the bookcase. "Never mind. I know. And if you didn't feel you have to be super-officious you'd admit it, too."

She didn't give him a chance to respond, but as she grabbed the doorknob he called, "Please be very careful, Ms. McKenzie."

• • • •

ESCAPE. AGAIN. KATE let the grateful joy course through her at surviving and leaving another murder site. Guilt colored everything, of course, especially since she'd never liked Sophia. But after the day's rerun of interrogation hours and fearing she would be locked up for a crime she hadn't committed, it was difficult to tamp down the happiness. Especially when she and Meg noticed Valerie climbing into a patrol car for the trip back for her Miata.

Life was joyous, that is, until Meg walked around the van and noticed black paint and a huge dent decorating the right rear fender.

"What more can happen to you?" Meg voiced Kate's thoughts, as they stared at the damage. "You not only have to play another round of verbal dodge ball with the cops, but your van gets bullied, too. You don't think this black paint is from one of the squad cars do you? Come on, let's go report this to one of the officers."

Kate shook her head. "Why bother? It's obviously a hit and run." She scanned the surrounding police cruisers. "None of these cars did it, and if one of the officers had seen it happen he would have pursued the runaway driver or at least taken the license number and told me. The back of the van seems secure." She gave the back door handle a sharp tug and the lock held. "Mainly cosmetic damage."

A glance through the rear window showed that the impact had tipped over the box of items from Amelia's desk. As tired as she was, she wanted to get the desk's paperwork to the lawyer's office to minimize her responsibility. Who knew what else might happen if she hung onto those papers? Not to mention the number the box played on her curiosity. It had taken tremendous restraint to keep from checking things out as she packed. Kate had no idea what kind of importance any of the paperwork held, but as a professional she had no right to peek.

She checked her watch. Quarter past five. "It's late, but if you don't mind I'd like to go ahead and stop off at the attorney's tonight, to pass along this personal paperwork of Amelia's. I just hope someone is still in the office."

"You're talking lawyers. Someone is always working late. But haven't you had enough fun for the day?" Meg's smile was weak, but her eyes still shone. "It's no problem for me, but your hubby might be wondering where we are and why he's the one keeping our kids occupied."

Kate shook her head. "I called him while I was waiting to be interrogated. After I calmed him down and made him promise not to run down here, I persuaded him to call Jane to help with dinner and the kids. He's probably getting ready to head to the radio station."

"What did he say about Sophia's murder?" Meg asked.

That was the funny thing. Kate thought about her husband's reaction when she said his employer was murdered, and how she heard no trace of concern in his voice. She came up with a number of theories why but wasn't sure she liked any of them. Instead, Keith saved all his oral histrionics for the fact she was in trouble again. *That's exactly what he said—You're in trouble again.* She mulled this over to herself, but aloud simply said, "He took it well. I guess his contract doesn't allow for murder to make an impact on his job."

• • • •

BY THE TIME THEY'D arrived at Charles Webster Walker's office, he and his two partners had left for the day. Yet, the place remained a hive of activity, with several paralegals, a secretary, and two associates. The associates, a dark-haired young man and an older woman who already had gray hair tracing through her short cut, took charge as Kate approached and explained their purpose in coming.

"Omigod!" said the young, female paralegal at the news of Sophia's murder.

"You found her?" The secretary clutched her throat.

"How did she die?" asked the male associate, his eyes gleaming as he added, "Was her death grisly?"

Kate shivered. "I'm not sure what the police want me to reveal, but the newspaper will likely cover the investigation in the morning edition."

The associate scoffed, "That rag never gets anything right. Sure you can't tell us more?"

"I'm sorry. I came to bring a box of papers—"

"From Sophia?" the man asked. His female counterpart turned and walked out of the room.

"No, Amelia Nethercutt's," Kate explained. "I've been inventorying her house for the will—"

"Oh, gosh," cried the secretary. "The reading of that will is set for tomorrow morning. We'll have to call things off under the circumstances."

"Why don't you get started making phone calls," the man said. Turning to Kate, he asked, "Do you need help carrying the box?"

"It's big, but I can manage," Kate said. She was sick of people at this point, and didn't appreciate his nosy, too-helpful attitude.

"Not necessary. I'll follow you out." He flashed sharp white teeth. "No sense in you having to come back in here."

"Don't I need a receipt?"

He smiled again. "You're right." Turning to the secretary, he said, "Get me a sheet of letterhead, Shirley. I'll write one up and sign it when I get outside." Defeated, Kate led the way to the van.

Meg had stayed to pile papers back in the box and stood waiting by the rear van doors. The associate extended a hand. "Scott Parker Pearson." Kate wondered whether his second and last names really began with the same consonant, or if he changed his middle name to emulate his boss.

The repacked box sat squarely in the middle of the rear floor. Kate caught Pearson's eye and waved a hand toward the cardboard container. "There it is. Big and unwieldy but manageable."

He hefted it for a second, then sat the box back onto the vehicle's floor and pulled out a pen. "This is pretty heavy. What did you say was in it?"

"The contents from Amelia's desk," Kate replied.

He squinted as he gave a half-smile. "Yeah, but you must have some idea..." His words trailed off, and he raised a questioning eyebrow.

"All I did was load up whatever I found, Mr. Pearson. I didn't read anything." She remembered Sophia's visit and added, "Oh yes, Daniel Nethercutt's coin collection is in there, too. Please note that on the receipt."

Pearson used the box as a table and wrote several lines in a slashing script across the page of letterhead before signing with a flourish. Wordlessly, he handed the receipt to Kate, picked up the box and headed back across the parking lot.

"I don't think he liked you much, Katie," Meg said, after they'd slammed the back doors and climbed into the front.

"I'll just have to send all my legal work elsewhere," she replied and turned the key.

· · · ·

QUIET, FINALLY, FOR the first time that day. With the dinner dishes loaded and washing, Kate headed up to her office to work on the final pieces for the next day's Book Nook presentation. Her collapsible luggage cart already stood loaded with show-and-tell items she used to explain her methods for easy and stress-free organization. Saree had offered one of the shop easels, and Kate had a nice collection of poster-sized displays printed up to illustrate specific points. Some were detailed how-to ideas, others bulleted sound bites of what she planned to discuss to help everyone remember the high points after her speech.

Deep in the middle of her notes on coping with kids' toys, Kate was at her desk arranging and rearranging cards when blond curls and blue eyes suddenly bookended her.

"Mommy, whatcha doin'?" Suze asked.

"Yeah, can we help?" Sam piped up.

She gave them a double hug. "Thanks, sweeties, but I really need to do this by myself."

Suze pulled away first and patted her hair back in place. Kate smiled as her daughter questioned, "Is it homework?"

"In a way," she said, with Sam still stuck to her side. Funny how different the girls were, no matter how alike they appeared to the eye. "This is work I'm doing at home, but actually, I guess you could call it work to try to get me some more work. It's for the presentation I'm doing at Saree's tomorrow night."

"Are you going to work for Saree?" Sam asked. "Can we work for her, too?"

Deciding these duties would have to wait until after the girls went to bed, Kate untangled from Sam and stacked the note cards. "No, sweetie, I'm not working for Saree. She has some organization books to sell, and I'm going to tell people how to organize their homes and lives."

"But how will that give you more work?" Suze scrunched her forehead. "If you tell them how to organize everything, and Saree sells them books on how, won't they just do everything themselves?"

Kate had already figured Suzanne for a future business leader, and the astuteness of her questions bore out this belief. "Well, some people come to hear about things, then get all excited at how new ideas can change their lives, make their lives better. But after trying it for themselves, they often realize they need help or don't have the time to do everything alone. For those instances, I'm hoping people will remember my presentation and call me."

Sam shrugged. "Makes sense to me." But Suze just pursed her lips.

Oh no, I hope that's not an indication of everyone else's idea on the subject, too. Looking at the clock, she asked the twins, "What are you doing in here, anyway? You still have another twenty minutes of cartoon fun left for the evening."

"Mommm," they groaned.

"It's not like we're little kids anymore," Suze added.

Kate smothered a smile and put a hand at the back of each head, walking them out the door. "So, what do you want to do for the next twenty minutes?"

"Go to the store," Suze started.

"And buy Sweetie Eaties for breakfast tomorrow," Sam finished.

Kate laughed. "Is it possible Sweetie Eaties was the sponsor of one of those cartoon shows you're getting too mature to watch?"

"Well, kinda," Sam said.

"But the cereal is really good for us," Suze explained. "Each bowlful contains vitamins and niacin, and, and...all kinds of nutritious sounding things. Sweetie Eaties will help us wake up in the morning, too. The guy in the commercial said so."

"With a name like Sweetie Eaties, I don't doubt that one bit," Kate replied. "Did he mention the sugar content when he was listing all those other good things the cereal contains?"

"Noooo."

Grocery shopping had been on the to-do list for the day, but after all the excitement she'd planned on shifting the chore to Thursday morning. Still, with ready helpers—regardless of their ulterior motive—the trip might be accomplished faster than usual. "Let me get my purse, and we'll head to the supermarket. Can one of you grab the shop-paks?"

"I will!" they chorused, taking off at a run and never slowing down until belted into the van.

The bright lights in the Bennington supermarket gave Kate a sense of security she hadn't felt in days. Despite the more populous community, evening shopping was less busy than during the day, and Kate relished being able to move through aisles with little likelihood of running across one of the small but growing number of Hazelton residents she knew.

Before pulling out a shopping basket, she helped Sam and Suze look for one of the miniature ones the manager kept ready for helpful and restless children. She knew the kid-sized carts were a marketing ploy to get parents to buy more, but Kate practiced her own method for making sure only the things she wanted to buy got into the smaller basket. Soon everyone was set, from Kate with her shop-pak full of coupons and pre-printed list, to the girls with their own small shop-pak and an equally pint-sized shopping list, along with drawn or expired coupons to pretend they were shopping like Mom.

"Okay, what are the rules?" Kate asked.

"We stay together at all times," the twins chorused, pent-up energy forcing their little Nikes to dance circles in the aisle as they waited to start the scavenger hunt. Though she had no doubt Sweetie Eaties would be the first item cannonballed into their shopping cart.

"Right, you're competing with me, not each other," she reminded. "How many items are on your list?"

Suze whipped the list above her head to keep Sam from grabbing it. As the designated better reader, Suzanne always assumed leadership in duties incorporating words. Kate chewed her lip, wondering whether she should intervene for Sam or if doing so would simply reinforce Suze's superiority in this task. But fate always had a way of stepping in, and while she worried the twins counted together, with quick-witted Sam shouting first, "Twelve."

Suze frowned. "A dozen," she responded, attempting to shift power her way through semantics.

"Exactly." Kate smiled at both girls, wondering if there was a course she could take that quantified for parents how much twin-competition was good competition. "You have plenty of room in your cart for everything. But work together to find exactly what is written on the grocery list. Sizes and quantities are marked for many of the items. And again, stay together."

"Ah, Mom," Suze groaned.

"Can we go?" Sam almost did a full pirouette.

"On your mark—"

They took off as one, tearing down the linoleum aisle.

"Don't run," Kate warned, and they slowed minutely. She smiled again and pulled her own list from the shop-pak.

She'd given up on those little multi-tabbed coupon holders years ago and created her own out of a half-sized, three-ring binder and a box of labeled sandwich bags that closed with plastic zipper tabs. By punching holes in the bag bottoms, opposite the zipper, then labeling in permanent marker an individual coupon category on the outside of each bag, one glance showed available coupons for a needed item. Best of all, different types of coupons didn't have to share space anymore. She added more bags for a new category. Even better, she could sort and shift the coupon bags anytime her regular stores changed aisle layouts. A friend in Minneapolis recycled her son's baseball card holder and used each pocket to hold coupons, but Kate liked her own system better since it allowed her to display shopping lists and sale ads for each store in additional front bags.

As she passed the cereal aisle the girls each clutched a box of Sweetie Eaties to her body and jumped up and down in delight. The rules of the scavenger hunt game required the twins return to Kate as soon as they found all the items on their list, and whoever's cart held the most items won. It was usually no problem letting her daughters come out on top, despite giving them the added chore of hunting sizes now that they read well enough to usually understand the differences in packaging. Mistakes offered a teaching experience Kate appreciated. She comparison-shopped with a vengeance and double-checked each coupon and rebate, cross-referencing to the sale ad, and she usually stayed one or more items behind the pint-sized shoppers.

The newly promoted produce man, a photo of his new son pinned to his green apron, smiled at Kate as she grabbed limes from the stack next to the mangos he sorted. She added a couple of rosy-peach-orange mangos to her cart, chastising herself for going off list. *I'll be better from here on.* But, if she did have to impulse buy, fresh fruit was better than cheese Danish, which was her own version of Sweetie Eaties. "Cute baby."

"Ah." The young man's face reddened. "My wife did this. I probably shouldn't wear it."

"I love the idea." Kate patted his arm. "How old is he?"

"Four months. He smiles and sits up and everything."

In the meat department she picked a nice brisket to crock cook for dinner Sunday. She caught sight of the twins as she passed the rice aisle, and they added a bag of whole grain rice to their half-filled cart. Kate was in the dairy section, getting milk for her and the girls, and soymilk for Keith, who watched his cholesterol. When she turned, she spotted Danny at the far end of the store, speaking to a pretty teenage girl.

Keep it casual. Kate moved back the way she'd come. While she didn't plan to break up the high schoolers' conversation, if she could pull the boy away for a minute she might get a chance to pursue a few questions still unanswered in her casebook.

Before she was even halfway to her destination, Gabriella Cavannah-Wicker appeared from the end of the bread aisle and grabbed the young girl's arm, pulling her away despite verbal protests from both teens. Kate wasn't sure what to do and waited to see if Danny followed the women. His face turned bright red, and he shoved a hand in one pocket to withdraw a piece of paper. He stared at the scrap, his jaw clenched, then he savagely fisted the paper, threw it on the floor, and stalked off.

She glanced around quickly, making sure no other shoppers were paying attention, then hurried down the brightly lit back aisle. The cart rolled up alongside the scrap, and she knelt to pick up the paper. A scribbled phone number but not a Hazelton exchange. Possibly a cell phone number.

"Why don't you let me throw that trash away for you, Ms. McKenzie."

Kate whirled and found herself face to face with Lieutenant Johnson, one hand held out, waiting for her to comply, the other holding a microwave dinner.

"I—I didn't see you when I..." Her words petered out with her courage.

He curled his fingers and waved them upward a couple of times, signaling he was still expecting her to put the paper in his hand.

And she did. As much as she hated to, she dropped the number into his palm.

"Thank you," he said.

"Anything to keep Hazelton clean," Kate replied, angry with herself. She didn't know the law, and it was entirely possible she had no choice. But something didn't set right down deep in her soul, and she knew the reason was because she hadn't even tried to argue.

"Are you following me?" she demanded.

"Just buying my dinner, ma'am." He gave her a brief salute and disappeared down the soda aisle. Kate decided she'd had enough of shopping and Lieutenant Johnson for the day and searched for the girls. They found her first, everything on their list checked off and nearly overflowing the mini-cart.

"Wonderful." Kate cheered, her anger ebbing away. "Let's go check out."

"We won, we won," Sam cried after counting the items in her mom's basket.

She pulled both girls into a hug. "You sure did."

As the checker scanned the items, she scanned what she could of the rest of the store's front, looking for Lieutenant Johnson. Apparently, he'd already paid and left with his one item, but she did spot Danny's back as he leaned outside against one of the plate glass windows.

Maybe she still had a chance.

Kate barely kept her mind on the prices, almost as antsy as the girls had been earlier, eager to start on her own scavenger quest of information. She had just slid her debit card through the reader when Suze cried, "Hey, look. There's Louie."

Indeed, at that moment their pizza delivery guy grabbed his change and exited the cigarette register. As Louie hit the automatic door, Danny bounced away from the window and walked over, putting his arm around the older teen's shoulders. The pair disappeared into the night, and with their departure Kate lost another opportunity to talk to Danny.

CHAPTER EIGHTEEN

STACKED IN YOUR FAVOR, LLC
KATE MCKENZIE, PRES.

<u>*TO DO FOR Thurs., April 15*^{*th*}</u>

• • • •

WORDS TO STAY ON-TRACK:

"Entrepreneurs are simply those who understand that there is little difference between obstacle and opportunity and are able to turn both to their advantage."

— *Victor Kiam* —

Goals for the Day:

- *Work on final invoicing, since job at Amelia's is shut down by order of state police.*
- *Presentation tonight at Saree's. Talk about making choices. Discuss how running late is a CHOICE, forgetting appointments is a CHOICE, wise time & resource managing is a CHOICE. Take family schedule calendar. Explain how each person is assigned a color, and appointments for each person are written on the calendar in the designated color so we can quickly spot who does what and when. (Also great reminder for bill paying—give bills their own color.) Suggest hanging in high-traffic area, like the kitchen or near the door everyone leaves by.*

• • • •

"SURE YOU'RE GOING TO be okay alone?" Keith asked, the girls already in the Jeep and his golf clubs standing ready by the front door.

The radio station planned to devote the entire morning drive hour to cover the latest crime spree in Hazelton. Scheduled experts would discuss how the violence trend continued widening ever farther from the urban areas toward rural locales like Vermont—something Kate knew wouldn't thrill town leaders. But with baseball season beginning, and hockey and basketball hurtling toward playoffs, the evening sports coverage remained set to continue without interruption. To that end, Keith was the man up to provide color for a special Thursday night fundraising baseball game in Burlington between the some of the Oakland A's and their Minor League team, the Vermont Lake Monsters, to support the children's wing of a Burlington hospital.

Pre-game, he and his station manager planned to add their own bit of color to their golf games. "I can call Jimmy and cancel."

"No." Kate waved a hand. "Go on. Meg and I have plenty to catch up on today even if we are no longer gainfully employed."

He walked over and circled her in his arms. "Not what I meant. Being close to a murdered—"

"Stop." Kate cut the sharpness of her response with a soft jab to his chest. "I'm perfectly fine about all of this, but I don't need anything resurrecting the memory." She pushed away. "Now go, before the girls decide to try driving themselves to school."

Keith scooped the cell phone out of the kitchen charger as he headed for the door. "If you think you're okay—but call if you need me later. Oh, and remember I'm staying over in Burlington tonight, and you'll have to pick up the twins after school."

"I will. Drive carefully. There's a chance of rain tomorrow, and the drive back might be slick."

He pulled her close and gave her a long kiss goodbye. "I may have had the reputation for being a little reckless on hockey ice, babe, but never on asphalt."

Kate followed him out the front door and waved to the girls as the red Jeep circled the cul-de-sac and disappeared onto the main road. The telephone rang as she locked the door.

"Hello."

"I saw everyone leave," Meg said. "Want me to come over and help you prepare our invoice or anything? I'll bring donuts and the newspaper. Gil made an early run this morning."

"Any new info?" Kate asked, smiling at the proprietary way all small towns want to learn everything about their own—good or bad. Especially the bad.

"Only new thing I noticed was about the rumors regarding Sophia's alleged involvement in some less than savory business dealings subsequent to the court ruling her husband incapable of handling his own financial affairs."

"He's not in for health problems, he's—"

"Ga-ga," Meg replied. "Put a fresh pot of coffee on, and I'll be over with donuts."

"Interesting. Sophia truly was in charge."

As the coffee brewed Kate scooped up breakfast dishes and added them to the dishwasher. She wiped off the maple syrup bottle and replaced it in the refrigerator, then took a wet cloth to the sticky area left on the table. A load of laundry churned rhythmically in the washer by the time Meg walked through the back door.

"I bring the most important of the basic food groups," Meg said, raising the flat box high above her head as if in offer to the carb-deity. "My men swarmed over these sweets like locusts, but I managed to keep two back before they devoured everything."

"My family had waffles with too much syrup, so both our offspring should be crashing right around first recess," Kate replied. "The girls originally wanted a new sugary cereal they *had to have* last night, but once they pulled out the prize they decided their dad's breakfast looked better."

Meg lowered the box with a flourish, and it landed gracefully in the middle of the table. "Then our work is done, my sister. Let us eat."

Kate laughed and set the coffeepot on a trivet. She pulled pads and pens from the drawer under the telephone.

"What are those for?" Meg asked.

"I've been thinking. We may not be able to work at the mansion anymore—nor do I want to," she quickly added as Meg displayed an alarmed expression. "But we do possess a pretty good knowledge of Amelia's eccentric taste and—"

"You do, anyway."

Kate shook her head. "And you, too. Your total hours in there nearly match mine, and you can't tell me you haven't absorbed more than a little of the crazy-quilt logic the couple used to buy what struck their fancy. Plus, you've seen enough in the rooms to be able to notice things which may belong in the Nethercutts' various collections."

"I'm not getting where you're going with this." Meg picked up a plump donut and bit into the glazed curve.

"I propose we go on a scavenger hunt today." When Meg raised a quizzical eyebrow, she hastened to add, "Check out area antique stores and malls for anything that might have belonged to Amelia and Daniel. Try to find out who brought the pieces in for sale and maybe discover who was stealing her stuff."

"Oh! What mother and the gossipy hens talked about at the garden club luncheon." Meg dropped her donut and almost knocked over a cup in her excitement. "I'd forgotten Amelia's mission."

"Well, we haven't exactly had the time to take it on while doing the inventory, but now we do have the opportunity and should recognize things that may have made Amelia's collector heart go pitter-patter. We know enough to be dangerous, anyway, to someone trying to keep his or her sticky-fingered crimes a secret."

"Speaking of sticky." Meg popped the last bite into her mouth and wiped her fingers on a napkin. "We could be placing ourselves in a sticky situation and uncover enough to get in more hot water."

Kate tore her donut in half and offered a piece to her friend. "I can't believe Meg Berman is suddenly getting super-security-minded. You've acted all along as if you're ready to launch into anything."

Meg snapped up the proffered fried dough and grinned. "Hey, I'm not turning cautious. I simply like to play devil's advocate once in a while. Speaking of Satan, you don't suppose the whole theft problem died yesterday with Sophia?"

"Maybe, but I've been thinking long and hard on this and every part of me wants to say no. I mean, yes. Sophia was swiping anything she could from the mansion, but was always out in the open about it, and she repeatedly claimed the items were willed to her. The thefts in question, however, began before Amelia died, and disappeared stealthily. Completely out of character for Sophia."

"True, but if she needed money for shady dealings—"

"We don't know she's short on funds, just that shady business rumors are flying. But if the woman needed cash, why not mortgage a property or sell something to put a lot of bucks in her bank account?" Kate took a sip of coffee to wash down the sugar overload, then walked to the counter and pulled her casebook from her purse, flipping a few pages before she answered. "Nope. According to what your mother said, Amelia found her stuff up for sale in an antique shop. Whether it was consignment or not, a Vermont antique shop isn't the best way to get top price or fast cash. With her connections she would have hit Sotherby's or Christie's for a more lucrative and timely payday."

"Connections in New York might offer the means. Remember she had to stay until Saturday on business when she and Keith flew there. Maybe the extra day was to arrange transport or something."

"Or something," Kate mused. "As much as I would love to say Sophia framed me, I can't make myself believe she was the thief."

"So, do you think it's Bill or Thomas?"

Kate shrugged. "No idea. The only thing to do is visit some shops and ask who brought in the goods."

"Any hints about starting places?"

"I wanted to ask Mrs. Baxter, but I called the phone number she gave me, and it's been disconnected. Apparently, she's moved out of her cottage, and I have no idea where. I guess I could try the attorney's office. They need an address to send a final check, or do you think Bill might be worth pumping for information?"

"I have a better idea." Meg pulled keys from her jeans pocket. "We go with the theme of your original thoughts and take to the highways and byways, my friend. Wander through every antique store we can find, and see what information gets unearthed. That's how Amelia discovered the scheme. Maybe we'll discover the schemer."

"Good idea. Any particular starting point in mind?"

"Bennington boasts a good concentration of antique emporiums located in and around the city limits. Close enough for the thief to get there easily, and far enough from Hazelton to make him or her complacent about the risk of getting caught. Come on, I'll drive, and you can ride shotgun."

"Shotgun, Meg, really? I think I prefer to be navigator."

"Yeah." Meg grinned. "But the other sounds much more exciting."

$$\bullet \ \bullet \ \bullet \ \bullet$$

THE BEST PART ABOUT her neighbor's adventure idea was getting to travel over several of the state's picturesque covered bridges. Kate loved the gentle *wap-wap-wap* sound tires made crossing the wooden floors, and the way the sunlight and leaf shadows danced in and out of the lattice-worked openings above the car. She sent up a wish with every crossing, her own personal superstition for blessing.

When the many shops in Bennington proper failed to provide a lead, the women hit the perimeter roads, finally heading north on Route 67A. It was at one of the three bridges off Route 67A, the one across Silk Road, where her wish came true.

The dark red barn sat off at the side of the road, surrounded by majestic hemlocks and various evergreens. Fallen cones lay scattered across the season's new grass, along with the short dark leaves that gave the hemlock branches their flat appearance. A crushed gravel drive and small parking lot completed the scene, with a rustic sign, URSULA'S ANTIQUES, swinging in the breeze. The loft held linens and bed things, sheet music, and antique camping and fishing gear. The lower level displayed kitchen and household items, books and tools, jewelry and music boxes—and one glorious puzzle box. Kate gasped. It was the same ebony and ivory inlaid puzzle box planted in Kate's house the night of Amelia's murder and returned to the mansion just days ago.

Meg picked it up, her mouth set in a firm line as she turned the box over. They nodded in silent agreement.

"A lovely little box," cooed Ursula, a white-haired pixie who rose from a needle-pointed chair behind a teak eighteenth-century secretary. "At least one-hundred-fifty years old. Asian. We just received it from a new vendor."

Kate took the box from Meg and shook it. Nothing. Whatever had been inside was gone. She wanted to learn the secret, for her own peace of mind if nothing else. "Can you show me how it opens?"

"Certainly." Ursula pulled open a thin drawer and extracted a hat pin. "Quite simple once the trick is revealed." She pushed the pin's point into an almost invisible hole near one seam.

Instantly, the top sprang up, revealing the empty interior.

"How interesting," Meg said. "This came from a new vendor, you say?"

"Yes." Ursula smiled. "I can't wait to meet her."

Kate's heart sank and knew from looking at Meg's face that her friend felt the same disappointment. "You've never met this person? This woman?"

Ursula shook her head. "I've only talked to her by phone. She sent the box by post, with an address to mail the check."

"Do you have an address?"

"Yes..." Ursula frowned. "Is there a particular reason you're interested in this vendor?"

Obviously we'll never make it as spies. Kate looked at Meg and received a shrug, taking that as agreement to go ahead and tell all. "You see, Miss, er, Ursula, we believe this item was stolen from an estate we've been working for. Various things disappeared over the past few months. You can see why we're interested in the person who sent the box."

"Stolen? My heavens." Ursula fluttered back to her chair and picked up a manila folder to fan her rapidly reddening face. "She said her name was Miss Wilson, and she had such a cultured voice. Of course, from what you say I assume her name is likely an alias, but I certainly had no reason to think so at the time or believe the item stolen."

"You said you have her address."

"Oh, yes." Ursula dropped her improvised fan and pulled a Rolodex closer. After picking through an almost endless stream of cards, she pulled out one. "A post office box in Wilmington."

The town just east of Bennington. Another let down.

• • • •

THEY WOUND THROUGH the picturesque roads back to Hazelton, both women unusually quiet. Meg's jaw was set and her knuckles white as she gripped the steering wheel. Kate wished they could check out more places, but the end of the school day was fast approaching with kids to retrieve. Additionally, she needed time to steel herself for the Book Nook organizing seminar in a few hours.

"This thing at Saree's tonight could do great things for your business," Meg said, as if reading Kate's mind.

"I just wish it were some other night. With Keith out of town, Tiffany is babysitting the girls."

"Well, at least there's no risk of any more surreptitious gifts appearing this time." Meg slowed as they approached a narrow, uncovered bridge.

"How do you figure?"

"You heard what Ursula said." Meg flashed a surprised look. "With Sophia dead, the theft problem is gone. Obviously, she was the one trying to pin everything on you."

"Hmm. You think she killed Amelia to cover her thefts?"

"I know you figured a whole 'why she didn't do it' scenario earlier, but the thief was a woman with a cultured voice. Plus, the death mask was at her murder and points toward her being the thief. She could have realized she would be caught and killed herself, sending you the text message to attempt one last try at framing you, using the mask to make things even more complicated."

"Not unless she was able to fatally stab herself, yet wipe her fingerprints off the knife before she died, and pose her body on the sofa after her own death. With those facts proven by the crime scene and forensics pros, it's highly likely the mask was placed after death."

"Posed after her death?"

Kate nodded. "The CSI guy told Johnson during my interrogation. The body was moved after death, and the mask had to be positioned after death as well. While the possibility exists that

Sophia could have been the thief, I'm convinced the murderer brought it in, planning to use the mask as another attempt to implicate me in murder. The only thing that saved me was Valerie running hard at my heels."

After chewing on her lower lip, Meg suggested, "What about Sophia as the thief and an unknown someone else the murderer of both women? The murderer spotted the mask in Sophia's house and put it on the dead body as a sick gag—murder victim and a death mask."

"Entirely possible, but we can't prove motive or opportunity, and until we do it's going to be difficult figuring out who the murderer is. Motives for Amelia's death could have been the will or her bossiness." Kate fished the casebook out of her purse. "Sophia was no sweetheart, but we don't have any idea how her life affected anyone else's. She and Bill had their fights, Danny avoided her, and every time we've seen Sophia and Thomas together they seemed unperturbed by each other. While notable in its lack of competitive atmosphere, hers and Thomas's non-hostile relationship doesn't give us any motive toward her murder. As far as money goes, she's married. Any money in her estate would likely go to her husband."

She flipped pages in the notebook, checking facts and ideas. After a few minutes, she closed it with a snap. "Nothing here to suggest any new direction, and nothing neatly connects. Something is missing. The person trying to make me look guilty may be the thief or the murderer, but..."

"What are you thinking?"

Kate gave a nervous laugh. "I'm sorry. I'm seeing conspiracy where there isn't any. You know, working through the puzzle again and again makes me put pieces together whether they fit or not. But the silly thinking does make a kind of picture appear."

"Quit apologizing and tell me what you're trying not to say."

"Probably the craziest thing you've ever heard."
"Try me."
Taking a deep breath, she said, "What if the woman on the phone with the cultured voice was Valerie?"

CHAPTER NINETEEN

STAYING ORGANIZED IN the Car

1) Use over-the-seat organizers on front seatbacks. Besides providing invaluable storage space for kids' stuff like iPods and books, the roomy pockets hold maps, umbrellas, and snacks for lengthy road trips—or just long errand days.

2) Keep food coupons in an envelope in the glove compartment. This way, they aren't sitting at home when you're at the restaurant.

3) Check flashlight batteries periodically to make sure you'll not be "in the dark" if you need light "on the road." In cooler months, keep an extra pack of batteries in the glove box—they'll stay fresh in low temps—but take them out during hot weather.

• • • •

"VALERIE? YOU'RE KIDDING, right?" Meg cried, almost running off the road in her surprise. She pulled onto the soft shoulder, in front of a white farmhouse advertising eggs for sale, and stared at Kate, incredulous.

"I don't have any specific idea to suggest, but Sophia never flipped all the right switches when I've deliberated over who planted the stolen items in my house and vehicle."

"Still, do you actually believe Valerie—"

"I don't know." Kate repeated, shaking her head as she tried to piece together her thoughts. "I must have gotten the idea from somewhere, but I can't figure out what makes me think it's a possibility. Regardless, I don't believe Sophia was the thief. I realize Ursula said the thief had a cultured voice, but really, most anyone can fake one for a telephone call. However, Valerie could have come by my house and planted the box that night, with Tiffany not even thinking about telling me her mom stopped by. The twins wouldn't see Valerie as a stranger, and I still need to talk to Louie—"

"Or Tiffany hid the box at her mom's request." Meg tapped the steering wheel with her index fingers and stared out the windshield. "As crazy as the idea sounded at first, it makes a scary kind of sense. No one could be more eager to be involved in this inventorying enterprise. We always assumed Sophia recruited her, but what if it actually happened the other way around? Remember, too, how she insisted on riding with us to Sophia's. What if she killed Sophia earlier, sent herself the text from Sophia's phone, and came back to work to establish an alibi for when the body was found? I didn't hear a ping, did you? Who's to say the message wasn't already on her phone, and she just waited for the perfect opportunity to 'discover' the summons?"

"Yes, and we only have Valerie's word she'd never been in the Nethercutt mansion before going to work with us," Kate mused. "She was livid that I got the organizing job. But could she really be the thief? Let Amelia spot the stuff in the antique shop so quickly?"

"Maybe she got sloppy right away and put the stuff in a resale place too close to Hazelton. After all, Ursula told us she'd just been contacted by 'Ms. Wilson' last week, and the merchandise arrived yesterday. Or maybe Amelia decided to go a bit farther afield to find new things to buy. If the Nethercutts traveled the world for the junk they bought, surely Amelia had hit all the antique shops in southwestern Vermont. It's all speculation until we discover which shop she stumbled into that was selling her stuff," Meg said, shrugging. "As far as getting into the mansion, we don't know how long our favorite decorator worked at Sophia's place. Who's to say she didn't tag along on trips to step-mummy's house?"

Kate thought back to the day of Amelia's murder. She had always assumed Sophia arrived alone and remembered driving around the silver-blue BMW convertible to circle out of the mansion's cobblestone driveway. The Beemer two-seater had been empty of any passenger, Kate was sure, and said so. "Not the day Amelia died. Even if Valerie ducked down in the car to hide as I drove by, I would have seen her."

"But she would have been able to slip into the mansion after Sophia did, right?" Meg prompted. "Didn't you say you went to the kitchen almost as soon as Sophia arrived? Valerie could have entered while you were out of sight."

"Yes..."

"Amelia had no butler or maid to keep an eye on the front door. Our Miss James could walk in without ringing the doorbell, and you would have never known she was in the house." Meg's eyes gleamed as she stacked damning possibility onto damning possibility.

"Why would Sophia not mention Valerie was with her? Johnson would have made sure to interview her with everyone else."

"Maybe Sophia did tell him. Or maybe Johnson skipped talking to Val."

Kate shook her head. She clearly remembered the day they discovered the mask's disappearance from the conservatory wall, then shivered when her thoughts shifted to where it had turned up yesterday. "No, the first time they met was the day Jefferson reported the mask stolen. The look on Johnson's face said she was just a new person to interview and an unrecognizable one to boot. Forget I said anything. The police checked our phones. If she killed Sophia and tried to manufacture an alibi, Johnson could prove she received the call long before joining us."

"But it was such a good scenario—"

"Nope." Kate waved the idea away like the perfume sample cloud that always hovered in mall department stores. "My imagination was getting the better of me."

"All our best laid plans." Meg sighed, then brightened. "Hey, the cameras. We'll get Meeks to let us scan the tapes."

"I thought everything went to digital files."

"Whatever." Meg turned the ignition. "I'll call Meeks when we get home." She tapped the car's clock. Two-eighteen. "We'd better make tracks if we're going to make it to Hazelton in time to pick up our little darlings at school. Are you all set for tonight?"

"Oh, yeah, no problem. Tiffany's coming at six-thirty, so—"

"Tiffany!"

Kate looked at Meg. "Well, yeah. Since you and Jane are going to be at the store to give me moral support, I called Tiffany and asked her to babysit."

"Do you think that's a good idea? I mean even if the Valerie angle is nothing more than creative brainstorming, we can't overlook a possibility—"

"Oh, for heaven's sake." Kate laughed. "Talking it out made me see how ridiculous the suggestion is. I'm forcing things to fit, nothing more. Valerie not only had to be at Amelia's on the day of the murder, but she'd also have to avoid Danny, his dad and uncle, and Mrs. Baxter—Oh, why didn't I think of it before?"

In duet, they cried, "Mrs. Baxter's the thief!"

"She had to be." Meg's curls danced as she nodded. "She was on the spot and had ample opportunity to steal the items. Besides, from what you told me she said during your visit, the woman vacillated between some strange friend/enemy, sympathetic/jealousy mood swings on an almost constant basis."

"A definite possibility. Twist the right emotion, and she probably decided Amelia had enjoyed the good life long enough, and she was sick of accepting the leftovers."

"Or she found out Amelia knew about the thefts and killed to save her job. No, that won't work. Valerie said Sophia fired Mrs. Baxter, and the cook went to live with her brother."

"What?"

As she signaled to turn left, Meg grinned sheepishly. "Sorry. You're going to fire me as your investigative partner, huh? Valerie told me yesterday morning before her temper tantrum. You were getting a glass of water."

"So where did Mrs. Baxter go?" Kate asked.

Meg shrugged. "That's what I asked Valerie, but she wasn't sure. Said Mrs. B. didn't have any relatives around here anymore and headed out of state to a brother in Texas or Wyoming. Some place cowboy-ie anyway. Apparently, she had a hissy at Sophia about having to leave, too. Valerie said Mrs. B. told Sophia she 'expected better out of Mr. Daniel's daughter' and 'Miss Amelia will spin in her grave at your turning me out into the cold.'"

Too much to process. A stress headache was coming on, something Kate didn't need before speaking to a crowd she hoped would become customers. She rummaged in her purse for the small aspirin bottle.

Three of their kids stood together on the sidewalk around the school's circle drive.

"Where's Mark?" Kate asked.

"Little League," Meg replied. "That's why I didn't take us on home to get your van. With one less kid, the car has enough seatbelts for everyone."

Meg couldn't stand the game of baseball—"Un-American, I know," she'd told Kate a month ago—so it was up to Gil Berman to support his eldest son and provide transport home after practice and games.

"It's great the paper gives Gil the flexibility to carve out the hours he needs to do this with Mark," Kate said.

"Uh-huh," Meg agreed. "And Mark really likes having time when his dad is devoted to him, alone. At the house, it's always the three of them playing catch or working on the boys' batting. On practice and game days, though, Mark has his dad's attention completely focused on him. We aren't dealing with as many stubborn fits anymore, and his grades have even improved. I wish we'd thought of this long ago."

"I guess the boys are pretty competitive," Kate reflected. "I've noticed tension growing between the girls, too. Maybe Keith and I need to do some talking and come up with some ideas. We try to give each of them full latitude in creating their own identities, but with both twins on the same teams and going to all the same events, maybe their fighting is actually related to wanting their own space and more individual time with each of us."

As she said this Jamey Hendricks walked by and said something Sam responded to with a smile and nod. A second later, Suze slammed a schoolbook across the back of her sister's head and Sam responded with a punch in the shoulder. A teacher separated the pair by the time Kate managed to jump from the car and get to them. Obviously, Suze's crush on Jamey Hendricks remained in full force.

• • • •

TIFFANY ARRIVED LATE for babysitting. Her mother hadn't been home, and the teen had to walk the few blocks. She wasn't as effervescent as usual, and Kate wondered what the personality switch signaled. One last round of orders to the twins and a reminder to do everything Tiffany said, then Kate ran over to get Meg. Gil was in the kitchen helping the boys finish off leftovers.

"Did you call Meeks? Can we take a look at the pictures?" Kate asked.

Meg shook her head. They stepped back into the cooler evening temperatures, and Kate was glad she wore a wool blazer. She put her hands in the pockets.

"The police already confiscated all his equipment related to the mansion. He did remember seeing, as he put it, 'a stout little lady puttering around the place that first night,' and is going to figure a way to make the police aware of our suspicions. Unless Valerie saw the box while we inventoried the parlor."

"Oh, stop." Kate backed carefully out of the driveway. "I told you my idea was seriously nutty. I'm sure it's nothing more than a subconscious desire to see her jailed for at least one night."

"Like an adult timeout for annoying the people who have to associate with her." Meg laughed.

"Someday when we rule the world..." Kate smiled as she flipped on the headlights. "No, more likely, Mrs. Baxter knew we'd started in the parlor, and after we had it inventoried, figured anything she took from in there wouldn't soon be missed. She looked in all the nooks and crannies and found the box."

"Well, that makes sense, too," Meg conceded.

Kate grinned. "Thank you. Sometimes I am able to look at things without seeing how I can implicate someone I don't like."

"I didn't mean—"

"I know." Kate laughed. "I know."

For the first time that day, Kate realized she was actually getting into a good mood. She'd been on edge all the time lately and worried what would pop up from around the next corner. Definitely within reason, to be sure, but exhausting nonetheless. Just laughing with Meg like this, though their conversation still revolved around the mess she had innocently landed in, was the release she needed. She wasn't even as nervous about speaking at the workshop anymore.

Nervous, but not so nervous.

"Did you get any information from Tiffany?"

She turned onto Main Street. "There wasn't time, but she seems preoccupied. Probably upcoming finals or boyfriend issues. She does have a new job at the ice cream place, and with her hours running Friday through Sunday, it can't help but put a crimp in her social life."

"Or she could have issues with her mom," Meg suggested, stopping Kate's retort by holding up a hand. "Don't say it. I'm simply stating the obvious again."

She recognized Meg was just needling, but her friend's words caused a shadow of apprehension to rise higher in her mind. As she pulled into the alley behind the Book Nook and parked her van next to the bookseller's lime green VW, Meg added, "Gil came home with information on Bill Nethercutt. Seems the scoop around the paper is Bill teeters on the verge of filing for bankruptcy, but he left Charlie-boy's office this morning sporting a huge smile."

"What did Gil and his newspaper cronies conclude from those facts?"

"Their cynical little minds decided that despite the postponement of the reading of Amelia's will, out of professional courtesy to Bill, C.W.W. spilled the beans regarding how the estate would be distributed. If true, information on what he stands to inherit would allow Bill to negotiate or renegotiate loans helping his business interests stay solvent. Naturally, such could be a relevant point in the police investigation. If you'll recall, old Charlie-boy said the will Amelia did not get a chance to sign had been changed to affect the timetable of the probate. Want to toss around theories about whether Bill killed her to keep the change from happening?"

"I think we've hypothesized enough today, but if you want my opinion, it doesn't work unless we assume he'd been planning to kill Amelia anyway."

"Hey, this is all supposition," Meg replied. "But let's face it, there didn't seem any love lost between Miss Amelia and the next generation. They thought she was tight and possibly hastened the death of Mr. Daniel, something to infuriate Bill and Sophia. Then there are the facts and innuendo we can apply to Thomas's father and his death. As quiet as Tommy-boy is, who knows how far down his emotions sit."

"But Joey's death was decades ago."

Meg responded with platitudes. "Still waters run deep, and revenge is a dish best served cold. There's a reason for clichés. They've encapsulated true situations too many times. The quiet ones are often those who let a hurt fester unchecked until an explosion erupts. And besides, he may have only recently learned what happened."

"If he knew anything at all," Kate mused. Before Meg could argue, she raised a hand. "We have nothing to prove whether or not he's ever been let into the loop over this bombshell. And I guess sibling rivalry would take care of the motive for Sophia's murder. But I like Mrs. B. for the thief. If only we knew for sure she left town and when, to determine whether she could have killed Sophia."

"I'll tell Gil to sniff around and see if he can learn anything." Meg opened her door. "In the meantime, come on. I'll help carry your stuff."

Inside, Saree had pulled out all of the stops for what Kate now called her Organizing Connection, hoping to connect with people who wanted her to personally organize their lives. Finger snacks and goodies tempted patrons from tables around the shop, along with three-by-five index cards for attendees to write questions and particular problems they wanted Kate to address. Saree and her helpers had rolled the middle bookcases closer to the perimeter walls to provide an expansive central meeting area for Kate to hold court, while displaying related books the shop had available for sale. Also in place stood a tri-legged display stand to hold the large informational charts Kate had worked on for months.

They finished lugging in the visual aids and handouts. Jane was already in the store. A second later, Saree swept close in a swirl of fire-tones and handed Kate a small, silver wand resembling a ballpoint pen. "Here, for you."

It was a laser pointer. Kate directed its dancing green light-dot toward the top poster board, which read TIME TO SPRING INTO AN

ORGANIZED HOME AND OFFICE in large type, with a smaller KATE MCKENZIE, STACKED IN YOUR FAVOR, L.L.C. printed in a smaller, but still highly visible font. "Saree, this is wonderful. Thank you. Don't let me forget to give it back to you before I leave."

"No, no." Saree waved. "'Tis for you." She smiled. "I dream many more nights like this one. Look—" She swept a hand toward the audience. "House almost full already."

One of the Book Nook's college-aged store assistants, Anna, a Nordic beauty with almost platinum waist-length hair, manned the register, but Saree took a seat in the back in case she needed to help. Before Kate began, Meg sidled up and pointed to the laser pointer, warning, "Make sure the girls don't get hold of this. Gil bought one a couple of years ago. Mark swiped it when we weren't looking and decided it would make a nifty light saber. Next thing I knew we were rushing Ben to the emergency room with excruciating eye pain and left with him looking like a little pirate wearing a patch for a burned retina. The ophthalmologist warned us we'd gotten off lucky. You wouldn't believe how fast you can blind someone using one of those."

"Eek!" Kate stared at the innocent looking silver object and vowed to lock it away in her office.

Several dozen chairs were already filled, mostly by women, but Kate was surprised to see Bill Nethercutt seated in the back. After returning his smile, she took a moment to ponder why he would show up at a Thursday evening presentation like this one. Especially with his sister recently murdered.

There were two married couples. The younger duo looked like real do-it-yourselfers dressed in flannel and Carhartts. Kate figured after her speech they would head straight home and tear into their closet, putting up customized shelves and racks to maximize space. The other couple, at or near retirement age, reminded her of a pair of birds. The wife a brown wren, busily twisting to talk to everyone, and husband a stalwart hawk, arms crossed, eyes sharp, waiting to get whatever he came for. A few more people drifted in and took seats. Kate greeted those she knew, and Saree scurried to bring extra chairs. The last to arrive was Gabriella Cavannah-Wicker.

Nervously, Kate shuffled through the question cards the early arrivals had filled out. Many were alike. As different as every American household was, most shared the same clutter dilemmas. She fingered through the posters on the stand, peeking to be certain they were in the right order.

Everything ready and everyone waiting, she couldn't put off the presentation any longer.

"Hello, it's nice to see such a big crowd here tonight. I'm Kate McKenzie, and I'm an organizational expert."

A spate of welcoming applause spread across the audience. Once it died down, she launched into her performance by slipping the top poster off the stack to reveal her FIVE-STEP ORGANIZATION START METHOD. Using her new laser pointer, she emphasized each point while discussing how this five-step, five-box method worked in every situation. "It may seem easier to simply take out items which go elsewhere and leave what stays in the room, but that method, while requiring less lifting, won't always work. By unloading the entire space and using the five boxes marked REJECT, RECYCLE, RESALE, RETURN, and REVIEW—" Kate shined a green dot on each as she spoke "—you replace only the things that truly belong, efficiently restore the rest to where they need to be, and will not fail to notice misplaced items tucked behind larger pieces."

The hawk-faced man piped up, "If a person's kitchen resembled the house-wares department at M—"

"Robert—" His little wren-wife fluttered, striking his shoulder with a small hand.

"Well, Margaret, it does," he countered. "You have everything from meatballers to ice cream makers. Even a heart-shaped waffle iron. Why do we need a heart-shaped waffle iron?"

"Valentine's Day breakfast for the grandkids," she returned. "And you always—"

Though Kate imagined variations on this scene played out almost hourly with this couple, she interrupted, "If you use an appliance regularly, then it earns its place on a kitchen counter. Take time to consider how often you need an object and whether another, more versatile appliance can do the job equally well. For example, my twins love fruit smoothies—"

"Twins!" A schoolmarmish woman jerked even straighter in her chair. "No wonder you're

an organizational expert."

After the laughter died down, Kate continued, "I have twin six-year-olds, and yes, their birth helped me to stay on the straight-and-narrow, organizationally speaking. But back to my story, they've been bugging me to purchase a smoothie maker." She held up a hand. "Don't think it's because they can't have smoothies at home because they can. We have a perfectly acceptable blender that creates excellent fruit drinks of every consistency. No, a smoothie maker wins out over the blender in their eyes because they want to press the lever in front and have drinks dispensed right into the glass. That spigot is the winning factor for my children."

Kate scanned the crowd. "Anyone want to be brave and admit to purchasing something your household could have easily done without? A special gizmo you acquired simply because it had a 'new and improved' extra you truly didn't need?"

Several women in the crowd tittered, but no one raised a hand until the hawk-faced husband snorted and uncrossed his arms to grab up his wife's left arm and hold her hand high. The crowd roared, with half joining in to show they, too, had purchased just such a treasure—or three. As courage grew in the room, more hands went up, until nearly everyone had at least one raised. Even Bill laughed and raised his right hand. The lone holdout, Gabriella Cavannah-Wicker, kept hers clenched in her lap.

"Yes, we buy more things on impulse, then hate to throw out the mistakes. But letting things fill your living space only because you don't feel you've gotten enough use out of it—and never will—only adds clutter and makes finding things you do need more difficult. Plus, unnecessary counter items add to cleaning time, as you must constantly move and wipe around each extra appliance. Save your money, people. If you don't use it, someone else might. Donate or sell it in a tag sale."

The husband, arms again tightly crossed, nudged his wife with an elbow. "See, Margaret,

I told you."

Kate quickly moved on to the subject of hidden storage potential. "Never leave the space under the bed to just the dust bunnies."

The group tittered again. She flipped to a detailed drawing of a box on wheels.

"Wheeled boxes are great for beneath the bed storage and can be easily made from disused or mismatched dresser drawers." She pulled a small, plastic wheel from her pocket. "Hardware stores carry a wide selection of wheels similar to this one. Attach it to the bottom, those cute guys at the hardware store can tell you how—" more titters, "—and the box or drawer will roll out and under the bed with ease, no matter how heavy and full. Large plastic storage containers that slide are lightweight and work equally well, plus they have the added advantage of stay-tight lids to keep out dust and crawly things. For economy, you can use those big clear zip bags blankets and sheets come in."

"What a good idea," one woman cried. "I can take care of my seasonal clothing that way."

Kate nodded, glad the audience was getting into the spirit of the event and shifted to another poster. "This is an answer for seasonal storage, but there is another way to get the most clothing stored in the least amount of space."

The next poster showed an enlarged shot of a white plastic bag filled with clothing, and a vacuum cleaner sitting alongside. From the puzzled faces, Kate knew she would win points here on sheer surprise. "By packing folded clothes in plastic bags, you can store them clean and ready for immediate use once the temperatures change. The only problem with plastic bags is they have a tendency to store air along with the clothing."

She flipped again and pointed the laser at a picture showing a hand tightly holding the neck of the bag around the vacuum cleaner's hose. "Once you get folded clothing into the bag, close the bag's opening around the hose of the vacuum and lean or lay across the packed clothes, flip the sucker on and—whoosh! All the air goes into the vacuum and your clothes package is nothing more than, well, *clothes*, with everything tightly packed." She flipped to the next poster and showed a blow-up shot of the 'after' picture, now compressed and easily stackable. "Air, and the extra space it takes, has disappeared."

Pulling out an example she'd brought of just such a bag, filled with summer clothes Kate hoped her family would be using soon, she watched as people came forward to *ooh* and *ahh*. They lifted the bag and grunted at its denseness and weight, marveling at the airless compactness. Many discussed how such bags could be stacked in cabinets and closets. One woman declared she couldn't wait to get home and try it for herself. "This will transform our walk-in closet," she said. "I'll actually be able to find things I want to wear."

Saree had said to expect a lot of working moms in the audience, and Kate saw most fit such a description. She moved on to zone cleaning to teach kids to keep rooms and clutter under control.

"Getting kids to clean their rooms and keep things neat isn't impossible if you teach workable methods and furnish the right tools. Even young children can learn to keep things in zones or centers for play and storage, like you see in daycare centers and elementary schools. For older kids, this method provides privacy and space to entertain friends, too."

She flipped to a bulleted zone chart. "Using zones, keep like and needed items where they are used most."

The poster showed four basic zones: sleeping, computing/homework, music, and R&R. Kate pointed to the first. "These zones stay the same throughout children's lives, whether they are two years old or twenty. For the sleeping zone, keep this for bed and bedding, and only things relating to time just before sleep, like stuffed animals and a small table with a lamp or nightlight.

"For the computer/homework zone, have a desk or table and chair, and keep this and the sleeping zone separate. Don't let kids start bad future sleeping habits by doing homework on their beds. They'll associate bed with work rather than rest. Make sure there is adequate desktop space to write on or add a separate PC table. Include game and educational CDs, pens and pencils, tablets or spirals for notes, research materials, and a good desk lamp."

She moved on to music, noting storage for iPod, CDs, and headphones. "If using rechargeable batteries, the charger stays here, too," she added.

For R&R, she suggested easy-to-shift chairs, like beanbags, floor pillows, or blow up furniture for reading and watching TV or DVDs. "Bookshelves work to store more than books, doubling to hold remote controls and other things easily misplaced."

From the basic zones, she moved on to activity areas which catered to specific age levels, changing to a chart that read—Let's Discover, Let's Pretend, and Let's Build.

"Okay, do you own a lizard or a guinea pig, or any other kind of pet that stays in your child's room?" Heads nodded throughout the audience. She tapped the first line and said, "Put the varmint and anything relating to the pet in the Let's Discover zone. This is the science zone. Add any microscope, binoculars, bug or butterfly collections, magnifying glass, flashlight, magnets, compass or camera your child uses."

As the mother of girls, the next had been a particularly busy zone in her house. Still was. "In Let's Pretend, keep all creative play items. Use hooks or a box for dress-up clothes and hang a mirror on the wall. Large bins hold props for playing house or putting on a stage production and can double as a place for puppeteers to hide behind for a puppet stage.

"The Let's Build It zone holds toys that evolve into larger projects. Give kids space to create by offering a carpeted spot to build a personal Trump Tower. This is also the spot for creating doll worlds, train tracks and landscapes, or loop-the-loop tracks for race cars."

She had their complete attention. Even the attendees of grandparenting age smiled, as if figuring how to utilize the information. "Once zones are established, provide the right tools for storage success. Small lidded plastic bins and boxes collect millions of pieces, like Legos, KNex, Hot Wheels, Barbie clothes, and other items that can drift unchecked through your house. Larger tubs and containers are great for blocks and balls, play dishes and larger trucks, train sets, and any kind of track system. Use see-thru containers or label what goes inside."

"But my children are too young to read," one mother interrupted. "I thought this was all about teaching them to do some of the picking up themselves."

Kate smiled. "It is. For young children, draw pictures or let them help you find photos of the items in magazines or catalogs. Or snap a digital photo and paste the print on the outside. Kids love putting pictures onto containers with tape or a glue stick."

Heads nodded all around, and the questioning mother seemed pleased with the suggestion. Kate moved on to closet fitness. "Hooks work best for very young children, and invest in sturdy plastic hangers rather than wire. Designate a certain color hanger or hook for all play clothes and another for school and church, and you might save the knees of dress pants from getting creamed during afterschool bike races." Laughter swept through the crowd.

Kate then suggested hanging a shoe organizer on the back of the closet door. "If kids don't have enough shoes to fill the pouches, use the extras to store umbrellas, caps, or other small items. Another organizer can be hung on the back of the bedroom door for toys, like cars or fashion dolls, or even small stuffed animals." As a hand went up, she anticipated the question by adding, "If your child is too short to use many of the door organizer's pockets, add a shoe cubby to the closet instead. Purchase one ready-made or do-it-yourself by asking your local grocer for one of the divided boxes laundry cleaners are shipped in. Cover with contact paper or let your kid play Picasso and paint it."

To growing applause, Kate covered adult and storage closets, family cleanups, morning no-battle routines, laundry low-maintenance practices, and gift and hobby storage. The crowd was on their feet as she concluded saying, "Organizing and de-cluttering are a lot like dieting. Pay attention before bringing an item into your house. Consciously decide you really need to pack those pounds around. When you de-clutter you truly are losing weight, both physically and emotionally. And like any change, it may not work overnight and can take long-term commitment, but believe me, it's worth it."

Several came by to speak to her and get a business card. In a wave, the rest of the audience moved to the display of books. Kate packed her things to leave.

"Can I buy you a coffee to thank you for a lot of terrific advice?" Bill reached out to steady the tripod as she pulled off her posters. Meg had a box of supplies in her hands, ready to head for the van, but Kate wasn't surprised her friend stayed grounded there instead. She knew Meg wouldn't want to miss a second of this exchange.

"Oh thanks, Bill, but I can't." She smiled to soften the rejection. Meg stood behind him and wiggled her eyebrows. Kate fought the laughter bubbling inside and turned away to stand the posters against the wall. "Coffee sounds wonderful, especially Saree's, but I need to get home and relieve my sitter."

"That's right, you have twins," he said. "And your husband works nights."

She collapsed the tripod and leaned it against the back wall. "Yep, you must be a sports fan."

"Not really," Bill replied, his smile shifting to the one she'd seen the first time they'd met.

The smile that failed to reach his eyes.

An icy chill slithered up Kate's spine.

"Well, guess Thomas and I will get out of here, then," Bill said in farewell.

Meg's eyes widened. Kate shared her surprise and said, "I hadn't noticed Thomas in the crowd."

Bill shrugged. "He came in to look for some gardening books." Craning his neck for a moment, he spotted his quarry and added, "There he is at the end of the aisle by the door. Well, I'll be seeing you."

"Goodbye."

As Bill and his step-brother left, Kate noticed Thomas was carrying a large Book Nook sales bag. She wondered if he bought the book in which she and Saree had read the information on lily of the valley. She couldn't remember whether she had touched the book. Though the volume was likely covered in fingerprints, it worried Kate that hers might be part of the mix.

CHAPTER TWENTY

NOTE TO SELF

To survive a meltdown:

- *Hug my kids.*
- *Go see a movie.*
- *Eat chocolate.*
- *Take a deep breath.*
- *Lean on a friend and don't panic.*

• • • •

MEG WALKED OVER AND stood at Kate's shoulder, watching Bill Nethercutt and most of the seminar crowd file out the front door. "That was kind of weird."

Deep breath. Don't panic. Kate watched a smiling Saree ring up sales as fast as the register allowed, having relieved Anna when the presentation ended. Did they have anything to worry about? If she only knew what book Thomas carried in his green bag. Headlights flashed through the front window as patrons drove away. Kate kept a careful eye on who still mingled. Gabriella Cavannah-Wicker strode out the door without speaking to anyone or making a purchase. Regardless, the evening looked like a big sales success.

Saree looked up and waved her over, but with a hand signal Kate told the bookseller they would be right back. She grabbed the posters, her purse, and the huge black carry bag and followed Meg. They moved toward the exit in the back of the store, and despite the dimmer lighting, the worries receded as she moved out of the store.

Who cares if my fingerprints are on the book. Saree will tell anyone how they got there.

Friends. She really had friends, good friends, who would stand by her for what seemed like the first time in her life. The most trying time in her life. She started to snap the rubber band on her left wrist, then realized it wasn't there, and couldn't remember the last time she'd worn the band—or felt like she truly needed it.

Keith is going to be amazed.

"Wonderful talk." Jane rushed ahead to open doors for the two. "And an excellent maiden voyage into the deep waters of business presentations."

"I think you're still in the throes of that cruise." Kate laughed. "But thank you. I don't know about maiden voyage, though. I'm not sure the butterflies in my stomach will let me reenter these uncharted waters."

"You were scared, Katie?" Meg asked, disbelief evident on her face. "I've never seen anyone appear more relaxed than you seemed."

"It was all an act."

"A very good one," Jane reiterated, as she opened the back of the van and stepped aside. "Anything else I can do for either of you?"

Looking at Meg, who shook her head, Kate replied, "I can't think of a thing, but I do appreciate your support tonight, especially given the fact none of this information is new to you."

"Might be surprised, Katie."

Kate patted her mother-in-law's arm. "Thank you for that, too. But it's late. You'd better get home before George is worried."

Jane looked at her watch in the dim light. "I would say that's good for him, but it is after 8:30, and I do hate to drive around once it gets so late."

After Meg set the box on the van's floor, Kate slid the posters between it and the backseat and placed her large carryall with the rest of her supplies near the door. She turned and hugged her mother-in-law. "The girls want to come over and see your cruise pictures."

"Bring them tomorrow evening, and they can spend the night."

"In that case, you really do need to go home and rest up," Kate said, smiling as she withdrew her keys and tossed her purse in the back with the rest of the stuff.

Meg slammed shut the back of the van, and Jane noticed the crumpled rear fender.

"What happened?"

"Somebody got too close," Kate answered, wistful as she rubbed a finger over the biggest part of the dent. "I haven't had a chance to contact my insurance agent yet."

Jane frowned. "Who did it?"

Kate shrugged, wrapped an arm around each of the other women's shoulders and headed back into the store. "It happened while the police interviewed us at Sophia's, and the van was parked out front."

"The person didn't even leave a note?" Jane asked, indignant, her words as forceful as her actions when she slammed open the shop's back door.

"No. Which means I'll probably have to pay a deductible to get it fixed."

Her mother-in-law shook her head but said no more as they reentered the bright bookstore. Saree rushed over and hugged Kate's neck. "It was rippin' good, eh?"

"Yes, definitely." Kate couldn't keep the smile from her face, and she felt true satisfaction at how few business cards she had left in her stack. She kept her fingers crossed the telephone would ring in the next few days with new clients.

Saree's voice called out happily, "Kate, Organized Queen, this night be a very nice hit. Come by tomorrow, I give free lunch. My treat. We gonna schedule another in summer, yes?"

Suddenly the butterflies were back. Speaking in public again? So soon? At all? Her smile slipped a little, but she forced herself to get brave. "Let me see how busy my schedule gets after the girls are out of school. Maybe we can plan a back-to-school workshop in August."

Nodding, Saree said, "Very good. And lunch tomorrow?"

"Again, let me see," she replied. "Keith's out of town tonight, and we usually try to meet midday when he's been gone."

"Ah, make a date with your mate, eh?" Saree flashed an insider grin. "That be the way, chickie, that be the way."

They all laughed, then Jane waved and headed for the front door. "Well, I really do need to go. I'll see you and the girls tomorrow."

"Bye, Jane." Kate looked around to see if she had anything left to load. "I guess you and I need to run, too, Meg."

With a sigh, Meg said, "Yes, home to see what kind of disaster my men have made this evening. Gil said the boys could make brownies."

"They might surprise you."

"Yeah, the kitchen might be worse than I think."

They climbed into the van and pulled carefully out of the alley.

"Can you stop a second at the mini-mart?" Meg asked. "Mentioning rechargeable batteries in your talk reminded me Mark needs double A's for some science thing tomorrow."

"I could lend you s—"

Meg waved her words away. "Nope, he'll never get them back home. I'd rather buy disposable, rather than replace your environmentally-correct ones later."

The Shop-A-Way, was as busy as ever, and Kate was pleased when a front space opened right by the fluorescent-lit entrance. Meg checked her jacket pocket. "Oh good, I thought I had a ten in here. Be right back."

As she waited, Kate counted more than a dozen people walk out, most with fountain drinks and cigarettes, and nearly as many who entered. She peered through the glass, checking out the store's layout, watching the patrons' traffic patterns, where congestion areas formed. Maybe she could branch out, propose ways for businesses to streamline and attract more customers through better stock organization. She decided to write up some notes on the idea later, as Meg walked out with her small paper bag.

"They actually sack one package of batteries?" Kate asked, as her friend opened the passenger door.

Smiling sheepishly, Meg shook her head. "I asked for it. I bought me a candy bar, too, for my morning chocolate attack, and I didn't want to share with the boys. I'll give you half, though, since I've had to confess."

"No. I'd rather save the information to blackmail you in the future."

"Okay. I'll risk the threat of blackmail if it means keeping all of my chocolate."

They left the parking lot, and Meg said, "It was kind of bizarre in there. I could have sworn I saw Thomas Lane in the back of the store, but I went to check, and no one was in the aisle."

"You're sure it was him?" She turned off Main Street and onto Wayfarer Road. The town couldn't afford to put streetlights more than a block past Main, and darkness engulfed the van. A new moon reigned over the black sky. Trees that lined the roadside, and seemed so comforting by day, delivered intense claustrophobia by night. The headlights did their job but delivered little further than the tunnel-strength of their beams. Almost like a new world was being created just before she drove into it.

"No. I'm not sure of anything anymore," Meg answered. "There wasn't any door he could have left through unless he crawled into one of the refrigerated cases, and I definitely didn't see enough room between those shelves. But I really thought I saw someone."

"He couldn't have gone around the aisle and ducked?"

Meg shrugged. "That would make the whole thing weirder. Maybe one of the store personnel resembles him. Maybe there was never anyone, and I imagined the whole thing."

"Sounds like you need sleep as much as I do." Kate frowned as she looked in the rearview mirror. "Is someone behind me?"

Meg turned to look between the seats. "Yeah, I think so. Somebody driving without headlights."

The hair on the back of Kate's neck stood at attention. "I don't like this."

"Just someone tired or distracted who forgot to turn them on. I've done that before. They'll realize and hit us with high beams in a second."

But the trailing vehicle remained shrouded in the blackness, only visible as a vague outline reflected from the van's taillights.

"We'll be in our neighborhood in a minute. Should I drive on? Not let them see where we live?"

"I'm beginning to share your heebie-jeebies, Katie. Look, the road to the maple syrup farm is coming up. It will take us back to town."

She started to hit the blinker arm, but Meg cried, "No, just turn. They're following close and will likely miss it. We'll know we have something to worry about if they come back again."

At the last second, Kate cut the wheel to the right. Glancing back through the mirror, she sighed in relief. "The car went on. I hope the driver isn't drunk or sick or something."

"Probably not paying attention is all. We were ahead and they could see our taillights. Their need for lights wasn't noticeable, but that will change. It kind of feels like you drive into a black glove when you hit Wayfarer Road."

"That's a great analogy." Kate said, remembering her own thoughts of only a few minutes earlier. "I think we need to petition the city council—" She caught her breath. "Omigosh. The car's back."

Meg jumped and twisted, then started speaking rapidly, "Okay, we can't panic. We're almost to the farm, and then it's a straight shot to town. We'll go to the police station and—"

"Please, calm down." Kate felt a lump forming in her throat. "You're talking so fast, it's making me even more nervous."

"Right! We'll call the police." Meg searched the floorboard. "I'll get my purse and—"

"No, we put our purses in the back." Kate shivered as she remembered.

Meg unfastened her seatbelt.

"Be careful." Kate leaned into the driver-side door, to give Meg more room. Her neighbor wiggled and shoved until she was through the space between the headrests. The first slam from behind came as Meg landed in the backseat.

"They're ramming us!"

"They probably figured out what you're doing. Buckle in and hang on!"

Stomping on the accelerator, Kate prayed a local cop had a speed trap set up ahead. The orange-red needle climbed slowly, but steadily. The next impact came as the speedometer read seventy-five.

Meg squealed as the van fishtailed a little. Kate pushed harder, nausea forming with her fear. She hoped no animal ran out into the road. There was no way she could brake in time. The van shook from trying hard to do what she asked from it. The glowing speedometer read ninety. Though wanting to charge even faster, she worried what might get hit if she continued at this great a speed. A couple of rural homes and yards lay along either side, but she couldn't see lights in any of the windows and didn't want to risk stopping to ask for help. Getting caught in a trap was too easy. Releasing the accelerator a bit, the needle retreated ten mph.

"What are you doing?"

"I'm afraid at such a high rate of—"

The next blow nearly knocked the van off the road. Kate panicked, metal on metal screaming in the air. Her grip on the wheel tightened to white knuckle level, and she willed herself to not let the steering veer again. Another slam came before she completely corrected from the first, but she stayed on the road. Barely. "Can you see what kind of car it is?"

"Dark and big."

Lights ahead signaled they were almost to Main Street. Kate let the van return to ninety. Just as she wondered what to do next, Meg said, "The car is gone."

"Did it turn into one of the driveways?"

"I don't know. One second the outline tailed us. The next it was gone.

"Well, I'm going by the police station anyway." Kate slowed at the stop sign. "My insurance company will want an official report to process this new damage. Now I really do need to call my agent."

"Two back-to-back hit-and-runs," Meg said. "I'd be willing to bet whoever did this tonight is the same person who hit your van yesterday at Sophia's."

"But why? What did he or she accomplish?"

"Were you scared?"

"Of course."

"Then, mission accomplished." Meg grabbed the paper sack and withdrew the Hershey bar. "I need this, and you're getting half."

"I won't argue."

$\bullet \bullet \bullet \bullet$

THEY GOT A POLICE ESCORT home but little more. The pimple-faced constable on-duty said he would have the report typed and ready for Kate the next afternoon. The women couldn't provide a definite description of the car or driver, so he offered no assurances.

"Can you at least tell Lieutenant Johnson of the state police? He should know this incident happened," Meg requested, but her tone really made it more a demand.

"I'll make sure he's aware of it, ma'am," the officer replied.

A patrol cruiser escorted them home, and Kate even made the officer wait as she dropped off Meg and loaded the twins to run Tiffany home. Luckily the damage to the van wasn't noticeable in the dark as long as she kept everyone away from the back doors and bumper.

"Why is a policeman following us?" Suze asked.

"He's making sure we stay safe since Daddy isn't home tonight." The quick fib satisfied them, and she sighed in relief at not having to do any more explaining.

They got back to the house and Kate kissed the girls and told them to run up to bed. She promised to come tuck them in, but they still had energy to burn so she knew there was no hurry. The message machine light wasn't blinking. She frowned. Nothing from Keith. Turning on the radio, she heard his voice still calling the game.

"Yep, we're in overtime, folks." Keith's voice traveled over the airwaves. "This'll probably run too late for a goodnight call, so I hope my wife and kids are listening. I love you, girls."

Her smile returned at the coincidence. Kate listened until Keith and his color-commentary partner resumed their baseball banter, and she became bored. She wished for his strong arms to hug her and tell her everything would be okay but was more than a little pleased to realize she actually felt fine.

Second revelation of the evening.

Maybe it had been some drunken teens out for a joyride like the officer suggested. Maybe it was her unknown assailant. Either way, she'd survived. She was home. She—well, she felt like Batgirl!

Chuckling, she prepared the coffeepot for next morning's single cup, rather than the three she and Keith shared, and headed upstairs to the girls. Lights out and eyes closed. Kate didn't honestly believe them already asleep but decided to play along. She would check for lights under the door later.

On the way upstairs, Kate had taken a brief census tallying the results of the girls' assigned tasks for the evening and was suitably impressed at the good job. She needed to commend Tiffany as well. "Thursday night pickup" was the McKenzie family's regular, all-together-now weekly routine used to keep from having to scrub on the weekend. Kate hadn't made the twins do any more than they usually did, promising to do hers and Keith's share in the morning. Sam and Suze had shot her a stern look before she left for Saree's with the admonition, "You'd better."

She smiled and closed their bedroom door, thinking about how to properly reward the pair for the follow-through. But knowing the vagrancies of the first-grade mind, she wasn't gullible enough to assume the habit was set and it would happen the next time.

The last chore before her own bedtime was to unload the van. And inspect the damage.

She'd backed into the garage, and had no trouble seeing the full effect. It could have been worse. The lock held and the doors stayed closed, but she was going to have to do without the vehicle for several days while it was repaired. Thanks to their black shadow on the way home, she had to do some tugging and prying to get the back open. It took just a minute to remove the visual aids and place them against one wall. She patted her jacket pocket and felt the laser pointer. Missing was the small plastic display wheel she'd used, the one that went on the box on her bedroom floor that currently sported only three wheels.

"Drat! Did I leave it at Saree's?" Suddenly, she remembered it falling to the pavement as they'd loaded up in the alley and how Meg had tossed the wheel into the back of the van.

Kate flipped on the overhead light and scanned the vehicle floorboard. She felt under the backseat and found something much bigger and bulkier than her objective. Sucking in a breath, she withdrew the satin covered journal from Amelia's desk.

Panic! Another item she shouldn't have in her possession that belonged to the murdered woman. After a moment, her pulse slowed with the realization the book must have slid under the seat the day before when the box of archived desk items spilled.

Oh, well, what's another trip to the lawyer's office? She bit her lip. Would it be terrible to take a peek first? Kate rubbed her hand across the cover. *No! This is private.*

Resolved, she renewed her search for the wheel and, once it was found, marched back into the kitchen and placed the journal on the counter by the phone.

She drummed fingers on the silky cover. Her alarm at finding the contraband item, no matter how innocent the circumstances, made her think she needed to tell the police everything. Yes, it was important to carefully word the tale, but the authorities needed to know about the stolen items and how she and Meg once again found the puzzle box during their antique store sleuthing. And the only way to accomplish the goal was to admit items had surreptitiously come her way.

Nevertheless, she couldn't do it. This was too much. Too confrontational for a person who always tried to operate under the code of live and let live. Yet, that was it, wasn't it? Mrs. Baxter, for whatever reason, had decided to steal and kill. She wasn't letting people live. Could she have been lying about not being able to drive, too? Could she be who had tried to run Kate and Meg off the road this very evening?

It didn't matter whether Mrs. Baxter was the phantom driver or not. Kate had to tell everything about the thefts and their suspicions.

Except doing so, besides muddying suspicions around her own actions, would ultimately implicate Meg, too.

"Maybe not." An idea formed, and Kate moved her hand to the phone, but she stopped short of taking it from the cradle. What if she mentioned the puzzle box found in Ursula's store as something she and Meg saw in the house? Not mention it was planted in Kate's home earlier. Johnson already knew about the thefts, he'd said so when they reported the disappearance of the mask. Sophia had raged about it. Yes, Kate could explain how the puzzle box had been in the parlor on the day of the funeral, how she'd noticed it by the plant, all without mentioning she'd been the one who'd hidden it behind the ceramic pot. Leading Johnson to watch the surveillance films and possibly catch Mrs. Baxter as she withdrew the item.

She searched the drawer under the telephone for Johnson's card, found it, and dialed his office number. As expected, she was connected to voice mail to leave a message or call his cell phone number to speak to him immediately. She wasn't brave enough for that. Voice mail was perfect.

"Lieutenant Johnson, this is Kate McKenzie. You don't have to call me back, but I have some new information to report." She delivered her facts, tips and suspicions, almost dropping the phone when her nerves gave way. Her hands still shook a full minute after she returned the telephone to the cradle.

There was still more to do. Once her voice strengthened again, she dialed Charles Webster Walker's office number and got his voice mail. Irrationally, she wondered whether her parents would be proud right then or disappointed in their only child. Despite her mom's and dad's brushes with the law, they had always been on the side they'd figured as right, and Kate decided in this case their views would mesh with her own.

"This is Kate McKenzie for Charles Webster Walker. Yesterday, I left a box of private papers at your office that relate to the Nethercutt estate, but I just found a journal belonging to Amelia which had accidentally fallen under my backseat. I wanted to let you know, on the off chance someone was looking for it." *And to tame my curiosity.*

The sooner she returned the journal, the better. She picked up the book and a scrap of paper slipped from the cover. "Oh, I have what appears to be a number to what looks like an account of some sort. It's labeled with the abbreviation 'G.Cay'. I'll try to get everything to you by mid-morning tomorrow. Goodbye."

She put the scrap back inside and stroked the satin cover once more. The draw to read was great, but it was too late. The day had been long, and she really was too tired for the temptation to last. She tossed her jacket back across the kitchen desk, deciding she'd spent too much energy on setting things straight lately and needed to play a little organizational hooky.

A rebel for just the moment.

As she climbed the stairs, she squeezed the wheel that would soon be in its rightful place under her bed.

CHAPTER TWENTY-ONE

WORDS TO LIVE BY

"Be sure you put your feet in the right place, then stand firm."

— _Abraham Lincoln_ —

"Or, in other words, don't let the bad guys scare you, Batgirl!"

— _Kate McKenzie_ —

• • • •

KATE WOKE TO THE PHONE ringing, seconds before the alarm.

"Hi, honey, did I wake you?" Keith asked, as the buzzer sounded.

Too many things at one time. She hit the snooze to keep from having to find the switch right away. "I miss you when I have to sleep alone," she told Keith, stretching with her free arm before pushing into a sitting position.

"I'm sorry. I miss you, too." His voice even sounded like he did, the words coming out a bit huskier than normal. She smiled, picturing him in a motel room bed with tousled hair and the phone wedged between his ear and the pillow. Then she heard chewing and road noise.

"Where are you?"

"McDonald's just south of Burlington," he replied.

Kate's stomach gurgled in hunger. "You're already on the road?"

"Yep," he spoke around a mouthful of what she knew was Egg McMuffin. "Proud of me?"

She hugged blanketed knees with her arms and cradled the phone in the crook of her neck and shoulder. "I sure am." Keith hated driving through anything that resembled morning traffic, always nervous in bumper-to-bumper snarls. It was something his former hockey teammates had ribbed him about mercilessly. "You drive carefully, and I'll be thinking about you."

"I was thinking about you last night."

"I know." Kate felt her smile broaden. "I heard you on the radio."

"When the game went into extra innings?"

"Uh-huh. We got home from Saree's a few minutes before."

"How'd the talk go?" He'd taken another bite, and the words came out muffled.

"Really well." Glancing at the clock, she rose and pulled on her robe. "Saree wants me to do another in a few months, and a lot of people went away with my card. Oh!" Kate suddenly remembered what she and Meg discovered. "We figured out who the thief is." She quickly filled in the details about the antique store trek.

Keith cleared his throat. "That's great, honey. Looks like everything's working out." She heard him take a quick sip of coffee, then clear his throat again. "Well, you need to get the girls up and going. I should be back in Hazelton by noon. Want to have lunch with a guy who loves you?"

"You mean you?" Kate asked, then laughed at his sharp intake of breath in surprise. "Of course, I do, handsome husband of mine. Where do you want to meet?"

"How about Giovanni's?" he suggested, a romantic Italian bistro Kate had fallen in love with soon after they moved to Hazelton.

"Mmm, sounds wonderful. Play your cards right, sailor, and I might even bring you back to my place for dessert."

"I was counting on it." Keith chuckled. "I love you. Give Sam and Suze a kiss from me."

She felt a sudden pang of loneliness. "I love you, too. And do be careful."

"Always. Bye."

"Goodbye." But he'd already hung up. She realized she'd forgotten to tell him about her frightening drive home and the damage to the van.

She smiled. *Guess I am getting braver.* Anyway, there was nothing he could do except worry all the way home.

The twins never got ready well when the morning routine was broken, and Keith's absence made everyone run late. Even bribed with a Sweetie Eaties breakfast and Kate following behind like a track coach, coaxing, challenging, and eventually warning dire consequences, they ran later than ever for a school day. Worse, a safety assembly was scheduled for the morning, the kids heading for the gymnasium first thing to meet one of Vermont's drug dogs, Rosie.

"Grab jackets, girls," Kate said. "Remember, the DARE officer is coming today with Rosie."

As she scooped up her own blazer from last night, Amelia's journal appeared beneath the coat. Kate almost picked up the book but stopped at the last second. The attorney's office wouldn't open until at least nine. No point in testing her resolve against peeking.

Still packing lunches into their backpacks, the girls remained coatless in the entry hall.

"Hurry," Kate warned, snatching up her keys. "Come on, get your jackets or we'll be late."

"Ah, Mom," Sam whined. "It's spring already."

Not in Vermont. Aloud she said, "But the mornings are chilly."

"We'll just have to carry them this afternoon," Suze contributed. "No one wears jackets now after school, except for the babies."

"Wow. You have to lug your coats all the way to the parent pick-up circle. What a job."

"Our friends laugh at us," Suze said, eyes downcast to perfect the sympathy appeal. "They say we're not true Vermonters."

Kate nearly gave in before she realized the eye shift covered a lie. Or at least an elaboration. Instead, she looked at her watch. "If you two aren't jacketed and loaded into the van in thirty seconds, you'll have to go to the office for tardy slips."

They streaked out of the door like a couple of pint-sized missiles.

• • • •

IT WAS AN HOUR LATER before Kate returned home, after being waylaid in the school parking lot by a mother who had been at Saree's the previous evening and couldn't wait to tell how the tips had already changed her life.

The phone rang as Kate inserted the house key into the lock. She raced to the kitchen, and saw Hazelton Elementary on Caller ID.

"Mrs. McKenzie?" a hoarse voice said, and the man coughed as if to clear congestion. "We have a woman here saying she's your mother and wants to take your children, but she isn't on the list of authorized—"

"What woman?" she cried. Her late mother's appearance was an impossibility, which only left Jane. Kate knew her mother-in-law would never remove the twins from school except in an emergency, and never without first contacting Kate.

Another cough came through the line. "A Mrs. Baxter—"

"No!" She headed for the door, carrying the cordless phone as she ran. "Don't release my children to her! I'm on my way. Please call 9-1-1 and report an attempted kidnapping!"

"Will do," the voice replied, and the line went dead.

She yanked keys from her jacket pocket and slammed the front door, not even stopping long enough to lock up the house.

At the school, she swung into the front circle and parked in a fire zone. As she ran for the building, she wondered how she'd beat the police cars and hoped they arrived soon. There was no way to know what Mrs. Baxter might do in a school filled with innocent children. She'd already killed twice. Would a child be any harder than adults?

Kate reached the front door, just grabbing the handle as a tall shadow rose and separated from the side bushes. An icy hand clamped around her wrist.

"Come with me, please, Mrs. McKenzie," said Charles Webster Walker.

Relief swept through her. "Thank goodness you're here, Mr. Walker. Please come with me and speak with Mrs. Baxter. She's trying to kidnap my children!"

"No, Mrs. Baxter isn't here." Walker pulled Kate toward the front sidewalk.

"Let me go." She struggled but could not break his grip. "I have to get inside. The woman has lost her mind. She killed Amelia and Sophia to cover her thefts, and now she's—"

"In Montana," Walker interrupted, shooting her the coldest look Kate ever remembered seeing.

"But the school called..." she faltered. "A man said..."

He coughed. "You mean the one who said Mrs. Baxter wasn't on the list of authorized people to take your children?" he asked, speaking in the same raspy voice she'd heard over the phone.

"You?"

"Of course."

She was too shocked to fight him, and he took advantage, easily dragging her several yards.

"And you talked with that antique lady, too," he said. "I called yesterday to make sure she'd received my shipment."

"You're the lady with the cultured voice?" Kate tried again to pull free.

"Did a lot of thespian work in college." He gave her arm a solid yank. "Came in handy all these years later."

Thoughts raced through her brain, but she forced herself to focus all energy on a fight for her freedom. They were on the side of the building, moving toward the cafeteria wing. Kate knew she was dead if he got her inside his car, and she could see it looming closer, parked slightly hidden beside the Dumpster. A black Lincoln with tinted windows. The front was hidden from view, but she suspected the grill and fenders were badly dented from bashing her van.

She fought hard, but despite his age Walker was stronger. *Why doesn't someone see me, come help me?* Her eyes lighted on the DARE van. Of course, everyone was in the gym. What irony. Police on the scene, and she was still on her own.

Kate tried to scream, but it came out as a series of aborted yelps. Yet, Walker took no chances. He grabbed both her wrists and held them in one of his large hands, then pulled a handkerchief from his pocket with his free one and shoved it into her mouth. His hand quickly covered it, and she couldn't expel the cloth. Another jerk and he'd pulled her body next to his.

They made their way clumsily the last few feet, with her unsuccessfully trying to trip him.

At the car, his body pinned hers against the metal, and he opened the back door. While one hand fumbled with the car keys, he wrapped the other arm around Kate's head, crushing her mouth against his shoulder. Her hands were free, but practically immobilized by his body. She tried her only chance. She reached for his groin.

"What the hell?" he roared, as her fingertips grazed the target area. Before she could follow through, he reared back and clipped her jaw with his right fist. She nearly lost consciousness. She fought to stay on her feet. He grabbed her jacket collar and hauled her up, twisting the car key at the same time.

Her mind screamed, *Not the car! No! Not in the car!* She tried to stick her fingers in his eyes. He pulled back suddenly, but not before her nails left four bloody slashes down the right side of his face. He hit her again, harder this time, on the side of her head. He smiled. Blood dripped onto his white collar.

Kate felt blood ooze from a cut at her temple. She spit the cloth from her mouth and screamed. He smacked her with the back of his hand, and the skin on her cheek exploded.

"Teach you to try any more foolishness." He laughed and held up his hand. Kate flinched. "I'm not going to hit you again, unless you try something equally stupid. Just wanted to show you this ring. It was Daniel's."

The large ebony and diamond signet ring matched the image of the heirloom Daniel wore in the portrait in his study. She watched the diamond flash in the sun, but her mind grew increasingly hazy. "Why?"

"Why kill them?" Walker asked, then laughed again. "Why not? Amelia took half of what I had in our divorce. Never mind we weren't married long enough for the marriage to hardly count. She didn't love me anyway. Loved that wimp boy. She comes back to town, pretty as you please, married again, and wants to hire me as her family attorney. Says Daniel agreed. I acted pleased at the compliment but began planning from that first moment."

"Planning what?"

"To steal everything they had, of course." He tried to pull the door handle, but Kate slipped her body over it, using every means to stall his progress. His face darkened. "Damn it, move. You've messed up everything all along, just like Amelia."

"How did—"

"She wanted to change the will. Take out the inventorying time." He roared, shoving her back toward the trunk and wrenching the door wide. "I had everything already started, but I needed those last sixty days to cover my tracks. Couldn't start divesting until they finally let me handle all the financials this year. Once they were both dead, that transitory period you were supposed to use for inventorying offered the escape time I needed. But you started investigating instead. I got to the office this morning and heard my messages, learned you'd found the journal and the offshore account number Amelia discovered with her snooping. I knew you read the damned journal and understood what was changing and why."

"The account number was the reason why—"

As she spoke he grabbed the discarded handkerchief, nearly pulling her to the ground as he held her arm. Kate thought it was to shut her up again, but instead he gave her a mighty shove and sent her flying into the rear seat, onto her back. A roll of duct tape lay in the floorboard.

But she had her hand free for the moment, and a moment was all she needed. As he ripped off the first strip of silver tape, her right-hand dove into her jacket pocket and came out with the laser pointer. One click and the beam shot directly into his eyes. It didn't take long, just like Meg said.

"Ahh!" he screamed. "My eyes! I'm blind!"

Walker tried to shield his eyes, and Kate made her final attack. With every ounce of strength, she brought her knees to her chin, and slammed both feet into his chest. There was a whooshing sound as air left his lungs, and he fell to the pavement. She scurried out the door, moving as fast as her wobbly legs could go. He grabbed blindly for her, catching hold of her jacket as he worked his way back to his feet.

Not this time.

She shook free of the coat and headed for the steel cafeteria door. But she couldn't get away from his long reach. As if by instinct, he moved, cursing and grabbing, then knocked her to the ground. She slammed a heel into his shoulder. She kicked off from the asphalt, her palms scraped and bloody. She screamed, but no one opened the doors. The cafeteria was her only hope. Closer. Closer. She was seconds away when he tackled her again, holding both of her feet this time.

Kate fell just short of the small concrete apron that served as the door's porch. Her hand rested next to the iron doorstop someone had left at one corner. As he rose to move on top of her, to pin her one more time, she grabbed the heavy metal wedge and swung in a ninety-degree arc, using the movement to bring all available weight behind the blow. The heavy doorstop connected with his left temple. Kate heard a sickening thump, and he fell away from her.

Laughing and crying at the same time, she rose to unsteady feet and pounded on the locked door.

"What the hell?" The door opened to reveal Valerie in a hairnet and floury white apron.

Kate collapsed into her arms, right before the world turned black.

CHAPTER TWENTY-TWO

ORGANIZE YOUR MIND for Clear Thinking

- *Think small. Take small bites, and you'll finish much easier.*
- *Focus on your objective. Don't let random chaos rule.*
- *Believe in yourself. Organization is a decision that you make.*
- *Don't let clutter trap you. You have power over your environment.*
- *Like the Nike ad says, "Just do it." Five minutes is better than nothing.*

• • • •

"IN A HAIRNET? VALERIE?" Meg hooted. "Tell me you're joking."

After the laughter died down at their table, Kate regaled Keith and the Bermans with the other details of her harrowing morning. Though Keith had made it back to town by noon, Kate had still been with the police and paramedics. After one of the cafeteria workers had run into the assembly screaming that a man was molesting women in the parking lot, the DARE officer had quickly taken charge. Charles Webster Walker had finally regained consciousness with Rosie standing guard over him, her German shepherd warning growl low and mean any time he tried to move.

"Yes, at first I thought I was having delusions from getting socked in the head, but it's true—our demon decorator volunteers in the Hazelton Schools food services division. One of the regular volunteers hurt her back and couldn't make it today. When Valerie heard, she offered to take the woman's place. Seems our gal Val is a regular helper at the high school cafeteria. Hard to believe, huh?"

"Valerie as benevolent servant?" Meg mused. "That's a toughie."

Gil swallowed his last bite of breadstick and said, "She's a big behind-the-scenes person for the community Toys for Tots each Christmas, too."

"I guess we've always looked at her through the wrong end of the telescope." Kate frowned as she carefully bit into a savory meatball. It still hurt to open her mouth very wide.

Ooh wonderful. The seasonings exploded across her taste buds.

"Well, not completely," Gil admitted. "She gets serious business mileage out of being philanthropic with her time, pitching decorating skills as she lifts a volunteer hand. It isn't all selfish. She does a lot of good, but she makes sure to self-promote at every turn."

"There's the Valerie we all know and tolerate," Meg said, and they laughed again.

Stabbing a slice of baked zucchini from his wife's plate, Gil mused, "Speaking of selfish people makes me wonder, with Sophia dead and her husband around the bend, so to speak, what's going to happen to the radio station?"

Keith chuckled. "You are not going to believe this. Story is when Mr. White's doctor and a nurse went in to tell him about Sophia's death, the old guy perked right up. They figured he didn't really understand what they were saying and planned to return later to try breaking the news again. Within an hour, he'd called his attorney—not Walker's firm, by the way—and was checking himself out. Said he wanted to go home and was perfectly fine. Said the whole thing was an act to get away from her and gain some peace for a while."

"Now, that I *can* believe." Meg clapped her hands.

Gil pulled another breadstick from the basket. With a glance around the crowded dining room, he said, "How'd we score a table here on Friday night during prime dining time?"

Keith shrugged. "Power of being a celebrity." Then he laughed and added, "Kate's celebrity status, not mine. I showed up here for lunch and waited until she finally phoned to tell me what happened. I ran out without even paying for my drink. I came back after I knew she was okay." He squeezed his wife's knee under the table. "They'd already heard what happened.

Management insisted I bring her back for dinner, on the house."

"How nice. And your parents were terrific to volunteer to babysit all our kids." Meg smiled, then looked closer at Kate. "Are you sure you're okay? You look a little pale."

As Keith and Gil turned worried eyes her way, Kate laughed. "I'm fine. Really. The paramedics patched up all my boo-boos. Just a few bumps, cuts, and bruises. Looks worse than it is. Besides, how can you tell what color I am in this light?" She waved a hand, taking in the romantically darkened dining room. "I counted on the restaurant's ambience to help me escape scrutiny."

Gil forked another bite of Meg's chicken cacciatore. "You look fine. My wife is letting her mommy genes work overtime."

"Hey, buster." Meg slapped his hand. "I can't help it if I care. And if you wanted to eat this dish you shouldn't have ordered lasagna."

He grinned at her, holding the delicious seasoned morsel poised at his mouth and asked, "Did Walker really confess everything in the parking lot? Word is he continued confessing the whole time the cop read him his rights. The guy's nuts."

Kate nodded. "Or trying to make it appear he is. On the day of Amelia's murder, Mrs. Baxter saw him on the front porch and thought Walker had just arrived. But he'd been there for a few minutes and already poisoned Amelia by then. When Walker first arrived, no one else was in the house, and Amelia let him. According to him, she then ordered him to go to the kitchen to act as servant to bring in the last cup of tea. He saw the lily of the valley, knew the danger from a lecture he'd once attended at the garden club. He claims it wasn't premeditated, that his anger at her made him act without reason. When he supposedly came to his senses he planted the stolen items to send suspicion my way."

"But why?" Meg interrupted. "Why not accuse a family member? Much more logical."

"He said he wanted the case solved fast and knew we didn't have the money for high-priced lawyers," Kate explained. "He'd used one of his fake voices to call for pizza delivery and waited by our back door for Louie to arrive, thinking he'd sneak in and hide the puzzle box. But Louie didn't just stand at the front door. Tiffany let Louie into the kitchen to use the phone, and Charles Webster Walker had to go to Plan B and use the fireworks as a backup."

"But how did he set off the fireworks and get back to your house unseen?" Gil cut in.

"He didn't," Kate continued. "He called that slimy Pearson guy from his office and said he needed to pull a prank to get someone out of a house. Pearson didn't ask any questions and brought firecrackers he happened to have left over from last year."

"Yeah, right," Meg said sarcastically. "Happened to have them lying around."

"Everyone ran into the woods, and Pearson ran away after setting everything off. That's when Walker took the opportunity to sneak into our home and plant the box in the laundry room," Kate finished. "He later swiped the van key out of my purse during the house tour, made a wax imprint like I'd guessed, and slipped it back in. The rest, as they say, is history."

Meg huffed. "Well, it doesn't surprise me Pearson was involved. He's the type to set

illegal fires and probably torch small animals."

"Quiet," Gil warned. "The guy's a lawyer after all. If he gets word you defamed him like that he'll—"

"I only said he was the type," Meg argued. "Besides, he did illegally set off firecrackers."

"But why kill Sophia, too?" Keith asked.

"I can answer that one." They all turned in surprise as Constable Banks walked up to their table. "I came by to make sure you're experiencing no ill effects from this morning's excitement, Mrs. McKenzie. Your mother-in-law told me where I could find you."

When Kate said she was fine, Banks faced Keith and continued, "Sophia remembered Amelia saying right after Daniel died how making everyone wait for a full accounting was silly. She also recalled how Amelia always worked out big things like her will ahead of time and wrote down her plans in her journal. Amelia's house may have been disorganized, but her mind wasn't. Earlier on the day Sophia was killed, she was at the mansion, and you found the journal, Kate. The book jogged her memory. That afternoon she called Walker and asked whether the journal, with all the notes documented in Amelia's own handwriting, could be used to validate the new will Amelia hadn't yet signed."

"He had to kill me, because he knew I had the journal," Kate said. "That's why he chased us after the bookstore event last night and rammed our van. Because the journal wasn't in the box of papers I took by his office the previous evening. He didn't know that I had no idea I still had it."

Banks nodded. "And after you called to say you'd bring the journal he was afraid of the reference you'd made to the offshore account. He knew Amelia had done some digging and thought you found the evidence."

"But why was Danny trying to pin blame on everyone?" Keith asked. "Was he working for Walker?"

Banks sighed. "Danny's problems predate the thefts and murders by many, many months. Unfortunately, he has friends just as rich and mixed up as he is. His little circle of trouble keeps me and a lot of parents on high alert."

"Including Gabriella Cavannah-Wicker," Kate said.

"Especially Ms. Cavannah-Wicker," Banks said. "She has a granddaughter Danny's age. Danny is known for keeping sales records written on his hand. Natalie Wicker's isn't the only name people have seen scribbled next to what can only be assumed is a quantity ordered or revenue owed."

"Drugs?" Gil asked.

Banks offered a weary smile. "They're all juveniles. I've probably already said too much. Especially around a reporter. Let's just say kids with large discretionary incomes are taxing our local police departments."

"We'll have to use that as a reason to turn the boys down the next time they ask for a raise in their allowance. It's our civic duty," Meg quipped. Everyone laughed.

Gil put down his pen. "Off the record. Just remember me when you have something you can comment on."

"It's a deal. Thanks."

"That's all so sad." Meg chewed her lip, and Kate knew she was thinking about kids and drugs, and hoping she never had to know firsthand. "Maybe Rosie the DARE dog needs to visit the high school, too."

"She does," Banks said. "And each trip has nothing to do with reaching out to kids in assemblies. She sniffs out trouble on a regular basis."

"Mrs. Baxter never had anything to do with the thefts," Kate mused, returning to the safer subject.

"Far as we know—no," Banks replied. "Walker said she was the original thief, but frankly I'm not ready to take his word for anything. She's currently out of state, and the family isn't even sure what, if anything, is missing. We're leaving that end of the case in closed status. The state police feel the same way. Johnson said as much before he left town this afternoon. Oh, but one thing I do need to tell you is we matched paint from your van to the damage on the front of Walker's car."

He handed Kate a police report with a yellow Post-it attached. "There's no doubt he was the one after you last night. You can give this to your insurance agent." Pointing to the sticky note, he added, "That's Walker's carrier."

"So Walker knew about the poison through the lecture," Kate mused. "Guess that means Saree and I worried over the book for nothing. I've been concerned that Thomas or Bill purchased it last night and had our fingerprints on the page. But it wouldn't have mattered anyway."

"And our talking about it in the van was enough to put the power of suggestion in my mind," Meg said. "When I ran into the convenience store for batteries, it was no wonder I couldn't find a place Thomas could have hidden. Our conversation made me see imaginary enemies and danger everywhere."

Kate patted her husband's hand. "Just like Keith always says, anxiety short-circuits the brain." The couple shared a smile.

"I still can't believe Walker spilled everything," Gil said. Ever the reporter, Kate noticed that he'd pulled out a small notepad when Banks showed up at the table and scribbled notes throughout the conversation.

"Yeah, you'd think a lawyer would keep his mouth shut," Kate said, relishing a sip of the delicious house wine. "Personally, I think he's going to go for an insanity defense. There's no other reason for singing like the proverbial canary."

"Or just get his confession thrown out," Keith mused. "He could say it was due to you bonking him on the head, and he didn't know what he was saying."

"None of it matters with Kate testifying about what he told her before she hit him," Banks said. "You are testifying, right, ma'am?"

"Absolutely." Confidence surged through her body with the words. "I can't wait."

Meg cried out, "I can't believe you said that! Katie, you're not being your normal, sweet, non-confrontational self."

"After a guy confesses to two murders, while he's trying to kill you, *after* he's made a hoax telephone call saying your children are being kidnapped..." Kate shook her head. "Let's just say making sure he stays behind bars is now at the top of my to-do list. After all, putting things in their place is my business." Everyone laughed.

Banks offered a small wave goodbye. "I'll be on my way. It's much nicer seeing people in this kind of setting than in an interrogation room."

As she watched his departing figure, Kate marveled at her own transformation over the past two weeks. For someone who knew nothing about criminal procedures, and had a tendency to over-worry about everything, she'd done a pretty good job at getting Amelia's murder solved.

Even if she'd never planned to get involved.

Just then, an older woman fluttered up to the table, someone who brought the word 'confrontation' to mind. The woman wore a brown dress and reminded Kate for all the world of a bird. That thought helped her recognize the wren-wife, Margaret, of the hawk-husband, Robert. "Hello," she returned the woman's greeting. "I'm sorry, I don't know your last name."

"Baker," the woman supplied. "Margaret Baker."

Kate made the introductions all around. "Margaret was at my presentation the other night. I hope you enjoyed it."

"It has kept Robert and me arguing nonstop," Margaret replied.

"I'm so sorry—"

But Margaret cut her off. "Think nothing of it. We argue all the time, but this gave us new topics. He's always griped about what I like and want to keep but got even worse after he retired. Your talk the other night set him off on a constant rant about what I need to get rid of, so I want to hire you."

Surprised at the woman's reversal, Kate clarified, "What exactly do you want me to do? Help you organize your house? Figure out what you can eliminate?"

"Heavens no." She gave a little bird laugh. "I want you to come in with a bunch of organizing shelves and box ideas Robert can start working on. My husband has wanted a workshop for a long time, and I think it's high time he got one. By the time he gets every closet and room organizer made, I figure he'll be too tired to complain about what he thinks I need to do."

"You're a very smart lady."

"After forty-two years of marriage you learn a few things," Margaret replied, smiling. "Well, I'd better get back before Robert has something else to fuss over. Lordy, I wish that man still had his corporate job."

The remark reminded Kate of the shocking line Amelia had said the day of her death, but she knew this woman was completely comfortable with her husband just the way he was. She looked over at Keith and smiled.

And that makes two of us.

Another client, how wonderful. She'd had a message earlier from a single father, an executive set to move his family across country, who wanted Kate's help to organize the endeavor. Things were looking up.

As Margaret Baker left, promising to call and schedule an afternoon consultation for the following week, a four-piece combo in the far corner struck up the Dean Martin classic "Everybody Loves Somebody." Keith motioned toward the small dance floor. "May I have this dance?"

Kate nodded. "This one and every one after, for the rest of our lives."

• • • •

THANK YOU FOR TAKING the time to read Organized for Murder. *If you enjoyed this book, please consider telling your friends or posting a short review. Word of mouth is an author's best friend and much appreciated. Thanks again!*

• • • •

APPENDIX

ORGANIZE LIKE KATE

<u>Top 3 Laundry Tips For Saving Time & Money</u>

- For presorted socks, choose white for all everyday needs. Get a mesh bag for each family member (these are the zippered bags normally used to hold and wash delicate items) and use a laundry marker to write each person's name on each one. Give every family member his/her own, to put dirty socks in after use. When washing and drying whites, throw in the whole bag. Socks are now presorted and bags can be left with each person's other laundry.
- Use white towels for every day, so it's always easy to get an efficient load of whites together when washing. You'll never again have to run a tiny load of just socks, underwear, or t-shirts.
- Save time and money by avoiding dry-clean only clothes. There are almost always washable alternatives available for business and sport. The same goes for bedspreads and curtains.

<u>Curing Closet Clutter</u>

- Install a closet organizer—styles and price ranges now vary widely.
- Keep Monday-Friday clothes in one area, casual in another, and elegant/Sunday separate.
- Install a second bar at half-height to double hanging capacity.
- Hang ties and belts near coordinating clothes. Keep inexpensive matching jewelry and accessories in a nearby

drawer, but remember that thieves are smart. Lock up your good stuff.

- A pocketed shoe bag on the door frees up built-in bins for sweaters and sweatshirts.
- Keep clothes untangled with plastic or wooden hangers—colors help kids remember which clothes are for play and which aren't.
- Use colored, stackable, un-lidded bins in kids' closets to sort clothing—socks in yellow, pants in blue, etc.
- Install hooks so small children can hang things up themselves.
- Store out-of-season clothes in under-the-bed, rolling drawers.
- Sort sheets into sets, placing a full set inside its coordinating pillowcase. This way bedding can all be quickly found, there is no need to fold perfectly, and sets are more easily stackable in linen closets.
- Attach towel racks inside a linen closet door to hang tablecloths.

Meal Organization

- Keeping clutter under control makes everything more organized and accessible.
- Organize and multi-task. Don't just read the recipe to decide what must be done first. See what things can be done at the same time. Example: chop veggies while water boils, or prepare sauce while pasta cooks.
- Begin cooking what takes the longest, chopping and slicing while waiting for oven or pan to heat.
- Clean while food is cooking, washing as many utensils as possible. If cook-time will be long, use this kitchen-time to organize the fridge or pantry. Fill pans with hot water and

soak dishes while mopping floors and vacuuming.

- Take meat out of the freezer to thaw overnight in the refrigerator, and you won't forget to pull it out during the morning rush.
- Cut up onions and peppers ahead of time to store in pint size baggies for the freezer, then add the desired amount right to the skillet whenever a recipe calls for them.

Plan meals ahead of time to cut down on the last-minute grocery store trips.

- When cooking to a recipe, put ingredients away as they are used.
- Cook once, eat twice. Cook a roast in the crock pot and divide leftover meat for a quick skillet dinner with vegetables and tomato sauce, or with beans for quick enchiladas.
- Freeze leftover broth, and additional meat can make a quick vegetable beef soup.
- Think big! Cook lots at one time. Bake chicken, boil chicken, grill chicken, and freeze for quick ingredients to casseroles or skillet meals during the week. Brown ground beef and make hamburgers all at one time.
- Pre-wash and separate lettuce leaves so they are ready for the week. Saves time making lunches and salads for dinner. Or buy pre-washed, prepackaged salad fixings for crunch times. While prepackaged costs more for the convenience, having salad ready and waiting in the refrig is usually well worth the cost for a fast meal ready on crazy days.
- Buy extra hamburger on sale. Divide meat into quart-size freezer bags, then flatten and freeze. It only takes minutes in the microwave or skillet to defrost the smaller servings, and they can be added to any dish. Another timesaver with

on-sale hamburger is to divide meat into patties and place, flat and not touching, in gallon-sized freezer bags. Lay bags in the freezer, patties in one bag stacked on patties in the next. When you need a quick meal, add either singularly or a whole bag-full, right to the skillet for fast burgers.

• • • •

WANT TO GET AN EMAIL alert when the next Organized Mystery is available? Sign up for Ritter Ames's newsletter today at www.ritterames.com

• • • •

ABOUT THE AUTHOR

USA TODAY bestselling author Ritter Ames writes the Organized Mysteries series, the Bodies of Art Mysteries, and the new Frugal Lissa cozy mystery series. These series and their varied locations give Ritter more opportunity to coax her husband into additional travel for "research." For more information about her and her books, visit her website at www.ritterames.com[1], and you can subscribe to her newsletter there—look for the gold signup box. Check her out on Facebook at http://www.facebook.com/RitterAmesBooks/ and her Twitter handle is @RitterAmes.

• • • •

---

1. http://www.ritterames.com

BOOKS BY
RITTER AMES

• • • •

THE ORGANIZED MYSTERIES:
<u>Organized for Murder</u>[2]
<u>Organized for Homicide</u>[3]
<u>Organized for Scheduled Sabotage</u>[4]
<u>Organized for S'more Death</u>[5]
<u>Organized for Masked Motives</u>[6]
<u>Organized for Picnic Panic</u>[7]
<u>Organized Mysteries: 3-Book Box Set</u>[8]
.

THE BODIES OF ART MYSTERIES:
<u>Counterfeit Conspiracies</u>[9]
<u>Marked Masters</u>[10]
<u>Abstract Aliases</u>[11]
<u>Fatal Forgeries</u>[12]
<u>Bronzed Betrayals</u>[13]
.

---

2.   https://www.books2read.com/u/bP5l1R

3.   https://www.books2read.com/u/3L0lrD

4.   https://www.books2read.com/u/mgrjWD

5.   https://www.books2read.com/u/mgrJwK

6.   https://www.books2read.com/u/4NGWZ9

7.   https://books2read.com/O4PP

8.   https://books2read.com/O4Box

9.   https://books2read.com/CounterfeitConspiracies

10.   https://books2read.com/MarkedMasters

11.   https://books2read.com/AbstractAliases

12.   https://books2read.com/FatalForgeries

13.   https://books2read.com/BronzedBetrayals

THE FRUGAL LISSA MYSTERIES
<u>Frugal Lissa Finds a Body</u>[14]
Frugal Lissa Digs Up a Body (coming soon)
Frugal Lissa Hunts a Body (available soon)

• • • •

---

14.   https://books2read.com/Frugal1

Don't miss out!

Visit the website below and you can sign up to receive emails whenever Ritter Ames publishes a new book. There's no charge and no obligation.

https://books2read.com/r/B-A-SNFC-XMWU

BOOKS 2 READ

Connecting independent readers to independent writers.